KELLY 'S QUEST

Book #2 in NYC Love Series

JENNIFER ANN

This is a work of fiction. The names, characters, places and incidents are products of writer's imagination or have been used in a fictitious manner. Any resemblance to persons, living or dead, actual events, locales or organizations is entirely coincidental.

KELLY'S QUEST (NYC LOVE #2)

ISBN: 978-0988390232

MYSTERY, SUSPENSE, & THRILLER
WRITTEN AS QUINN AVERY

www.QuinnAvery.com

CHILDREN'S BOOKS
WRITTEN AS JENNIFER NAUMANN

bit.ly/dogsdonthavefins

Prologue

JEWELS PETERSON

BEFORE NOW I didn't have a full understanding of what the saying "walking on clouds" meant, but I'm about to move into a brownstone in New York City with the love of my life, so...yeah.

For a Saturday morning, our small neighborhood tucked away in Murray Hill seems relatively quiet; the mixed odor of the city and summer smells thick in the stifling air. The little Irish pub on the corner, lined with dark hardwood inside like most of the others we've visited, doesn't open until noon, though I've heard it doesn't draw in much of a crowd during normal party hours. The constant hum of traffic along Park Avenue still takes some getting used to, but I wouldn't want it any other way. Aside from a few joggers, dog walkers, and residents going in and out of their brownstones, my best friend and I are the only two around.

I've only been here a few times since Adam first surprised me with the news that he purchased us our very own piece of New York with an inheritance he received from his beer mogul grandfather. We were quick to pack our things in Wisconsin and move into a rental for a few weeks while the final papers were processed for the brownstone. We spent the last few weeks picking out a college, findings jobs, and shopping for furniture as neither of us has owned so much as our own mattress outside of our childhood homes.

My face nearly splits in two when I take another long look at our new home. The narrow, tan building blends in with the others sandwiched beside it, but the dull shade of red I chose for the front door gives it a subtle kick from the other lower-level entrances. Our wrought iron gate is tall and rather heavy, giving me an extra sense of security even if the gate is only for show.

Inside is a work in progress with leaky faucets, cracked plaster, floors that need refinishing, and a kitchen that's a complete eyesore. But it's ours, and we plan to fix it up over time. The ground-level back-yard is exactly the kind of getaway I've been dreaming of since I took the road trip to the city with Adam earlier this summer.

My best friend, Kelly, wipes at her sweaty fore-head from the unrelenting heat the morning already brings. The incredibly short shorts and low-cut tank top she wears fit her curvaceous body like they were custom tailored for her. Without a stitch of makeup, she looks younger and exhausted. Her large brown eyes show the stress of the grueling weather wearing her down. She twisted her long brown hair into a sloppy bun this morning, but pieces have already fallen out around her supermodel-like cheekbones. Only Kelly could make natural look incredibly sexy. Whenever I try that kind of look, I resemble Whitney Huston during her days on crack.

I was somewhat thrown off when Kelly insisted on flying out to help us move. When I reminded her moving meant doing *physical labor*, she mumbled something about getting away from her sisters. After spending her summer as a counselor at her family's camp, I think the restrictions of being around her overbearing sisters really wore her down.

Kelly pushes her pouty lips out farther than usual. Moments like this I see why all guys seem to be drawn to her. "Does Adam seriously expect us to stand here and do *nothing* until he gets back? I don't understand why we can't just go in. I swear I've lost ten pounds in sweat."

I nod, feeling my ratty Alice in Chains t-shirt cling to my chest. "You're right. Let's take a few things in. I'm sure it won't hurt anything."

I slide in next to her and unlock the back gate with the keys Adam had me hold on to until his return. The van is filled with a few dozen boxes, a bed for the guest bedroom, an armchair, and the dresser from my childhood. Most of our furniture was newly purchased, thanks to Adam's inheritance, and should be delivered later in the afternoon. All I care is that we have our bed up by the end of the day. Tomorrow's my fourth day working at the market down the street, and I want a good night of sleep. Standing on my feet all day has been particularly draining, considering it's been over a year since I last worked at one of the clothing stores managed by my mom.

The first tangible object within reach is Adam's flat screen. Together, Kelly and I wriggle the monstrosity free and shuffle toward the steps.

"Don't even think about it!" a voice yells out. Theo, my relatively new friend, swoops out of nowhere to my side, grabbing my end of the TV. "You had strict orders not to go inside on your own, remember?"

I turn to him, smirking. He's so predictable. In running clothes soaked with sweat, headphones blasting hardcore rap, it's like looking at the same temporary neighbor we met just months ago in these same streets when Adam and I were renting a place and still trying to figure out what to make of our tumultuous relationship.

Considering Theo hit on me, buck-naked, mere *minutes* after we first met, it's actually a small miracle to think just how good of a friend he's become to both me *and* Adam. And I still laugh every time I see him dressed in designer suits for his swanky job as a television producer.

"Look who finally decided to show up to help," Kelly snorts, struggling with the TV on her end. "Pretty sure you could manage to carry this whole thing on your own, big guy."

Theo moves his hand down the flatscreen further until her face relaxes with relief. "That better, or you need me to carry you, too?" he teases with a playful smile.

Kelly rolls her eyes to the sky. "Back it down a notch. Not everyone is automatically charmed by your massive muscles."

"Oh, I can charm the pants off anyone, Cavenaugh. All you have to do is ask."

I moan, shaking my head. This has become their usual banter since they first met two days ago. Theo flirts, and Kelly pretends she's not interested, although I caught her giving him some pretty dopey-eyed glances. I think a part of her is afraid of what will happen if she lets herself fall for him since she lives in Wisconsin. I'm secretly hoping something *will* happen between them so maybe she'll decide to move to New York. It's going to be hard not having my best friend around, considering she's always been the one I can count on when things turn to shit.

Theo and Kelly disappear down the narrow steps to our newly acquired brownstone, just four streets down from Theo's. Taking a deep breath of the heavy air, I study the peaceful neighborhood. A warm rush of pride and excitement fills my gut. Until now, I've never felt like I was exactly where I'm meant to be. My life suddenly feels right on track, like this is exactly how things are supposed to play out.

Theo and Kelly emerge from the ornate door, her bright giggles endless. Theo catches me smiling like a goober at the building behind the van and folds his massive arms. "Where *is* Loverboy this morning? I think this is the first time I've seen the two of you more than five feet apart in the last two weeks. Shouldn't he be helping us?"

I snap from my trance and reach for the pile of blankets that were covering the TV, throwing them into Kelly's arms. "It's not like he can actually carry stuff anyway. And he had to meet with a professor."

Dealing with Adam's Type I diabetes was at first incredibly stressful on our relationship, especially when he was ready to accept possible death over being with me. By the time we met he'd been through so many surgeries and awful procedures—leaving him regrettably scarred and broken—that he didn't have the mental strength to endure any more. Though he insisted that we'd never be anything more than friends, we fell in love and he realized our relationship was worth fighting for. He's come a long way on his recovery, yet it's still slow going.

Kelly snorts as she heads back to the steps with

her arms full. "Who meets with professors on the *weekends*? He's such a nerd."

"He's *trying* to make sure all his credits are accounted for before fall semester starts," I scold her.

Kelly scoffs before disappearing. Theo crawls up inside the back of the van to sort through our sparse belongings.

"You should probably stick to the lighter stuff until James gets here," I suggest to him. "I'd hate to see you develop a hernia while Kel is in town."

Luckily, Theo wasn't the only overly muscular, tattooed friend we made in the city. His buddy, James, was quick to volunteer his help when he heard we were moving.

Theo peers around the corner of the van, his expression broad with hope. "Are you saying she *is* into me? I mean, she's a total knockout, and any friend of yours *has* to be worth my time. C'mon, give me something to work with."

I shrug coyly. "I never said anything of that sort, though she did make a comment about your perfect ass, and the only time I've really heard her giggle is when she's around you. If you say anything to her, though, I'll totally deny it. I can't have you breaking my best friend's heart."

"I don't plan on breaking her heart, I just want to get to know her. C'mon, throw a guy a bone here." He crouches down until we're closer to eye level.

"How can I impress her so she'll agree to go out with me?"

A familiar pair of arms slip around me from behind, molding against me like it's where they're meant to be. "Offer to take her on a trip across the country. It worked for me."

I whirl around in my gorgeous boyfriend's arms. I didn't see him sneak out of the rental this morning, but it's no surprise he's looking as hot as ever in a button-down that matches the hue of his baby blues. His hair doesn't have the usual spiky flip going, which is typical when he has to get up early. He's growing stronger with every day and has more of the boundless spirit from when we first met. I lace my fingers through his hair and drag him close, pressing my lips to his for a deep kiss.

Theo coughs behind us. "You'd think that'd grow old eventually."

Adam stops kissing me to beam at Theo. "Once you find the right one, it never grows old, my man. You wait. You'll figure it out one day." He kisses the tip of my nose. "Have you been inside yet?"

Theo jumps down onto the street with a big box in hand. "No, she hasn't, and you can thank me. I caught her just as she was trying to sneak in."

"I wasn't trying anything," I say, rolling my eyes with feigned annoyance. "The man's a chronic liar."

Adam's eyes sparkle. "Are you ready for your surprise?"

I lean in to kiss him again. And again. "Does it involve locking Kel and Theo out to give us a little privacy?"

"I'm sure we could make that happen." Adam smirks before sucking on my bottom lip.

"I've developed a whole new level of sympathy for your new neighbors!" Theo hollers over his shoulder.

We follow him inside, hands held, my excitement skyrocketing through the roof. The first level of our new place looks halfway decent sized without any furniture, but I know as soon as the couch and deep armchair we picked out arrive, the living room will shrink back down quickly. The wooden floors, bleached and cracked, just need a little TLC once we've saved up a bit more money. The kitchen, however, could use a wrecking ball. The crooked cabinets have rotted out in places, and small chunks of the laminate countertop are missing. It's unattractive, but at least Adam was able to afford *something* in this neighborhood. After we've fixed it up, we'll probably come out ahead *if* we ever decide to sell.

Adam's adorable dimples flare when he pulls me toward the drapery-covered patio door, past our friends playfully arguing on their way back outside. Before Adam pushes the doors open, I already have an inkling of what I'm about to find.

What was once a small area with short, chain-linked fencing and the world's saddest patch of grass has transformed into a backyard wonderland. Dozens of twinkle lights are strung beneath a draping canopy that does an excellent job of filtering the sunlight. Three outdoor sofas with red cushions circle a stone fire pit inside a new, walnut stained fence. Ornate stone covers the ground inside the intimate gathering area in a swirling pattern, with a patch of fresh sodding in the far back. It's incredibly charming. I can't believe it's ours.

"Ohmigod, Adam!" I drag him over to one of the couches, sinking back into the giant pillows. When he collapses on top of me, I kiss him. Hard. "It's exactly what I pictured! When did you have time for all of this?"

His lips trail down my neck. "Davis was only visiting as a ploy to keep you busy while I had to put in 'extra time' in therapy."

I spent the better part of the last week running around the city with Adam's cousin from Minnesota. He's an artist and has been in New York dozens of times for shows, so *he* actually showed *me* some of the insider tips I've missed. "So he really *isn't* thinking of moving out here?"

"I think deep down he's actually considering it, but you never know with him." Smirking, Adam bends in to cover my neck with kisses. "Want to know the best part about this setup?" His hands wander down my thigh before reaching up my shorts to gently stroke the part of me that will always want him. I inhale sharply, delighted. "With this ingenious cover over our heads, I can do whatever I want, *whenever* I want, to my girlfriend in the privacy of our backyard." He kisses my lips. "Just don't let out one of your screaming orgasms, or the new neighbors will likely call the cops."

"Could you be any more amazing?" I cling to him, dusting the tip of my tongue against his lips. "We better send Theo and Kel away. I have a feeling we're going to be back here a while."

"By all means, don't let me stop you," someone calls out sarcastically.

Adam and I turn around at the same time to find the very last person we'd *ever* expect to see standing in our new patio doorway.

It's almost impossible not to acknowledge that Adam's brother, Erik, is just as hot as my boyfriend. Their square faces have the same exact shape and angles in addition to their eyes being nearly the same beautiful shade of blue. Even their hair is styled in a similarly precarious way. Last time I met Erik, I wondered if I'd be able to tell the difference between them in the dark, aside from Adam's surgery scars marring his otherwise smooth stomach.

But Erik's abrasive personality makes him a thousand times less charming. He reminds me of one of those preppy assholes in 80s movies with his turquoise designer polo and striped khaki shorts. The arrogant smirk against his full lips is something

I've come to expect, even though we've only met once before. I've heard Adam call him a "prick" or "asshole" enough times to know he's a piece of work. Plus there were the inappropriate comments Erik made about me being too hot for Adam and how he'd be around if things didn't work out just seconds after we were first introduced. Needless to say, the brothers aren't close, and very rarely communicate.

I scramble to adjust my clothing and hair before Erik can make some kind of gross comment about what he caught us doing.

"What are *you* doing here?" Adam yells, pushing me off his lap. "How did you know where to find us?"

"I hired a PI," Erik says, shrugging one shoulder.

Adam bolts to his feet. "You *what*?"

With a jolly chuckle, Erik strolls toward us. "Holy shit. Back it down a notch, bro. I'm not *that* interested in finding you. Mom gave me your address. I was passing through on my way home and thought I'd stop by." He sinks into the other couch beside me, stretching his long arm across the back as he assesses our backyard. His musky cologne makes my eyes water. "Nice pad."

"Thanks." I reach up to pull Adam's hand until he's back down on the couch at my side. All the muscles in his upper body are tight with tension. I lace my fingers through his and squeeze. My gesture doesn't seem to take the edge off as I had hoped.

"Don't make yourself too comfortable," Adam tells his brother in a low, almost threatening voice. "Next time you should considering calling before making a surprise visit."

Erik rolls his eyes with an arrogant flair. "I would if you actually gave me your number. I figured you would've reached out to me sooner, considering we're only living *minutes* from each other now."

Theo sticks his head out the patio door and nods at Adam. "Delivery truck is here. They need your signature." His expression changes when he tips his head at Erik. "Hope it's okay that I sent him back. You didn't mention you had a brother, but I figured there's no way he's lying since the two of you could pass as twins."

"I'm not exactly his favorite person," Erik replies smartly, a tight smirk curling his lips.

Adam turns to kiss my cheek. "I'll be back in a minute." When he stands, he passes a poisonous look to his brother. "Be nice to her. I mean it."

"I'll be a perfect gentleman," Erik insists, crossing his legs. He throws me a sickening wink as Adam joins Theo in the doorway. Once they're out of sight, Erik leans in closer, his eyes narrowed. "It seems you have my brother whipped. He nearly blew his entire inheritance on this place. My parents don't seem too concerned, but they're idiots. Give me one good reason I shouldn't think my big brother has snagged himself a little gold-digger."

My jaw drops. I figured his rude side would rear its ugly head eventually, but hitting me with a 2 x 4 would come as less of a surprise. "I...are you high?" When his suspicious gaze doesn't change, I cross my arms. "I *seriously* can't believe you just said that. You don't know a thing about me. And whatever Adam chooses to do with his inheritance isn't any of your business."

A low chuckle rumbles in his throat. "So you're not going to deny it, then?"

Both flustered and appalled, I bring my hands up to cover my face and moan. Just when it feels as if things couldn't possibly become any more awkward, Kelly comes skipping out to join us. "Jewels, what'd you think? Isn't this fucking amazing?"

"*Hello, beautiful,*" Erik sings, popping to his feet. He offers his hand to her, using a sudden charm that makes him almost appear civil. "And you are?"

She takes his hand with a suspicious gaze. "I'm Kelly, and *you* must be mistaking me for someone who is easily charmed."

I stand at his side with a wide-eyed stare, hoping to pass a silent message. "He's *Adam's brother, Erik.*"

Kelly's eyes also burst wide when she understands. "*Oh!* The infamous brother. *Right.*" She drops his hand like a hot potato. "What are you doing here? I thought you and Adam weren't simpatico."

"He's just leaving," I say, crossing my arms.

"Do you live in the city?" Erik asks Kelly, unfazed by my blatant hint. "We should really meet for drinks sometime."

Kelly runs her fingers along the torn hem of her shorts, suddenly looking peaked. "Actually, I..." Her voice trails off and she wets her lips, glancing back at me, her brown eyes perplexed.

I know my best friend's mannerisms better than my own. There's something she's holding back because she knows it will upset me. I'm wrecked with guilt. She's had to walk on eggshells ever since my high school sweetheart was killed in Afghanistan last year, sending me into a deep depression. Before I met Adam, my life was a total mess. Kelly was always there to pick up the pieces.

"Kel, stoping making that face. What's going on?"

"Shit. I've been meaning to tell you since I got here, I just haven't found the right time, if there even *is* such a thing." She lowers her head like a scolded puppy. "I bought a one way ticket here. I'm staying indefinitely." Her jittery hands raise to the sky, and she smiles in mock enthusiasm. "Surprise."

Chapter One

DECIDING to drop my life in Wisconsin and move all the way out to New York City was an extremely rash decision—probably ranks up there as one of the dumbest ideas of all time considering I have no real *plan* now that I've arrived. I mean, I haven't even *been* to New York before now. I don't know that I would've ever pictured myself living in such a colossal place. Still, the decision to come here came at me with such blinding clarity that I threw hardly enough of my belongings into a suitcase to last me a week, let alone however long I end up staying.

The idea first popped into my head when Jewels told me she was moving to the city with Adam. She made New York sound so damn exciting. Of course it started out as a thing of grotesque jealousy—the type that a girl would never dare admit to her bestie —but after I put some thought into it, I decided moving away was the best way to erase my foolish past and start fresh. I knew it would be incredibly exciting, too.

Spending the first two months of summer working alongside my annoying, nosy, and sometimes pretentious four sisters just solidified the fact that I needed to get the hell away from Wisconsin. I booked the ticket online before I had time to change my mind.

Jewels stands next to Adam's smoking-hot brother, her jaw literally dropped, pale blue eyes frozen on me. As much as I wanted to share my news much earlier, I was afraid of how she would react to my poorly executed decision. What if she sees me as a leech for deciding to follow her across the country? In hindsight it seems I *did* latch onto her dream in an attempt to find the kind of happiness she found with Adam. What if I'm just too much of a coward to devise a dream of my own?

I grab my friend's arms. *"Jewels,* you're freaking me out. Surely there must be *something* you want to say to me."

"So I guess you *are* going to be living around here," Erik says with a sly smile. "That's the best news I've heard in, well, *forever.*"

Looking away from Jewels, I meet his intimate gaze and suddenly feel like sex on a stick despite the fact that my hair is a mess and I'm all sweaty.

Erik is undeniably sexy—even more so than his

reserved big brother. He's the type who defines the very definition of a "pretty boy": the type you'd expect to rule at a fraternity house. Long eyelashes, high cheek bones, pouting lips, eyes that make you forget anything else exists. I can just about imagine what he can do with his full set of lips. Or his long fingers that look as if they've had a recent manicure. A hot guy *and* a full bank account? Puh-lease.

Jewels warned me he's trouble, but I'm a firm believer that sometimes a girl needs a bad guy in her life to show her a good time. Then I remember that I resolved to come here to change my ways and let out a frustrated sigh.

Jewels finally snaps from her trance to gather her thick blond hair behind her head. "Erik, could you give us a minute? Better yet, maybe you should leave before I tell your brother what you just said to me. And quit leering at my friend. She's not interested."

Erik replies with an arrogant hum. "I didn't hear *your friend* protesting."

I somehow manage to press my lips together and flash him a stiff smile before I say something that would piss Jewels off further. She's obviously irritated by her boyfriend's brother, and I'm not going to push the issue. I stand tall, trying to appear assertive even though I only have so much restraint when it comes to incredibly good looking guys. "What she said."

Erik turns to leave, flashing Jewels a darker look. "I'll be back another time."

Parts of me throb excitedly with his words—the parts that always seem to take precedence over whatever rational thoughts may be milling around in my head. The guy may be totally wrong for me, and it would probably put a ginormous wedge between me and my bestie if I were to actively pursue him, but *damn* I bet he's a tiger in the bedroom.

Once we're left alone, Jewels flashes me what I affectionately call her "motherly" gaze. Her blond eyebrows furrow with worry, her lips turn down at the edges. I've always pictured her becoming a school teacher despite her resolve to stay far away from little kids. "Seriously, that guy is trouble. Don't even *think* about hooking up with him."

Irritation stirs in my gut. "Wait. You're just going to assume that I want to hook up with him? Could you maybe give me a *little* credit?"

She waves her hands through the air like a madwoman. "Can we focus on the fact that you just told me you're *staying* in New York? How? Where? When did you decide this? Why didn't you tell me sooner? Does this have anything to do with why you just randomly quit Facebook?"

"Sure. You like it when *Adam* surprises you. Why can't I pull the same shit?" I take a deep breath and wander over to one of the new outdoor couches, sinking into the plush cushion. "Are you mad?"

Jewels plops down at my side, slapping a hand on my bare leg. "Are you kidding? I love it that you're going to be here with me! I just wasn't expecting it. You're seriously *moving* here?"

"*Here* as in your backyard? That would be a little awkward, don't you think?" When she doesn't smile, I roll my eyes and let out a low grumble. "A lot of shit happened this summer while you were away. I wanted to tell you everything sooner, but you had your own issues to wade through. It just never seemed like the right time." I feel a sharp sting behind my eyes and quickly push it back down. I'm not a crier. Crying is a sign of weakness, and I'm Kelly Fucking Cavenaugh.

Jewels takes one of my hands in both of hers. "God, I'm so sorry. *You're* always there when I need *you*. Whatever it is, I want to know. I want to return the ten thousand favors I owe you from all the times you've scraped me off the ground."

"There's no reason for you to apologize. I'm pretty sure getting your boyfriend to agree to a life saving surgery trumps my petty drama."

"It can't be *petty* if it made you want to permanently leave Wisconsin." She draws me in with one of her pleading looks. "C'mon. I want to know what happened."

My stomach becomes a mess of nerves. "Shouldn't we be helping the guys carry stuff in?"

"Theo and James can get most of it. It's not like we have a lot of things."

Blowing out a long, stuttering breath, I look to the patio doors. Friends and family back home are the only ones who know the whole story, and I haven't had to tell anyone else before now. "Do you have any beer, or wine, or anything that will make this process less painful?"

Jewels slumps in the couch. "Shit, that bad?"

"Two bottles of wine should do the trick."

With a bright smile, she sits taller. "Wait, I have a bottle of champagne I was going to drink tonight once we're moved in. Since Adam isn't really supposed to drink with me anyway, I may as well share it with you instead of drinking alone." She leans in to kiss my cheek. "Stay here. I'll be right back."

I lift my hands up, smirking. "I *literally* have absolutely *nowhere else* to go."

As I watch her disappear inside, I let my shoulders fall, ready to drop the façade I've worked so hard to keep the past few days, and finally let myself fall apart. The brutal look of disappointment in my dad's eyes and the anguished cries of my mom are still too raw. They settle in the pit of my stomach like a ball made of concrete. I made the right decision to come out here indefinitely. A fresh start is exactly what I need.

"Taking a break already?" Theo asks from the doorway. "Afraid to break a sweat, Cavenaugh?"

Surprised by his sudden presence, I let out a quiet gasp. His dark, deeply set eyebrows looming over his hazel eyes always have a way of turning my insides to pudding. I'm not usually one to fall for a guy with a military-like haircut, and I really don't get why Theo keeps it up considering he's moved on from the Marines to the entertainment world. Still his sculpted mouth and sharp jaw highlighting his square face makes the look actually rather fitting.

When I saw him standing on the steps to the brownstone my first day in the city, I thought Jewels and Adam had changed their mind about hiring a moving company, because he's so well built that I'm sure he could move a couch with the strength of his pinky. Then I realized he's the guy I'd seen in pictures with Jewels and Adam from their trip to New York at the beginning of summer. The fact that he can volley back and forth with me without batting his dark eyelashes makes him even hotter. I've always considered it to be a good sign of character when a guy can keep up with my sarcasm.

I sigh under my breath. Why is my best friend always surrounded by crazy hot guys? I mean, I get that she's a natural knockout, and she's fun to hang around because she's funny and sincerely cares about her friends. I get that hot guys are naturally drawn to her, but the sight of Theo's bulging muscular arms does things to my sexual desires that should be considered indecent in public. Jewels told me she once "caught" him naked, and said that his entire body could be declared a national treasure. I lick my lips when I try to picture whatever it was that she saw.

Theo regards me with the same hot desire, one of his dark eyebrows raised. "You okay? You need...something?"

Although we've been alone for a minute or two before, I'm hyper-aware that we're standing in the romantic backyard Adam created for Jewels. The *private*, romantic backyard where anything could happen, and the neighbors wouldn't see. Feeling an excited pang down below, I shift my legs.

Theo's exactly the kind of guy I should be avoiding: the self-absorbed type who works out for show, and goes through women the way I once went through men—enjoy and discard. The last time I fell for someone like him, it started the downward spiral that landed me here.

I'm not here to have sex. I'm not here to have sex. I'm not here to have sex.

Yeah, right. No matter how many times I chant the mantra, I can't shake the image of mounting the insanely hot, former soldier-turned-television producer. The Marine Corps symbol tattooed on his calf muscle makes me wonder if there are more tattoos on his body that I could explore. With my tongue.

"Don't you have some cars to bench or something?" I ask, irritated by his relentless ability to turn me on.

He grins, his eyes smoldering. "Sweetheart, I could bench *you* if you want."

I lick my lips again, feeling the onset of a panic attack. This is new, incredibly dangerous territory. I'm well accustomed to guys wanting to get it on with me, even some who were as delicious as Theo, but those days are over. So how in the *fuck* do I say no to an offer like that?

"What makes you think I'd be interested in such a thing?" I retort, my voice sounding the exact opposite of confident.

Theo strides across the patio toward me, his grin growing wider. My eyes flicker down to his shorts to discover his grin isn't the only thing enlarged. "Because I see the way your body responds to mine." He stops, tilting my chin up with his sausage-like finger. My skin flushes expectantly with his touch. "And I see the way those gorgeous brown eyes size me up."

"There's an awful lot of you to...*size*." I attempt to swallow, but fail miserable. It feels as if a bonfire has been set inside of me. Holy shit, I want to do things to this hottie that would make my married sister flush.

His thumb brushes along my lower lip. "What do you say you and I make a little magic?" I close my eyes, unable to stop myself from responding to his touch. "How many days do we have before you leave the city?"

With his last question, my eyes pop open. Maybe I've become über sensitive with all that's happened in my past and Jewels's recent assumption that I wanted to hook up with Erik, but since Theo thinks I'm about to leave, and only wants a one-time fling suddenly makes me feel dirty and disposable.

I lean away like I've been backhanded. "What makes you assume I'd want to 'make magic' with you?"

"I'm sorry, I thought that's what we were hinting at here." He blinks several times, appearing blown away by my question. "And Jewels said—"

"Fuck what Jewels said!" I spring to my feet and dart to the patio door, struggling to find my breath. I can't pretend it doesn't hurt that my best friend would sell me out like that. I throw Theo a resentful look over my shoulder. "And you can forget it, because I'm not going to *fuck* you!"

"Wait a minute," Theo calls after me. "That's not—"

I move past Jewels and Adam who are busy directing the movers where to put the new furniture. Jewels has the bottle of champagne in her hand, but she doesn't seem to notice me as I sneak past the living room. I grab my purse off a moving box in the entryway and slip out the front door.

My mind's racing as I dart inside the tavern at the end of the block. The dark quiet of the place offers exactly the kind of refuge I need to clear my head, and a good dose of alcohol will help calm me down.

After all I've done for Jewels, all the times I picked her up when she fell down, all the times I let her cry on my shoulder, she had the nerve to tell Theo I was good to go for a one-night stand? The sting of betrayal swells inside of me, festering into a deep rage.

I guess it really shouldn't come as a surprise. I've spent a lifetime being less than stellar in the eyes of those I love. Of the five daughters my parents raised, I was their biggest disappointment. The first couple years of high school I maintained a pretty decent GPA like the rest of them, but I wasn't president of the debate team like Megan, or a starter for the basketball team like Sarah. I didn't place as a runner-up for junior beauty pageants like Glori, or sweep state records for hurdles in track and field like Ella.

It was always challenging to get past the fact that I was unaccomplished in my parents' eyes. As the youngest, my far less notable achievements were swept under the rug to make way for my far more gifted sisters. By my senior year, I became more concerned with locating the next big party, and setting my sights on the biggest hottie of the bunch to become my latest conquest. I was obsessed with the idea of finding someone who would treat me special, burning through guy after guy and never really having a boyfriend.

Because my grades took a considerable dive, my chances of being accepted to some of the most prestigious colleges in the country that I once had my sights set on were shattered. By that point, however, I really didn't give a shit.

I wish I could still say I didn't give a shit, but the way my parents and everyone else sees me now really stings.

"What'll ya have?" a short redhead asks from behind the bar as I settle into one of the dark green stools. She's exceptionally spindly with bright green eyes set close together, and smiles tightly like she knows it's the only way she'll score any tips.

I pull out my wallet and flash my ID. "Whiskey sour. Better yet, just Jameson on the rocks. Make it a double."

I hear a low snicker behind me. Rather suddenly, Adam's brother slips onto the stool at my side, his baby blues flashing down to where my shirt dips low. "I would've pictured you as a daiquiri kind of girl."

Suddenly I wish I would've taken my sister, Ella, up on the can of mace she offered to send along. I tend to be a magnet for douchebags, and apparently Erik is no exception, even if he *is* infuriatingly attractive. "When you suggested we get together for drinks *sometime*, I never would've guessed that was code for *ten minutes*. Are you stalking me?"

"Last I checked, bars are considered a public domain." He peers into the glass of clear liquid in his hands, snorting. "And I needed a drink, apparently just like you."

Narrowing my eyes, I whisper, "Aren't you, like, eighteen or something?"

He leans in close, his warm breath tickling my neck. "Twenty in a few months, actually. And newsflash, it doesn't take much to get your hands on a legit ID. I would even venture to guess you had one not too long ago."

I lean away, clearing my throat. "I picture someone of your *stature* having a little higher standards than this place." When the bartender sets a glass in front of me, I add, "No offense."

She shrugs. "I only work here. That'll be ten dollars."

"For this?" I ask, gesturing to the small tumbler glass.

"Welcome to New York," Erik tells me, tossing her a crisp $100 bill. "I've got this."

"Thanks, I guess," I mutter before knocking the drink back in a series of large gulps. Shivering, I slam the glass back on the worn wooden bar and nod at the bartender. "I'll take another, please."

Erik chuckles. "Slow down there, Lohan. Whatever got your *panties* in a bundle isn't going to be solved with you stumbling your way around the city."

I don't miss the heavy sexual undertone he uses for the word "panties." Recoiling, I curl my lip. "Back off. Just because you bought me a drink does *not* mean you can fantasize about my panties." The whiskey burns its way down into my stomach, reminding me it's nearing lunchtime and I have yet to eat today. At this rate I'll be drunk in no time.

"That's rather presumptuous of you. Do I look like the kind of guy who would indulge in sexual fantasies?" He watches me with a rather obnoxious smirk that, for some reason, wedges its way beneath my skin.

My phone buzzes with a string of texts from Jewels asking where I went. Silencing it, I motion for the bartender to refill my glass. "All I know is the way you were trying to get a look at my tits just now, it's safe to assume you're not gay."

"That automatically means I fantasize about you naked?"

"I thought we were talking about my panties." I set a $20 bill on the bar before turning to him.

"Look. I'm not interested in hooking up with you. So you can stop this flirting thing before you exhaust yourself."

With a delightful grin, he runs his fingertips across my arm, bringing goosebumps the the surface of my skin. "I love an assertive woman. They're usually capable of some mind blowing skills in the bedroom."

"You can forget it. I'm not going to start messing around with someone my best friend clearly doesn't approve of."

I down the next double shot of whiskey and bring it back down on the bar, welcoming the glowing burn that settles in my bones. Drinking when I can't deal with my emotional turmoil is never a good idea as it almost always leads to more problems, but I need to quiet the delusional part of me that believes I deserve to be treated this way.

I exhale slowly and nod to the bartender. "Another."

"She's had enough," Erik tells her, holding his hand out. The woman rolls her eyes and leaves us to wait on an old man a few stools down.

"*Excuse* me? What are you, *my fucking dad*?" I ask, hearing the subtle slur to my words. "You don't even know me!"

"I may not know you, but I know you're a naive girl from the midwest with an ax to grind over something that really pissed you off, and I'm not going to let you get loaded and wander around the city all alone." He grins into his glass of alcohol. "'Cause I'd *really* like to join you if that is, in fact, your plan." He takes a long drink before setting the glass down to stare at me.

The hot fire blazing between us is impossible to ignore. I want to wrap my fingers in his thick hair, and forget whatever Theo and Jewels think of me. The alcohol filling my blood stream only intensifies my desire to be with him.

My phone bursts out with Sir-Mix-a-Lot's errant ramblings. It's incredibly obnoxious in the otherwise relaxed bar, and quite frankly, embarrassing. Jewels thought she was *so* clever when she changed my ringtone the night before. Grumbling to myself, I silence it.

Erick chuckles, his eyebrows raised. "Avoiding someone?"

I know without looking that it's Jewels, angry that I'm ignoring her texts. Once she knows the truth, she'll be eager to lecture me on how immature I'm acting, and demand I come back. "Fuck this," I mutter under my breath. I turn to Erik and touch his taut thigh. "You win. Let's blow out of here."

Erik calls Adam from the private car to let them know we're together and that I need some time to cool off. Jewels must ask him what exactly I need to "cool off" about, because he tells her, "It's none of my business. I'll let her explain when she returns."

Knowing how pissed and confused Jewels will be to hear I'm randomly keeping Erik's company after the warning she tried to pass along, I feel a small wave of satisfaction. For all I care she can think we're having wild sex back at his place. It sounds like that's exactly the kind of thing she expects of me anyway.

I do what I can with my hair, trying to smooth it out before we head into a swanky sports bar in the heart of Manhattan. An entire soccer team from Brazil dominates the place, telling stories of seeing the city for the first time in broken English. Somehow I'm drawn into their circle and become an active part of their conversation. They're highly entertaining, easily taking my mind off Theo and Jewels. For a short time I'm actually able to pretend my life isn't one big catastrophe.

The players buy me and Erik round after round, even insisting that we take a few shots with them. A couple of them try to hit on me, wrapping their arms around my waist and pulling me closer, but I just laugh it off and playfully push them away. Erik is reserved around the players, saying very little and watching on with his smug smirk. This goes on for hours before the players decide to head back to their hotel.

As we step outside of the bar, I wait for Erik to

announce our next move. The drinks have loosened him up considerably, making his comments far less snide. He looks carefree and even somewhat alluring as his hair blows around in the warm breeze.

He leans dangerously close, filling my lungs with his musky scent. "It's time we soak up all this booze. Let's go. I'm buying you lunch."

My phone buzzes on vibrate for the hundredth time since we left. Though I'm well on my way to a state of inebriation and Erik's enticing smell makes me suddenly want him in a urgent way, I'm blindsided with how immature and irresponsible it was to storm away without giving Jewels any explanation. As infamous as I've become for running from my problems, I promised Jewels that I'd help her move, yet here I am, getting blitzed with one of the few people in this world she can't stand.

"Thanks, but I think I should go back and face the firing squad."

Erik brushes his index finger along my forearm. "What you *should* do is get some food in your stomach. We're both going to be in deep shit if I bring you back like this."

I briefly gaze at this mysterious man, wondering if there could possibly be someone sweet deep down, or if he really is the total asshole he's been labeled as. Then I realize I'm judging him based on what other people have told me, which is basically the story of my life. What if he's just looking for someone to come along and give him a chance?

"Fine," I finally give in. "But only because I'd hate to be a witness to your murder. Not that I care, I just hate the sight of blood and guts."

With an amused smile, Erik takes my hand.

Chapter Two

HALF of the dozen round tables adorned in red and white checked tablecloths are filled with patrons, all of them appearing to be couples. Soft Italian music plays over hidden speakers, and despite it being bright outside, the heavy curtains pulled over the restaurant's two windows make the perfect atmosphere for the glow of candles at each table. The smell of pasta gets my stomach rumbling beneath the gallon of alcohol sloshing around each time I move.

A pretty, petite waitress wearing black and white attire approaches our table once we've settled and sets small plastic menus in front of each of us. "Hi, there. I'm Lucinda and I'll be your server today. Can I start you with something to drink?"

"Two waters," Erik tells her with a nod.

"And a cup of black coffee," I add.

Erik nods with approval. "Make that two."

After she leaves us, I shut my eyes and use the tabletop to steady myself. Everything has taken on a slight sway as the alcohol consumes my bloodstream. I'm a seasoned drinker by all accounts, but it's embarrassing how I allowed myself to become this hammered with a group of strangers. When I take a moment to really think about it, everything about my actions today have been less than stellar. I groan under my breath.

"Hey," Erik says. "Are you going to hurl, or what?"

I open one eye. "My life's a mess," I blurt, feeling a wave of tears brewing deep down. As if the day isn't humiliating enough, it appears I'm going to break down in the middle of a restaurant. I press on my eyes, waiting for the ridiculous feeling to pass.

"I refuse to believe someone who looks like they'd be their daddy's little princess could have it that bad. I challenge you to prove your life is worse than anyone else's."

"I assure you, I'm not my father's princess. Quite the opposite, actually." Taking a long, steadying breath, I open my eyes. "I decided to move out here on a whim with virtually *no* plan. No place to live, no job, no nothing. I don't even know if I'll even get to finish school." I push my hair behind my ears, moaning. "By the end of the week, I'll be sleeping in Central Park with newspapers for a blanket."

He chuckles, though the sound of it comes out as being humorless. "You really *are* trying to escape a rough past."

"Something like that."

"What were you so fired up about when I found you trying to drown your sorrows?"

A warm flush covers my face. I'm not going to delve into my sexual history with him or go in to detail of Theo's proposal. "Long story. Jewels said something that really pissed me off."

"Why doesn't that surprise me?"

I cross my arms and glare back at him. I'm not going to let anyone speak ill of my bestie, even if I *am* still incredibly ticked at her. "Jewels told me you accused her of going after Adam for his money."

"What? Like it's not true?" He lifts an eyebrow, the arrogant smile on his lips growing.

"Jesus, of course not!" I bounce forward on my seat with a flash of white-hot anger and set my hands on the table. "Your brother nearly broke her heart when he told her he wasn't going to have the transplant, and her heart was pretty messed up to begin with! And Adam bought that place as a surprise for her birthday! She didn't even *know* about his inheritance!"

I look around the restaurant, ready to crawl under the table when I realize I've drawn the attention of everyone. I take a minute to compose myself before leaning close to Erik. "You should spend time with them before you judge her like that," I say in a low voice. "They're both so crazy in love that it's literally nauseating."

"Okay," he says with a chuckle. "I get the idea. No need to be so sensitive."

The waitress sets our steaming cups of coffee in front of us. "Ready to order?"

"We'll take two plates of your four cheese ravioli," Erik tells her, gathering the plastic menus. When I frown, he laughs. "You don't like ravioli?"

"I *am* capable of reading a menu."

Erik hands the menus to the waitress, dismissing her with, "Thank you."

She flashes us both a polite but stiff smile before scattering away, most likely wondering if we're on a date from hell.

Setting his chin on his fist, Erik regards me with sparkling eyes. "So maybe your friend isn't the gold digger I assumed. I guess I'll have to take your word for it."

"Yeah, you most definitely will."

"So you're homeless and broke in the big city." His cocky smirk makes a comeback. "Fortunately, you can't throw a designer heel in New York without finding *some* kind of job, even if it's only temporary and pays shit."

"I never said I was broke." I have a good-sized

savings for the apartment Jewels and I were going to rent in La Crosse this fall. "Being *homeless* is my biggest worry at the moment. I know housing out here can't be cheap, and I don't even know where to begin looking."

For a minute he just stares at me, his face drawn into a serious, thoughtful expression. "You could stay in my spare bedroom."

"*What?*" I half-yell. "Forget it! That's a *terrible* idea."

"Why? Just because my misguided brother says I'm a jerk? I'm not offering for you to move in with me indefinitely, just until you find a job and a more permanent arrangement. Besides, I need someone to clean the place. My staff recently quit on me, and it's always a challenge to find someone I feel that I can trust. We could take it out in trade."

I inwardly balk at the idea of cleaning someone's apartment. Most guys I know are complete pigs, especially if they're living alone. And I haven't exactly done a whole lot of cleaning in my lifetime. What makes him think I'd even agree to do such a thing? Do I even want to know why his "staff" quit?

Although Adam and Jewels have a spare room, asking to stay with them would feel like a complete invasion. They're moving in together for the first time. They're still fresh into their relationship and have *a lot* of sex. Like all the time. I'm not convinced that I could take all the flirty looks and perversion on a daily basis.

"Well?" Erik asks, frowning.

"I'm thinking." I press at my temples.

Am I that desperate to take him up on such an offer? I would have more than enough money to stay in a hotel for a week or two, although the thought seems incredibly lonely, and it seems like a waste of cash. Erik has lived out here for a year and would be able to teach me the ins and outs of city life. But am I really ready to live with someone who has such a horrid reputation? Then again, I remind myself of the unfair way Jewels sees me.

I have to give him a chance.

I blow out a long breath. "I'd have to talk it over with Jewels and Adam before making any kind of a decision."

A sudden light fills Erik's eyes. "I knew you couldn't resist me."

"Dude, I'm not saying yes." I cross my arms over my chest, frowning. "I could be a crazy bitch for all you know."

He raises his eyebrows as he takes a sip of his coffee. "And for all *you* know, that's exactly my type."

"Listen," I say, leaning in once again, my expression hard. "*If* I'm insane enough to take you up on your offer, it would only be with the understanding that *nothing* will ever happen between the two of us."

I wag my finger between us. "You and me, it ain't gonna happen. Does the offer still stand?"

For the first time since we met a few hours ago, a full smile graces his lips, popping a small dimple into his cheek. "Whatever you say."

All at once I understand how frustrated Jewels must've felt when Adam first insisted that they be nothing more than friends. The Murphy boys seem to have a way with women. So why the hell do I have to open my big mouth and insist on a platonic relationship?

The moving van is gone when we return to Jewels and Adam's brownstone. Guilt rushes through me with the force of a speeding train. I grip the door handle, trying to control my breathing. One thing's for sure: I'm getting pretty skilled at fucking things up.

"If I came with you, they could aim all their hateful energy at me," Erik offers.

"Thanks, but that sounds like a really shitty idea." I turn to study him, realizing how pitiful I must seem to this rich kid who rides around the big city in a private car, wearing designer clothes. "Jewels was planning to have me stay for a few days while I was in town. If I decide to take you up on your offer after that, I'll call."

For a moment I consider leaning in to kiss his

cheek to thank him for his company, but don't want to give him the wrong idea. Better yet, I don't want to give myself the luxury of touching him in an intimate way. There's no promise I could stop with an innocent kiss. I offer him a sincere smile instead. "Thanks, for lunch and...everything."

"I hope to see more of you," he tells me. From the strange pitch to his voice and the lost look behind his gaze, I suddenly get a glimpse behind the hard shell Adam and Jewels don't seem to have broken through.

Erik Murphy is lonely.

I point my finger at him, squinting. "As *friends*."

He lets out a low laugh. "You're filled with never-ending assumptions."

I leave the car and enter the code on the keypad to the brownstone, strolling in to find Jewels perched on the edge of the new living room couch, her expression sour as she fidgets with her cell phone. Adam sits behind her with a stoic look, rubbing circles into her back. My heart sinks with the sight of my friends looking so despondent because of something asinine I did. I swear under my breath.

Jewels jumps to her feet when she sees me, her eyes wide, mouth tight. "What the *fuck*? You've been with *Erik* this whole time? How did you even find him? Do you know how worried I've been? What were you *thinking*?"

"I'm sorry," I say, on the verge of tears. It seems

one way or another, today will be the day I break down and sob like a baby. "It's a long story. But I know it was shitty of me to take off without saying anything."

"Damn right it was!" she says, bounding forward to wrap me in her arms. "I was so worried! At one point I thought maybe Erik actually kidnapped you! Why do you always have to disappear on me like that?"

I squeeze her tightly, glancing at Adam over her shoulder. "Can you give us a minute?"

He throws me a small smile nearly identical to the one Erik kept flashing over lunch. "Sure. I'll be upstairs unpacking." He stands to kiss Jewels on the temple, closing his eyes like he's passing all his love to her through his lips. He nudges my arm before leaving the room. Why can't I find a guy like that who's head over heels for me?

Jewels takes me by the hand to sit on the couch. She's starting to look less relieved, and more angry. "What's going on in that dimwitted head of yours?"

"Do you think I'm a slut?" I blurt, swallowing the little bit of pride I have left.

Her eyebrows draw together. "*What*? Shit, of course not! Where did that come from? Why would you say that?"

"Your buddy Theo hit on me after Erik left. He made it sound like you told him I was okay with a one night stand." I study her expression, trying to gauge her true reaction. Jewels is one to often wear her emotions on the outside, and it never takes much to figure out what's going on inside her head.

She looks confounded. "Oh my god, no way! The only thing I told him is that I would never forgive him if he broke your heart. I would never say *anything* like that to *anyone* about you! Did he *say* that?"

"Not in so many words."

"There was obviously some kind of misunderstanding going on somewhere. Theo's not like that. And I seriously can't believe you think I'd say something that shitty about you." Her lips twitch with a small smile. "Can you *please* do me a favor next time and *ask* me straight up what's going on instead of running away? You've been an amazing friend to me with all the shit I've dealt with the past couple of years. I really hope you know just how much that means. I want to be here for *you*, Kel, whatever that entails. Talking things out, giving you a place to crash until you get on your feet, you name it."

Erik's offer rises to the surface of my thoughts. It's on the tip of my tongue, but yet I don't feel ready to drop such a bomb on Jewels. Not now. Maybe I can subtly get her to invite him over, let her get to know him a little better first.

I move in to hug Jewels tightly. "You're right. I'm sorry. I should've known better. I don't know what I was thinking."

"I love you, Kel," she says into my ear. "You ever think that ill of me again and I'll kick your ass."

A loud laugh bursts from me. "I love you, too."

The next morning I wake to someone patting my cheek. Jewels stands over me in a green polo shirt and a matching baseball cap. It's so unlike my care-free, concert t-shirt wearing friend that I giggle-snort. And I almost never "giggle," so the strange noise surprises us both. "Are you here to deliver a package?"

"Stop," she whines, shoving my shoulder. "It's hard enough to put this on the way it is. I don't need you to remind me how ridiculous I look. I'd try to find somewhere else to work where I didn't have to dress like a baseball player if there was something better just as close."

I try to straighten my grin. "It's not ridiculous."

"Yeah, whatever." Rolling her eyes, she takes a minute to adjust her ponytail through the hole in her hat. "I just wanted to let you know Adam has a doctor's appointment later this morning, and I have to work until three. I asked my friend, Chloe, to show you around the city. She's a hoot—you guys will get along really well. She'll be by around ten to pick you up."

I prop myself up on my elbow. I'm all for adventures with new friends, but I still feel the need to make it up to Jewels for being such an ass the day before. "Wouldn't you rather I stay here and unpack?"

"I want to help so I know where everything is. Besides, I've seen your idea of unpacking. I *still* can't find my favorite DVD from freshman year."

"Whatever, you big baby. You probably loaned it out to someone and forgot."

"Right. Just like you decided you loaned your straightener to someone, you just don't know who." She starts for the door. "Chloe's lived here most her life, so she said she's up for showing you whatever you want. It'll be good for you to go around by foot and get a feel for the city, figure out where everything is. I'll see you later this afternoon. Adam and I plan to take you somewhere fun for supper. Have fun today!"

With a comical flick of her baseball hat, she's gone.

I grab my phone off the nightstand to see a missed call from Erik late in the night, as well as a text from a few minutes ago that simply reads:

Well?

I'm grinning like an idiot when I type back:

· · ·

I should probably see where I'd be agreeing to stay

Little bubbles appear instantly as he types a response. In less than a minute he sends me an address, then a separate message saying:

I'll be around most the day

I quickly map out the distance between the brownstone and his apartment. He lives on the north size of Central Park, which I'm guessing would make for an extremely long walk. The map shows a subway ride that would take about 27 minutes, but I'm not about to take my first ride solo.

Looks like I have a special request of where I want Chloe to take me.

After showering and changing into a strapless tank top and lacy jean shorts, I wander down to the kitchen where I find Adam cooking up a pan of eggs among the clutter of unpacked boxes. It's hard to look at him and not picture his little brother as the two of them look so much alike. When he's healthy, Adam works out at the gym at his doctor's recommendations. He's broader in the shoulders than his brother, and even more top-heavy. When I was hanging out with Erik, I decided he must be a runner as his muscles are lean rather than bulky. But both guys have incredibly perky butts, the kind that must be amazing to grab onto during wild sex.

When it dawns on me that I'm checking out my best friend's guy in *that way*, I clear my throat with a ridiculously high-pitched noise, ready to slap myself.

Adam turns around, grinning. "Mornin'," he greets me in a throaty voice. I find myself wondering if Erik's voice sounds that sexy early mornings. "Did you sleep okay? It took us a while to get used to all the noise outside."

"I slept great," I say, settling in one of the high-backed metal stools at the bar. "Didn't hear a thing."

"You should know Jewels felt like shit after what happened between you guys. She called Theo after you went to bed. Sounds like there were a lot of misunderstandings all around. Theo might come off a little strong, but he's like a big freaking teddy bear underneath and swears he didn't mean to offend you. He asked Jewels if she thought you'd let him take you out for dinner one night to make it up to you."

"Hmm," I say, tapping my chin. "I suppose I could be persuaded to forgive him with the promise of good food." I run my fingers through my long hair, sighing. "*Ugh*. I can't believe I created so much drama. It's going to take a lot of favors to make it up to Jewels."

"I wouldn't worry about it. This morning she was back to her old self. She couldn't stop talking about how excited she is that you're staying in the city." He uses a spatula to move the eggs onto a square, white plate, and hands it to me with a fork. "You know you're welcome to stay here as long as it takes."

"Thanks." I decide to leave my answer at that for now. I dig into the eggs as he sets a bottled water next to me, surprised when my taste-buds go wild. "Mmm, I didn't know you were such a good cook."

Chuckling, he dishes himself a plate. "My skills in the kitchen are limited, trust me."

"So...routine check with the doctor today, or is something wrong?"

"It's just a consultation. They're getting ready to hook me up to an insulin pump. It'll be better than daily injections. Nothing too major."

I throw him a frown as I twist the top off the water. "Want some company?"

He waves me off. "Nah, I'm good. I hear Chloe is going to show you around today. It'll be a good chance for you to check out some of the different neighborhoods and see where you think you might want to live."

"Erik told me he lives on the Upper West Side. Do you know much about it?"

Adam visibly stiffens with the mention of his

brother's name. "Jewels and I drove through there on a tour. It's a nice neighborhood with a lot of families. I think my parents said a lot of kids from Columbia rent apartments in the area." He wipes his fingers on a napkin, pretending to act all casual, but I can see the tension in his muscles. "What did you and Erik do yesterday anyway?"

"Hit a bar before we grabbed a late lunch." My face heats with a flush. What does he *think* we did? "He could tell I was upset over something, and offered his company. He was a lot nicer than Jewels has made him out to be."

"His *niceness* only goes so far. He was a real ass to me over the years. I'd be careful around him, Kel. He's only tolerable when he wants something from you."

What if the thing Erik wants is simply someone to be his friend? I can't erase the look of loneliness hidden behind his gaze when he dropped me off.

"How was he an ass to you?" I ask, crossing my arms over my chest. "You mean like normal brother stuff?"

A dark look flashes across his beautiful eyes. He looks away. "He's the type to go out of his way to make sure everyone is just as miserable as he is. I'm just saying you really don't want to waste your time hanging out with him." His gaze meets mine once again. "He'll end up hurting you one way or another."

It's clear Adam's only saying these things to protect me, but it suspiciously sounds like he's holding onto an old grudge that may never be settled. A deep resolve hinges against the pit of my stomach. Maybe it's time someone gave Erik the chance his brother refuses to give him.

Chapter Three

WHEN THE BUZZER sounds at the door ten minutes after ten, I find a small bundle of energy waiting on the other side, a cup of coffee in either hand, bright smile on her face. "Hey! You must be Kelly! I hope you like your coffee black." Her voice is kind of high with a slight east coast lilt. She hands off a cup to me before breezing past. "It's already fucking unbearable out there. Like walking on the surface of the sun. When it's this hot you have to drink your weight in water to keep from falling over, although I'm not always good at remembering that. Autumn can't come any sooner, I swear to god."

I close the door and turn to her. Chloe's incredibly petite and at least three inches shorter than I am with shoulder-length, jet black hair and bright blue highlights in her bangs that look stunning against her pixie-like face. Her dark brown eyes seem incredibly large in proportion to her smallish nose and pale pink mouth. She wears a drape-necked tank top with the name of a heavy metal band that puts her extensive tattoo work running up her right arm on display and shows off the top swell of her giant boobs that could very well topple her over.

There's a mischievous fire in her eyes, and the way she stands relaxed yet confident, it's obvious she's no pushover. Though I'm definitely a guys-only kind of girl, I find her incredibly attractive in the most adorable way. I seriously want to put her in my pocket.

Her heart-shaped lips quirk into a smile. "Jewels tells me you're looking to stay in the city for a while. You ready to get a tour of your new hometown? We don't have a *ton* of time to sightsee, and it's imperative we take a break from the heat every so often, but we'll work out another day to go again. You wanna start out with the Statue of Liberty and the touristy shit on the south end, or take the subway up to the Upper West side around Central Park and work our way down? Your call."

My ears perk with the mention of Central Park. "Upper West," I say quickly, afraid if I don't get my choice in now, she'll start to talk again.

"Works for me." she takes my untouched coffee and sets it next to hers on the counter. "Forget it. I don't know what in the hell I was thinking. It's too hot out for that shit. They're selling one dollar waters on every corner for tourists riding the double deckers. We'll grab a few of those. Let's head out. We'll get to know each other while we walk to the subway."

The minute we step outside, I realize Chloe wasn't being factious about the extreme weather. Just as the day before, the damp heat quickly soaks through my shirt and lines my forehead with perspiration. I can't get over how stifling the heat becomes inside the concrete jungle compared to back home where there are ample trees and open spaces for the air to escape.

Despite Chloe's legs being *inches* shorter than mine, she walks at a hurried, even pace. I have to nearly jog to keep up. "Where do you live?" I ask.

"Staten Island. The city's way too expensive for me. Jewels is lucky she found Adam or there's no way she could afford this neighborhood." With everything she says, she uses grand hand gestures. "These places run millions of dollars. I had a cousin who was a computer expert or some shit, and bought a smaller place a few blocks down for five mil. You don't live in a place like this without being incredibly wealthy."

We reach a crosswalk and stand behind the crowd waiting for the light to turn. Most people are looking down at their phones or casually speaking with their friends. A few in suits stand tall and appear anxious to get somewhere. I'm so busy studying the crowd that I hardly notice Chloe babbling on beside me.

"...street fair through the week if you want to stop by. Jewels tells me you've never been to the city before. Are we just scoping out the neighborhoods, or you interested in the sights, too? There's lots of time for that if you're sticking around, unless you're excited to see them, of course. I'm game for whatever shit you want."

I bite my lip as I look down at the incredibly energetic girl. She's friendly in a way that makes me want to trust her, and I'm dying to discuss Erik's offer with someone neutral. "So I know we just met and everything, but do you think you can keep a secret?"

She flutters her thick lashes that look to be the product of professional extensions. "Depends. If it involves something illegal, I don't even want to know." The crowd moves ahead and Chloe follows without missing a beat, even though she isn't watching where she's going. "There was this guy I used to date who told me about the time he robbed his uncle's store. I had to testify in court just because the asshole told me all about it. I don't do court. I've mostly been a good girl my whole life and can't take that kind of bullshit."

Laughing, I shake my head. "Nothing illegal, I swear. It's just...Adam's brother offered me a place to stay until I can get on my feet. He lives near Central

Park, and I was hoping to take a look at his apartment today. See if it's worth considering."

"Why's that a secret?" She glances over at me, narrowly escaping a collision with a little kid on a scooter. She pivots gracefully like she's avoided similar accidents a million times. "Unless he's offering it to you for sexual favors, I don't see a problem."

"Trust me, I made it crystal clear nothing would happen between us if I move in. He said I could live there in exchange for cleaning the place. It's only a secret because Adam and Jewels *hate* Erik for some unknown reason."

"So you're not planning to tell Jewels?" Chloe fidgets with the back of her hair. "I haven't known her very long, so I'm not sure how I feel about that. I mean, I can keep a secret, but if she pressures me to give her a no bullshit answer, no promises. If you decide to live with him, how are you going to hide something like that from your best friend?"

"I haven't thought that far ahead. I'd have to tell her eventually, I guess. It's just that I don't want to create any more waves between us after we had a stupid fight yesterday. And I haven't figured out what exactly they have against Erik. I only knew him a few hours before he volunteered his spare room to me. He seems to be a pretty decent guy. It's no different than considering an ad on craigslist for a roommate, right? Or do you think it's weird that I'm even debating this?"

"Weird? No. You're right. People put out ads for roommates in this city all the time. Fucking *risky*? Maybe. I mean, what do you really know about this guy? Is he rich and hot like his brother? It's understandable if that's the case, because who wouldn't be tempted by someone loaded who looks like that? Still, he could be a total whacko. What if he gets off on chopping people up and storing them in his freezer like that guy from your neck of the woods?"

"You mean Dahmer?" I ask, unable to suppress a smile. Chloe's bubbly personality is contagious, to say the least. I already love hanging out with her.

"You never know who's two cents short of a full buck. Good looking and well bred guy like that could just be looking for a way to project his mommy and daddy issues like those wealthy brothers in Beverly Hills who killed their parents. I've watched a lot of documentaries on serial killers. Started out as something I thought maybe I could go to school for, get a degree in criminology or whatever, but now it's just kind of a sick hobby. Most of them start out as normal people, like you and me. Just sayin'."

"Yeah, he's really hot and rich, but that's pretty much all I know about him. Jewels once mentioned he's pre-law, so there's that. At least he must be smart. Adam and Jewels offered me their spare room as long as it takes, but there are so many reasons it just doesn't feel right. They were really looking forward to having a place of their own together, and they're still in the highly physical stage of their relationship. I'd feel like some kind of creeper, knowing they have to be quiet on my account. You know?"

"Ugh, do I ever. I once had a roommate who was dating a stripper and they'd go at it, like, all hours of the day." She waves her hands in front of her like she's trying to erase the memory. "Drove me fucking *insane*. The guy was crazy hot, though, so I couldn't really blame her. She kicked him out after I accidentally walked in on them one time and he asked if I wanted to join in. Total sex addict. The stripper, not my roommate. She moved on to marry a broker and moved to Jersey to pop out a couple of kids."

I can't stop laughing under my breath at the way Chloe carries on. She continues chatting until we reach the subway station, only stopping long enough to show me how to purchase a pass and slide it through the turnstile. She directs me for a good five minutes on how not to advance through the turnstile before the green light signals my card has been read because she had a friend who once cracked a pelvic bone charging through, and how not to stand close to the subway cars because people have been pushed off the edge and died.

I only half listen to her as I'm more intrigued by a cute guy around my age playing Jack Johnson on an acoustic guitar a few yards away. He catches me staring and throws a playful wink.

As soon as the next car stops, we find an open seat across from a group of young boys who seem rather boisterous. The subway is everything I imagined it to be from watching movies. Fairly clean, minuscule to someone like me who's borderline claustrophobic, faintly smelling like pee and dirty feet, filled with a handful of people of different ages and races. Since I arrived in the city, I've had to remind myself on several occasions that not everyone speaks English. Coming from a small town with only a handful of minorities, it's going to take some getting used to.

Chloe stops talking long enough to look me in the eye. "Back to this Erik guy. Given that he's related to Adam, he can't be all that bad. You plannin' on giving him a chance even if it pisses Jewels off?"

"Depends. I was hoping you'd come with me to check out the place, see if you think it's worth the trouble."

"There's all kinds of real estate in Manhattan, which can be both good and a crock of shit. If you can find a decent place for little to no cost, consider yourself lucky. I'll definitely let you know what I think. By the time I take you back to Jewels's place, you'll know exactly what you plan to do."

Somehow, I don't doubt that, and I can't stop grinning the rest of the way.

The Upper West Side (or UWS as Chloe keeps calling it) turns out to be clean and even enchanting. A wide variety of shops and small eateries from all corners of the world pepper the retail sector. We're greeted on the sideway with smiles and head bobs, making for a real light, casual atmosphere. Once we get into the residential area filled with apartments, we're bombarded with kids playing in the street, running their bikes along the sidewalk, and even a group of little ones splashing through a fire hydrant. The neighborhood seems quite friendly in general.

"This is it," Chloe announces, pointing to a tall, tan brick building at the end of a quiet block. "No doubt about it, this boy of yours has serious cash flow. Now let's get your skinny ass up there so I can decide if he has the charm to go along with it."

I shoot Erik a text to let him know we've arrived. An older doorman who appears completely miserable in dress pants, a burgundy jacket, and hat, greets us with a bright smile despite the sweat covering his forehead. He doesn't hesitate to ring Erik right away, ushering us inside once we're given his approval.

Chloe and I both sigh happily when we're blasted with cold air. Tan marble covers the old-world lobby from floor to ceiling, the smells of fresh wax and disinfectant strong from a recent cleaning. We find a set of ornately decorated elevators and head up to Erik's floor. Chloe gives me a play-by-play of the quality of the place, from the antique chandeliers in the lobby to the old style of the slow-moving elevator, loosely estimating the building's value to be near a billion.

I'm too busy to really listen, instead psyching myself up for whatever we're about to find as we step out onto his floor. Erik's apartment is the last one at the end of the bright hallway. Smaller version of the chandeliers in the lobby light our path to his beige door marked with gold numbers. I suck in a deep breath and raise my hand to knock. The door swings open before I have a chance.

Erik stretches one long, muscular arm against the door frame with his other hand buried in the pocket of his cargo shorts. From the small preview of his smooth chest beneath his trendy, black button down, there's no doubt he's in excellent shape. He smells musky and fresh, as if he just stepped out of the shower. When I look into his intense blue eyes, the lust I keep denying myself stirs once again.

"Kelly?" he asks, smiling brightly despite the frown to his eyes. "Is that really you? I'm sorry, you look a bit different from the person I met yesterday. Did you do something with your hair?"

Yeah, so I guess I looked *that* bad while we were bar hopping. There's no chance in hell I'll traipse around New York like that again without even a stitch of makeup. I ignore his dig. "Erik, this is Chloe. She's a friend of Jewels's and volunteered to show me around today since Jewels had to work."

"Friends with Jewels?" Erik asks, quirking his brow her way. "You have my sympathies."

"I guess it really is true what they say," Chloe answers with a surprised look. "A person learns something every day. I never would've guessed you could afford a place like this doing stand up comedy. I had a friend who couldn't even buy his groceries off the shitty wages he earned performing in Times Square. You must draw a loyal following."

As Erik brays in a low laugh, I try to peer behind him. "Are you going to let me see this place of yours or what?"

He opens the door wide, the arrogant spark to his eyes flaring. "Come on in."

Chloe and I file in, barely making it before he closes the door behind us. I'm thrown off by the relaxed feel of the brightly lit loft apartment, and the pleasant aroma of vanilla hanging in the air. I suck in my breath with the sight of the giant arched windows framing a breathtaking view of Central Park and the skyscrapers beyond. There's a bachelor pad vibe from the dark leather furniture and black curtains, burnt brown brick walls, and sleek, worn wooden floors, yet it's still incredibly classy and upscale. The small kitchen opens into a slightly bigger living room where the couches gather around a large flat screen television mounted to the wall.

And just like that, I'm in love with the place.

"The bedrooms are back here," Erik tells us, swiftly moving to the right. We trail behind him. My heart skips excitedly against my ribs.

"Would you get a load of this freaking place?" Chloe says to me from the side of her mouth. "If it were me I'd move in so damn fast his head would spin. I'd *kill* for the chance to live in a place like this. And normally I'd say I mean that figuratively, but...*damn*."

I'm in so much awe I can't even form a complete thought to answer her. We reach a short hallway with three doorways, the first leading to a cramped bathroom. There's a glass door on the shower, showing two nozzles and a stone interior. The walls and floors are done in the same expensive-looking brown stone. The second door leads to a room that's very orderly and bare with a twin bed in the far corner, a nightstand at its side. A single window over my head lets in only a small amount of light.

Across the hallway, a four poster bed with smoky gray bedding and a sleek black dresser covered in personal items both appear small in comparison to the set of large windows exactly like those in the living room. Chloe and I stand sandwiched together, taking the rooms in with appreciation. The guest room, while pretty small, is cozy. I could easily see myself living there.

"That's what I'm offering," Erik says, jabbing his thumb at the spare room. "I'd expect you to keep the place clean at all times, especially your room. That means your bed always made, no *panties* on the floor, that kind of thing." Not surprisingly, he smirks with the mention of panties as if it's now our little inside joke. "Look, this is New York, and your chances of finding an affordable place within a few months is pretty slim. I'd be willing to let you stay as long as it takes *if* you follow my rules and keep the place presentable. I'm not going to live with a complete slob."

I cross my arms and cock my hip, trying to appear indifferent when in fact I've already resolved that I want to make this work. I'm pretty sure this is every small town girl's dream set-up. "What kind of rules are we talking about?"

"Besides keeping the place immaculate?" His smoldering eyes lock with mine, releasing a hundred shivers to creep through me. "No sex in your room. I don't want to worry about having to fumigate the apartment once strange guys have paraded through."

With the mention of sex falling from his lips, I feel a sudden burn between my legs, and can't look away. He bites his lower lip slowly, almost taunting me.

Damn, he's sexy.

For a moment I completely forget that we're not alone, and that I previously warned Erik that the two of us would never hook up.

"Those rules seem simple enough," Chloe pipes in, most likely sensing the sexual tension buzzing between us. "You gonna make her sign a contract or something? What if she finds a job? Are you gonna charge her rent? Even if you're well off like your big brother, this shit can't be cheap."

"I'm pre-*law*," he tells her in a matter-of-fact tone, finally tearing his eyes away from me. He looks down at my new friend like she's a moron. "*I'll* take care of the details. It's unnecessary to worry your pretty little head over such trivial things."

His cool attitude toward her tears me from my sudden sexual trance. Does he just not know how to deal with people in general, or is he simply earning the reputation of an asshole? Thankfully Chloe taps away at her cell phone, appearing un-jilted by his crudeness.

"The no sex thing *won't* be a problem," I declare, clearing my throat. "I have no intention of 'parading guys' through your apartment." I press my arm into Chloe's side. "Hey. Would you mind giving us a moment? I need to talk to Erik about his brother and Jewels, and I don't want to drag you into it any more than I already have."

"No problem," Chloe answers, already in motion as she pecks at her phone. "I gotta call my boss at the tattoo shop anyway. Turns out there's an emergency he wants me to cover tonight. Ozzy can be a real dick, and I gotta do whatever it takes to make him happy. I'm still under his apprenticeship and can't afford to blow this. I've got a few months left until I can operate my own booth." She glances up at me long enough to wink. "I'll wait for you down in the lobby."

After there's a click of the front door, Erik turns back to me, his brows stitched. "She talks too fucking much."

My resolve breaks the moment we lock eyes. I step into him, wrapping my fingers in his tousled locks, and kissing him. His lips are soft, but demanding. He immediately nudges his tongue inside my mouth, devouring me until I'm unsteady on my feet. His flavorful mouthwash bursts against my tastebuds as his tongue massages mine, making me so hot that I'm ready to implode.

Hardly a full minute passes when he hoists me up by my waist and hauls me into his bedroom, slamming me into the mattress with the weight of his body. His full lips possess me with a force so strong I'm sure my own lips will be swollen for hours.

Erik grinds up against me as we kiss, his massively hard package rubbing against my bare leg through the coarse material of his shorts. When I realize just how *large* he must be, I moan softly against his mouth. One of Erik's hands darts up my shirt, his long fingers teasing the exposed tops of my breasts.

My desire kicks into over drive when I imagine him naked and inside of me, filling me to my core. I reach for his shirt and begin to unbutton it, shivering in delight with the feel of his sculpted muscles beneath my fingertips. A deep hum vibrates from his throat just before he intensifies the kiss. He reaches back to slip his hand beneath my shorts and underwear, cradling my bare ass cheek.

He stops kissing me to press his lips against my ear, his breath hot against my skin. "Here's what's going to happen. I'm going to climb off you now, and you're going to strip naked for me."

Stunned by the unexpected dominance, I suck in a deep breath. Trailing kisses down my neck, he backs away, watching me with a dangerous fire behind his eyes. He towers over me like some kind of freaking mythical god with his gorgeous chest exposed, all tanned and muscular. I don't break the connection our stare as I reach down to unbutton my shorts. My body tingles excitedly with what's to come.

Then for some ungodly reason that I'll forever live to curse upon, I picture the disappointment in my best friend's eyes when she hears I've slept with the only person she's ever warned me to steer clear of. I may as well be dunked in a bathtub filled with ice water.

"Shit." I drop my hand to cradle my head. "I can't do this. It's a really bad idea."

"Ideas are only bad if you don't want them, and who are you kidding?" He continues staring down on me, his heated gaze unrelenting and oh, so seductive. "You know you want me."

Clicking my tongue, I slide off the bed and straighten my disheveled shirt. "Wow. Conceited much?"

"I only say things if they're true. You want me, and I want you, so what's the problem?" Damn it, the way he's so confident makes his sex appeal shoot off the charts. And the enormous bulge in his pants hasn't subsided any.

Shit.

I'm the poster girl for flustered as I stumble out into the hallway. My head and vagina are on two separate stratospheres, both vying for my complete attention.

"The *problem* is that your brother and Jewels told me to stay away from you! And I already *told you* this thing between us isn't going to happen! I don't need to get into a complicated relationship where I wonder if I have to fuck you in order to have a place to live!"

"Who said anything about a relationship? We're adults. There *is* a such a thing as consensual sex."

I cackle a bit too boisterously. "Right. Ask your brother and his girlfriend how well *that* goes."

"Would you stop bringing my brother into this? You and I? We have absolutely nothing to do with him. Or Jewels. We're two very attractive people. There's nothing wrong with us being drawn to each other. I'm not saying we have to do this in order for you to live here. It would just be an added bonus. For *both* of us."

I look away, my heart racing, crotch throbbing. He's right, and I can't stop picturing us having sex together. I imagine it would be a new level of hot that would put all my past conquests to shame. Something about his irresistible physique and king of the world attitude makes me wonder if I'd remember my own name after being with him.

I bite my lip and pull my phone from my back pocket for something to distract me. "My life's already a mess without this added complication. I came out here to become a different person. I'm not about casual sex anymore. Anyone who wants in my pants is going to have to wine and dine me first."

"Really? You're going to pretend that's what you want, and make me draw this out? I can do things to you that will never make you see sex the same way again." His words, low and sultry, ping around inside my brain with excitement. "I'm worth skipping the pretenses for."

I frown, ready to pull my hair out. "Jesus. You are *completely* full of yourself."

"Listen. I normally don't offer myself up like this to women." He spreads his arms wide. The hard muscles of his chest shift with the gesture, about making me cream my underwear. "Are you interested, or not?"

I pull my jaw tight. "Fuck this. I'm out of here."

Before he can try to stop me or say anything more, I spring from the apartment and practically jog down the hallway. My trembling fingers poke at the buttons in the elevator, pushing more than one and making the ride down to the lobby way longer than necessary. Feeling like I could punch something, I cross my arms and grumble.

Who *exactly* does Erik Murphy think he is? The kid's only nineteen, for fuck's sake. Not only does he act like he's lived in the big city his whole life, but he thinks he's some kind of superhero in the bedroom. If Jewels knew about any of this, she'd be ready with a big old "I told you so" look that would make me feel all of three feet tall.

I must still look flushed when I catch up with Chloe. She leans away from the marble wall with the sight of me, raising her eyebrows with a little smirk. "Well? Did you make any decisions?"

"You're right, the place is amazing." I hook my arm through hers, smiling as I pull her along to where the doorman holds the door for us. "Only a total idiot would turn down an offer like that."

As we launch onto the sidewalk, I realize I don't have a lot of options right now. I dug this complicated shit up all on my own when I decided to drop everything and hop on an airplane to escape my problems. Erik's offering me this incredible place to stay, free of charge. I'll just have to find a way to see him as being unattractive, even though I've seen just how phenomenal he looks without a shirt. Regardless of what anyone else thinks, I *am* capable of self-control.

Or so I hope.

Chapter Four

By the time Chloe and I return to the brownstone, Jewels has showered and dressed for our night out—surprisingly *not* in the usual baby doll t-shirt and torn shorts. She wears a peach, fluttering tank top that flatters her skin tone paired with a flirty short skirt and a bunch of coordinating jewelry. Maybe the big city's fashion is already rubbing off on her.

Not surprising, however, is that she appears to be finishing a hot and heavy session with her boyfriend. They're each adjusting their hair and clothing as Chloe and I step into the living room. Jewels hops off the couch to join us, her flushed cheeks smiling brightly as if it can divert us from the fact that they likely just had sex. It only reminds me why I seriously can't stay with them. "Hey! How'd it go? You guys have fun?"

"We spent most of the day checking out the Upper West Side," Chloe says, kicking off her thick sandals and sinking into the couch across from Adam. She massages one of her feet. "We checked out a street fair, and grabbed lunch at a Mexican eatery. I showed her the ropes in the subway so she can find her way around on her own. At least she'll recognize one corner of the city. It's not much, but it's a start. We'll have to take her to see all the touristy shit another time."

"I finally understand why you fell in love with this city," I say, slipping my arm around Jewels's shoulders. "And I owe you for setting me up with the best tour guide out there. Seriously, Chloe was amazing."

Jewels wraps her arm around my waist, hugging me for a brief moment. "I knew you two would get along. Can you join us for dinner, Chloe?"

"I wish, but I have to fill in for one of the guys at the shop tonight. Some shit about his wife having the stomach flu and no one to watch his baby. Sometimes I think they just like to take advantage of me because they know I have to get my time in. I swear they're always calling me in on my rare days off. It's like I have a fucking sign on my head that says *gullible* or something." She jumps to her feet, slipping back into her sandals. I get the feeling she doesn't sit still for much longer than that. "You guys should come down to The Sticks tomorrow night on 23rd Street. My band will be playing at nine."

"We'll be there," Jewels assures her, grinning. If there's one thing my bestie would never miss, it's the chance to see a live band. She runs over to hug Chloe. "Thanks again, I owe you."

"We had a good time." Chloe shrugs, turning to smile my way. "I think she'll do just fine in this city. I look forward to hanging again." After throwing me a wink and exchanging goodbyes with Adam, she disappears down the stairs.

Jewels flashes me this ridiculously toothy smile until we hear the front door click. "Did she drive you crazy?"

"No," I say with a shrug. "She's a talker, but she's also a lot of fun."

"Good. I knew you'd like her." She becomes preoccupied with her phone for a moment. "So I hope you won't get mad over this, but we invited Theo to come with us tonight."

"Jewels," I whine, twisting my hair around my finger. "*C'mon.*"

"Kel, he really wants a chance to start over with you. He's embarrassed that you thought he just wanted a one-time fling. That's totally not what Theo's about. He's a flirt, and I know just exactly how blunt he is when he's attracted to a woman, but he's a total sweetheart once you get to know him." She reaches out for my hands, batting her thick eyelashes. "Pretty please, will you give him another chance?"

"You're like a pathetic puppy dog with those dopey eyes. Are they supposed to make me cave in or something?"

"Of course." She flutters her lashes again like a cartoon character. "Say yes."

I catch Adam throwing me a hopeful look, and remember what he said about Jewels being crushed over our spat the day before.

"*Fine,*" I cave, pushing her away. "If you're going to make me go on an actual date, then I need to get ready. Put my sexy face on."

"That's the spirit!" she says in her old cheer-leading voice. "Yay, Kel!"

"Can you say that again, exactly the same way?" Adam asks her, wiggling his eyebrows. "Although maybe jump around this time."

"You two are like a bunch of newlyweds," I moan. "I'm outta here." As I slip away to the guest room, my gut pangs anxiously. Tonight I'll have to tell Jewels and Adam that I'm going to move in with Erik. I can't put it off any longer.

The restaurant they choose is small and charming, but reminds me far too much of the Italian bistro Erik took me to the day before. It makes me all the more nervous about breaking my news to them. I'm chewing on my straw and tapping my knee against the bottom of the table by the time Theo joins us, looking mighty fine. Jewels told me he looks amazing in a suit, which I have yet to see, but *damn* he can really rock the shit out of a casual button down and chinos shorts.

"Hey, big guy!" Jewels greets him eagerly.

His sincere gaze meets mine as he dips his chin. "Hey. You look beautiful tonight." He stuffs his hands in his pockets and tilts his head toward the small bar. "Join me for a quick drink?"

"We'll order some appetizers," Adam suggests.

"Get the prosciutto crostata and pancetta focaccia twists," Theo tells him as he helps me slide my chair away from the table. He gently touches my arm while we walk over to the small bar at the far end of the restaurant. We settle into the only free stools in the middle.

"What's your drink of choice?" he asks, signaling the bartender.

"Jameson on the rocks," I blurt, knowing I'm going to need some liquid courage to confront Jewels and Adam by the end of the night.

Theo lifts his eyebrows, smirking. "Really?"

"Why does everyone expect me to order something with an umbrella?"

"No judgments." He turns back to the young guy behind the bar. "Two double shots of Jameson, on the rocks."

The bartender nods with a smirk. "You got it."

Theo turns his stool so his knees press to the side of my legs, and casually drapes his large forearm against the bar. "I wanted to thank you for giving me a chance to apologize. I was an ass. I wasn't trying to suggest that you were *easy*. Jewels made it sound like you might be interested in me, and I wanted to let you know that I was definitely into you. I knew the long distance thing wouldn't be ideal, but I saw it work for a couple of my buddies when we were overseas. Now that I know you're going to stick around, I'm *especially* interested in getting to know you better."

"Yeah, well, if I hadn't jumped to conclusions and run off like that, maybe there wouldn't have been such a colossal misunderstanding." I set my hand on his massive bicep, quivering a little with its firmness. "I'm the one who should apologize. I've been through a lot lately, so I guess I'm a bit more sensitive than usual."

"Anything you want to talk about?"

"Not especially. I haven't told Jewels all the sordid details yet. All you need to know is that I'm not interested in a casual hookup. I came to New York for a fresh start. Maybe to figure out who I am without my parents, or sisters, or anyone else defining me."

"I can respect that."

The bartender sets our drinks down and Theo

quickly pays him and holds his drink out to me. "Here's to fresh starts."

I clink my glass with his. "Thanks. I hope I didn't bruise your ego by turning you down. Don't get me wrong—I really am interested in getting to know you better."

His eyes widen. "Does that mean I can take you on a real date?"

"Sometime. I'm not quite ready to go there yet."

With his eyes twinkling, he holds his glass up. "You know where to find me when you decide that you are."

The mood between us turns light and playful as we join Jewels and Adam. I catch myself biting my bottom lip when watching Theo tell us work-related stories. As much as he appears to be the complete package and as much as I'm attracted to him, he doesn't get me going the way Erik can. I curse myself out under my breath. Erik's just a *kid*. Theo's as manly as they get. He served our country and has a stellar job that could eventually lead to parties with celebrities. He earned his money instead of having it handed down to him like a spoiled rich boy.

The night's filled with amazing food, a ton of laughter, and enough drinks at the bar down the block from the restaurant that I feel tingly and loose-lipped by the time we agree to head back for the night.

As we near the brownstone, Theo slows his pace at

my side, letting Adam and Jewels—who have their arms wrapped around each other—get a decent lead on us.

"Wanna come over to my place for a drink or two?" Theo asks in a low voice.

I reach out to touch his toned arm, because apparently I can't keep my hands off his marvelous body. "And how's *that* going to work with our agreement to take things slow, exactly?"

"I can be a gentleman," he says with a rather devilish smirk.

I brush my fingertip across his forearm. "Maybe so, but I don't know that I trust myself around you."

"Then don't," he says, taking my arm to stop me in the middle of the sidewalk. "This *can* be about more than sex. If you let me kiss you, maybe we'd both make it through a few dates before we decide to cave in and take things further."

I wag my finger at him, grinning. "Don't you know kissing's a gateway drug?"

"I have a high tolerance," he says, leaning in closer. "I once had to tread water in the ocean for two hours straight. It takes a lot to break me."

I shove him lightly, pretending to be offended. "Agh, do you have to make yourself even hotter? Seriously, Theo, let's just stop this now." My head spins from all the drinks I had, and I can't help but feel incredibly guilty for even *considering* kissing Theo when I almost took things too far with Erik earlier. "I don't want our friendship to be tainted by our alcohol-fueled hormones."

"Okay, fair enough." He backs away, hands held up at his sides. "But if I promise to keep my hands in my pockets, will you at least let me kiss your cheek before we say goodnight?"

It's actually kind of sweet how he doesn't want to part without having kissed me in some way. "Would you settle for a hug?"

With an ear-splitting grin, he leans into gather me in his arms, bringing me close with his arm hooked around my neck. I feel like a little girl with my face pressed to his chest. I feel his nose skim against the top of my head.

"Are you sniffing my hair?"

He pulls away, slowly letting go. "Can't help myself. You smell like sunscreen. It's driving me wild."

"It's coca butter scented shampoo."

"I like it." His eyes light up, and he reaches down for my hand, bringing it to his lips for a soft kiss. "Goodnight, Cavenaugh. I look forward to seeing you again tomorrow."

I agreed to let him take me to see Chloe's band, figuring it would be safe to double with Adam and Jewels again. But as he strolls away, whistling, I can't decide if canceling would've been a better idea. My head's such a mess. Is there something *morally* wrong with simply being *attracted* to two guys at once?

I find Jewels by herself in the kitchen, drinking from a bottled water. "Adam said to tell you goodnight. He's wiped."

"I never got a chance to ask him how it went. Are they going to install the pump thingie?"

"Yeah, it's all good. He's set up for the procedure next week. You and Theo have a good time?"

I grin happily with the memory of his hug. "Yeah, we did."

She offers me the bottle with her eyebrows raised. "You want to hang out in the backyard and chat, or are you ready for bed too?"

I take a swig of the water before handing it back, and hook my arm through hers. "I'm up for a girl session. We haven't had much time alone since I got here."

She grabs a bottle of wine from the fridge before we head out.

The night has taken on a significantly colder feel, although there's still a heavy humidity that settles around us like a dense fog. Jewels flicks the switch to bring the twinkle lights to life beneath the canopy. The beautiful sight of the white lights shining against the dark night brings on the feel of a mix between a fairytale and a stunning wedding reception.

Jewels crosses her legs once she's on the couch and settles against my side the way she always did in our dorm room as she works on twisting the top off the wine bottle. "So! What'd you think of Central Park? We'll have to go running through there some time. I've only been on the edge of it a couple of times with Adam, but Theo keeps inviting me to run the trails with him. I guess the park is huge." She hands me the bottle. "Speaking of, how'd it go with Theo just now?"

"We didn't kiss, if that's what you're hinting at."

"So you're not interested?"

"Are you kidding? Of course I am. He's one of the hottest guys I've ever met. He's really funny and kinda sweet, too. I'd be stupid not to give him a chance. He's the total package."

"You don't seem convinced."

"I'm just really not ready to start a relationship when I have other things to worry about, like finding a job, and figuring out what I'm going to do here, if I can find a way to finish college. What if I *don't* find an affordable place to stay, or a job that pays enough for me to live here?"

Jewels begins playing with strands of my hair, something she only does when completely inebriated. I didn't realize she had so many drinks tonight. "It'll all work out, Kel."

"And if it doesn't?"

"Then you move back to La Crosse. Or somewhere else in Wisconsin. But you should stop worrying about it so much *right* this minute." After taking another slug of the wine, she sets in the bottle in my lap and snuggles into my side, wrapping her arms around herself and closing here eyes. "You've got all the time in the world to figure this out. Just enjoy life while you're here."

"Jewels?" I ask softly, wondering if she's sleeping. She hums with her eyes still closed. "Have you ever wanted something that you knew wouldn't be good for you?"

"Does falling in love with a guy who wanted to give up on life count?"

I look down at my sweet friend, reminding myself she's been through hell and back with Adam. My drama is like a stroll through the park compared to all she's been though.

I stroke her head gently. "Yeah, that counts," I whisper, listening to her breathing slow into soft snores.

I'm going to have to sort out my living situation and feelings for Erik on my own.

Chapter Five

JEWELS, Adam, and I spend the entire next day unpacking. Yeah, the two of them are a bit sickening to be around at times, but they're so in sync with each other's emotions and every move that it warms my heart. They're the first couple I've been around where it's obvious they're meant to spend the rest of their lives together.

I'm caught up in the excitement of my best friend settling into her very first place off campus with the guy she's head over heels in love with, and completely forget about my meeting up with Theo later. Erik sends me a text while I'm getting ready, asking when he can expect me to move in. The reminder that I still have to tell Jewels *something*, even if it isn't the truth, weighs down the excitement of going to see Chloe's band perform. I quickly type:

. . .

Come 2 The Sticks on 23rd St tonight after 9. I'll fill u in.

The city's alive with locals and tourists as Adam, Jewels, Theo, and I wander down to the hip bar just before nightfall. You'd think it was the weekend rather than a random weeknight the way an excited vivacity buzzes through the crowd on the sidewalks. For the most part it's easy to pick out the visitors from the residents the way some stop to take pictures frequently while others carry along at a steady pace, filled with laughter and conversation. I find myself wondering if I'll ever fit in with the locals, or if I'll always be overwhelmed by the constant movement of the massive city.

As we wait in line to enter the bar, I occasionally feel Theo's warm breath on my neck as if he's staring down on me. My body tingles in anticipation despite my resolve to take things slow. As much as I want to change my ways, it still feels good to be wanted. And I can't deny a part of me wants him just as much. The fire rippling between our connected hands has the feel of holding on to a live wire.

Once inside The Sticks, I let out a sharp laugh. The interior is eerily similar to the rural bars back home, complete with log-lined walls covered in tin signs, only there's just a touch of modern added with stainless steel lights and bar stools, and it's filled with fashionably dressed patrons rather than flannels. A decent crowd gathers around a small stage at the far end where a three-person band plays a punked-out cover of some 90s song, their guitars ripping through the bar with a boisterous charge that vibrates against my chest. The four of us join the cluster of people waiting to put in their order at the bar.

"Holy shit, they're playing Blind Melon!" Jewels squeals, jumping up and down. No one is surprised to hear that the musical genius knows the song playing. She tugs on my arm. "I freaking *love* this song, but I've never heard it played like this before! C'mon, let's dance! The guys can join us after they buy our drinks!"

"Yeah?" I confer with Theo, raising my eyebrows in question.

"Go ahead. She's not going to let you say no to her anyway." He winks, flashing me one of his million dollar smiles. "Besides, I know what to order."

"Thank you!" I yell, allowing my friend to drag me away.

The intensity on the designated dance floor matches the thrum of the power cords blasted over the speakers. I dip and grind with Jewels as we've done a hundred times before, letting the excitement of the music lift my worries off my shoulders.

When the song ends, Jewels jumps up and down,

sticking her fingers in her mouth to let out an ear-shattering whistle. The band switches to an even more energetic song with an undeniably sexy beat. Jewels squeals excitedly with the sound of the new tune, jumping around with such force that her long blond curls sway over her face. She closes her eyes, losing herself in the music as always. She doesn't even notice when a wall of dancers barge their way between us, jumping and clashing into each other.

Giggling, I shift my hips along to the electric beat, letting myself also get lost in the notes. Each strum of the bass guitar makes me feel more sexy, confident. I close my eyes, feeling the deep staccato of the drums vibrate inside my chest.

A pair of hands slip around my stomach, cradling me. I spin around, expecting Theo, but I'm met with Erik's seductive blue gaze. Incredibly turned on by the intense way he's looking at me and still holding on to my waist, I let out a low gasp between my parted lips. His mouth slowly curls with a pleased smile as he presses up against me, sliding his hands along my side as he dances, slow, tantalizing.

I'm too focused on the pulsating swell between my legs to remember that I'm supposed to play it cool with Erik, that I'm not going to become involved with him, no matter how insanely sexy it feels to be dancing in his arms. I rest my hands against his lean chest, locking my eyes with his as I slide up and down him like a feral animal. Not only do his eyes shine in approval, but I can feel him growing against my leg when I straighten back up.

I've hooked up with a lot of guys over the years, but I've never felt as wildly attractive around anyone the way I do when Erik's looking at me with his commanding gaze. He slips his hand beneath my shirt to tease the small curve of my back with his fingertips. His touch is like hot coals against my skin.

He pulls me close. "Come with me."

My heart's racing at dangerous levels as I allow him to pull me away, undetected by Jewels. I should dig my heels down and refuse to leave with him, but once again my hormones dictate my actions, and I find myself exiting through a back door at his side. The small parking lot out back is filled with half a dozen smokers lined up against the back side of the building, laughing with one another. The smell of nicotine and the warm city air add to the excitement of the impulsive moment.

Erik doesn't stop pulling me by the hand until we're around the corner, sandwiched between another side of the building and a rusted out conversion van with the name of a catering business on the side.

I'm breathless when he tosses me against the hood of the van, his lips colliding into mine, making way for his warm tongue to sweep through my mouth. Our hands eagerly grip onto each other as our bodies mold into one hot mess. Erik eagerly slides his hand against my bare stomach, popping a button off my shirt. He stops at the swell of my breasts when he finds the small barbells pierced into my nipples and gives them a swift tug, none too gentle. I moan with pleasure, and our kisses become more ignited.

He stops to grab my hand away from his chest, guiding me down to the button on his shorts. I reach down to release him, nearly coming come undone when I discover he's commando. I use both hands to ease him out of his shorts, delighted. I've been with some good-sized guys before, but *damn*.

His lips cover mine once again, claiming me with a kiss so deep I'm surprised I don't gag with the probing of his tongue. It's the hottest make out session of my life. And it only gets hotter when he reaches beneath my skirt to rip my thong from between my legs with one hard pull, pressing two fingers into me as if to check to make sure I'm wet. With the flash of his hands, he stops to reach for a condom from his back pocket, and rolls it on, tossing the wrapper down to the parking lot. Maybe I should be concerned by just how easily he does it, as if having sex is something he does on a daily basis, but instead I'm mystified at the skill.

Then he enters me swiftly with the sounds of the smokers around the corner still dancing through the air. He pulls at the hardware on my nipple while guiding my hips and biting my bottom lip. A low grunt vibrates against his throat as he pushes into me repeatedly.

"Holy shit," I gasp against his mouth, wondering how I'm able to fit all of him inside me without splitting in two. I dig my fingers into the roots of his hair, pulling the soft tufts as I ride him. Intoxicated by the unexpected thrill of the moment, my head swarms with each thrust.

Sex is my drug of choice. The satisfying friction created from bodies grinding together, the cosmic kisses, the electrifying build of the orgasm that brings me to a euphoria unlike anything else. If someone told me there was something I could take that produced the same satisfying release, I'd become an addict.

I lean back to watch Erik. There's an intensity to his eyes, as if he's determined to give me all he's got. Paired with the satisfied smirk plastered on his lips, it's intoxifying. As his hips bend for one long, final thrust, I realize the satisfied look is because he came.

I'm still on fire and rather disoriented as he lets go of me to pull up his shorts, buttoning them with the smirk still tilting his rose-colored lips. "I'll tell my doorman you're moving in tomorrow."

Then he walks away without another glance, or a kiss goodbye.

. . .

After ten minutes of an internal battle with my darkest demons, I slither back into the bar with a messed-up walk of shame from the women's room, where I tried to freshen up and fix any signs that I just had sex in an alley. What in the *fuck* did I just do? Not only did I break my resolve not to sleep with any more guys until I've fallen in love, I screwed up the entire living situation with Erik. As if things weren't complicated enough before.

The minute I find my friends alongside sweet, handsome Theo, waiting for me near the bar with their expressions a general mix of confoundment, my insides painfully shrivel. I've perfected the metamorphosis into the kind of slut I'm trying so desperately *not* to be. I've proven my family and everyone else to be right about me.

"I lost you out there!" Jewels hollers above the noise. "Where'd you go?"

Theo hands me a glass. I thank him and take a quick gulp, hoping to calm my frayed nerves. "I had a smoke with some girl," I tell her. While in the past I've tried a few cigarettes, I've never really understood how someone could enjoy making themselves sick and smelly for a brief buzz. The lie really sucks, but it still beats the truth.

Theo's thick brows bend, giving me one of those looks a person emits when they're judging your character. "You smoke?"

I shrug, grateful for the dark lighting. The way

he's studying me closely, he may be able to see the after-sex glow on my cheeks. "Not really. I've only tried it a couple of times. She was nice, and I didn't want to offend her when she offered one."

Adam wraps his arms around Jewels from behind, grinning. "This is *New York*. You're bound to offend *someone* at some point. May as well get used to it."

From the unsatisfied glint to Jewels's gaze, I know she isn't buying it. She tilts her head to the dance floor, only half looking me in the eye. "Chloe's band is about to play. Let's go work our way up to the front row."

Theo waits for me to trail behind the other two, setting his fingers on the curve of my back. I stiffen when I think he's trying to take a whiff of me again. Is he looking for the smell of the shampoo, or trying to validate my story?

As we work our way through the crowd, it sinks into my skull just how badly I screwed up by having impromptu sex with Erik. Now if I tell Jewels I'm moving in with him, no strings attached, I'll be lying. I can't lie to her. Not about this. How can I expect her to take it without freaking out on me?

And I really *am* interested in dating Theo because I know he'd be good for me. I'd be a fool to pass up someone who served our country and has the kind of job most people would dream of having, plus he's sweet and really fucking hot. He's exactly the kind of guy I need in my life. But if he discovers I banged another guy in the alley while he was buying my drink, he'll believe the reputation that I've now earned.

I'm the whore everyone accused me of being.

Someone makes an announcement into the microphone and everyone around us cheers in approval. I feel Theo's hand on my back. The bodies surrounding us suddenly seem too close. My head spins with the brutal dose of reality I was stupid enough to bring upon myself. My vision blurs in and out before everything turns to black.

"She's awake!" I hear someone yell above brash, seemingly angry music.

My eyelids flutter open. Adam and Jewels watch over me, their expressions a mixed bag. I'm propped against Theo in a booth near the entrance of the bar. The hardness of his chest and musky scent of his cologne are like a zinger to my already daunted conscience. I try to move away, but his arms hold me in place.

"Take it easy," he whispers into my ear. "You passed out on the dance floor."

Jewels hands me a sweating bottle of water. "Drink!"

With shaking hands, I take it from her and down nearly half its contents.

"It's my fault," Jewels tells me, leaning against

Adam. "I should've been on you to drink more water since you got here. I swear I drink a glass every hour in this heat."

"I'm a big girl," I insist, waving her off. "And *duh*, I usually drink more water than *you*, Jewels."

I peer past my friend to see Chloe on center stage, rocking a blue electric guitar the same color as the streaks in her bangs. A tattooed guy with gages in his ears stands at her side, dressed like he stepped directly out of the grunge era, and a skinny drummer who looks 16 or 17 slouches behind a set of drums, his arms a blur of movement as he plays. Their music cuts through the bar like knives as Chloe's sultry voice screams out indistinguishable lyrics. It reminds me of some pretty, tattooed rocker chick Jewels always listens to that sings a dark song about a being some guy's whore. Maybe after tonight it'll become my theme song.

And then a thought occurs to me: Erik ripped my thong in the alley. I feel the color drain from my face. Underneath my skirt, my world is exposed for all to see.

Damned if my bestie ever misses a single thing, Jewels leaps forward to grab my wrist. "What's wrong? You gonna pass out again?"

I yank her closer. "Did anyone see...*anything* when I passed out?"

"I'm pretty sure *everyone* around us saw you pass out, girlfriend." She peels my fingers off her arm, giggling. "But don't worry, Theo dove down to catch you like a scene out of a war movie. I feel like we witnessed him taking a bullet for you."

I exhale deeply with my eyes closed. It doesn't sound like I put on an X-rated peep show after all.

"I wasn't letting you get a concussion on my watch," Theo says, his breath hot on my face. "Can I take you back to their place now? You need to rest."

My insides twist with the idea of being alone with Theo. I doubt he'd try to kiss me after I collapsed in front of him, but my dirty secret feels like the weight of an entire planet resting on my shoulders. How am I going to look him in the eye without conceding to the truth?

"I can go back with you," Jewels offers.

I shake my head, knowing if I pulled my music-loving best friend away from a live band, it'd be the equivalent of sacrificing a small animal. "Nah, I'm good. Everyone can stay, I'll just take a taxi."

Theo rises to his feet, lifting me in his arms. "No way. I'm going with to ensure you make it back. Someone needs to stay with you."

"*Set me down*," I hiss between my clenched teeth, holding my skirt tight against my legs. Enclosed in his bulging arms, I feel like a five year old. And with each insanely kind gesture he makes, it's like adding more fire to my already burned psyche. "I *can* walk."

Theo doesn't budge. "No use in arguing, Cavenaugh." He tips his head at Adam and Jewels. "I'll stay with her until you get home."

Although I'm quite aware we're in the most populated city in the entire nation, and it's safe to say that no one will ever recognize me as the pathetic girl who couldn't walk out of the bar, I cover my face as Theo carries me outside.

To say I'm mortified by the situation I've created for myself would be a major understatement. After Theo sets me down on the sidewalk to hail a taxi, my mind becomes a garbled mess of thoughts and feelings. I keep my distance from him on the ride back to Jewels and Adam's place. I'm unworthy of his affection.

As we head out to their backyard with bottles of beer in hand, I swear I can feel a shift in the air between us. Theo's eager to take things a step further. I wait until he's seated until choosing the couch across from him. With my feet tucked underneath me, I take a long sip of the bitter beer, making a note to buy a bottle of Jameson.

"Seems like a waste that they put this canopy up," Theo comments, looking up at the twinkle lights. "Nice night like this? We should be looking at the stars. When I was a kid, I memorized all the constellations so I could point them out to my baby sister."

"You have very many brothers and sisters?"

"Just her. We're real close, though. What about you?"

"Four sisters. And it was exactly the kind of nightmare you'd expect growing up in a household of women. I think my obsession with animals started because it felt like I was living inside of an actual zoo."

He grins with delight, his beautiful eyes lit with the glow of the lights above us. "You're obsessed with animals?"

"I wouldn't say *obsessed* so much as *fascinated*. At one point I was considering becoming a veterinarian. Now I'm leaning toward zoology. Who knows if I'll ever actually finish my degree now that I'm here."

When I take another swig, my lips sting from Erik's rough kisses. Guilt and shame burns through my core with the speed of a roman candle. I peel the label off the bottle of beer, telling myself it's best if I avoid eye contact with Theo. But really, I'm just ashamed.

"Theo, there's something you should know."

"Lay it on me," he says, his voice soft and low.

"I'm, like, *really* screwed up. I came here to escape my messy past, but it seems it followed me." I blink back a sudden bout of tears stinging my eyes. "And you seem like a really great guy. Trust me when I say you don't want to get involved with this natural disaster. I'm sure you deserve better."

"Hey, they call it 'the past' for a reason. I have

some pretty ugly skeletons in my closet, too. It doesn't define who you are now."

"It actually does." When I look up at him a lone tear breaks free, sliding down my cheek. "I'm trying like hell to change my ways, but it seems I'm destined to be a fuck-up."

He shakes his head like I'm wrong. "Of all the things Jewels told me about you, none of it was bad. Whatever's haunting you, maybe I can help."

A blatant, ugly laugh shoots out of me as I wipe at my face. "I'm sorry. It's just...you're part of the problem. I should be avoiding hot guys in general, but I don't seem to have the willpower. I know I'm the only one who can change things, but sometimes I wonder if I'm just playing into the expectations of my family and everyone I know. You know how they say if you're told something enough times, you eventually start to believe it? That could be my mantra." I run my fingers through my hair, sighing. "Jesus, could I be any more pathetic?"

"You *aren't* pathetic." He leans forward to rest his elbows on his knees, lacing his hands in front of him. I expect a judgmental look to kick in, but his expression remains calm and rather serene as he stares me down. "Look, I appreciate that you're being honest with me, so I should come clean. Until this summer, I didn't have a lot of time for a social life. Most of my friends are either a bunch of guys and their girlfriends, or the actors I work with.

Those rare times when I meet a woman with potential who isn't in the industry, trying to make it big or using me for my position, I tend to jump at the opportunity with a little too much vigor. To be completely honest *with you*, I haven't been laid in a really, *really* long time. So it would seem *I'm* the pathetic one here."

My eyes grow wide. "How long we talkin'?"

"Brooklyn left nearly a year ago."

"And you haven't been with *anyone* since?"

"Like I said, I've been busy." A half smile tilts his mouth.

"Ouch," I say, flinching. "That's gotta hurt."

He shakes his head slowly. "You have *noooo* idea."

I run my hands through the hair on both sides of my head and let out a frustrated moan. "This is completely ironic. Our problems couldn't be any more opposite. What are we going to do?"

He raises his thick eyebrows. "Are you open to suggestions?"

"Sure. Let's hear it."

"I like you, Cavenaugh. A lot. I don't care if your past is trying to bring you down. I say we keep hanging out, take it slow. No pressure. If you decide you want to take it any further, I'll take you on a real date, just the two of us. If you decide you just want to stay friends, I'm cool with that too. I'll let you be the one to decide our fate."

"I don't deserve for you to be this understanding." When I close my eyes and shake my head, I see Erik all over me in the alley. "You could do so much better."

"That's where you're wrong. Don't sell yourself short."

I open my eyes to find a dazzling smile on his face that could one day destroy me.

Chapter Six

I'M groggy as hell the next morning since I hardly got more than a couple hours of sleep. I was sick with self-reproach for loosing myself to Erik, then letting Theo convince me to give him a chance just a couple of hours later.

Theo stayed until Jewels and Adam came home sometime after one in the morning. Hanging with Theo was so relaxed that I slipped into a comfortable pair of yoga capris and a tank top, even let my hair down. He told me stories of his adventures in the Marine Corps, and I told him some of the nightmares of being a camp counselor. We did nothing more than hug before he left, though it still felt like the ultimate act of treachery considering I had just slept with someone else.

Of course the biggest problem contributing to my

restlessness is the fact that Erik expects me to move in with him. I really like Theo, and I want to give him a chance. There's no way I can do that if I'm living with someone who drives me sexually insane. I'll just have to find a way to tell him I changed my mind, which means I'm back to being homeless.

I shower and dry my hair before heading to the kitchen where I catch Adam and Jewels making out. She's sitting on the counter with her fingers wrapped in his hair, and he's pressed against her, his hands cradling her face. Although there's nothing vile in the way they're holding each other, I still feel like the world's biggest pervert.

I *definitely* can't stay here any longer.

I clear my throat with dramatic flair.

Adam springs away from her. "Mornin'!"

"Sorry," Jewels tells me, her eyes wide and shoulders hunched. She's flushed, and her lips are puffy. "I thought I heard the blowdryer still going."

I roll my eyes. "Don't worry about it. It's not like I haven't seen the two of you make out before."

Adam drapes his arm over Jewels's leg. "Since it's your last free day without school or work, why don't you take Kelly out, show her more of the city? There isn't much left to unpack. Pretty sure I can handle it by myself."

"And this is one of the million reasons why I love you," Jewels says, leaning in to kiss his cheek. She beams across the kitchen at me. "Theo gave me the number for a realtor who's known for finding hidden gems for rent at low cost. Maybe we could check out a few places."

Just like that, I'm filled with a renewed hope. Maybe there's another option after all.

Six hours later, we're standing in the third and last "gem" Barbara Bernstein had to show us, this one in Hunts Point. Outside of the apartment building, there was a crowd gathered where two homeless men were violently fighting over something, and a spindly young girl asked if we wanted to party. I'm not sure if she was offering sexual favors or drugs, but she was far too young to be suggesting either one.

The "apartment" isn't any bigger than my bedroom back in Wisconsin, and smells like old cheese. There's a hole in the plaster next to the refrigerator where it looks like someone either chucked something big, or found a way to release their anger. The sounds of screaming children, a woman yelling, and multiple sirens blend together, sounding as if they're in the room along with us. At least there don't seem to be any rats, unlike the last place she showed us.

Fear sticks in my throat with the thought of

staying somewhere like this all alone. I was raised in a house with five girls. There was always someone stealing someone else's things, someone on the rag who'd threaten to murder you over an ill look, or someone who was devastated over some guy. I can't begin to imagine what I would do by myself all the time.

Barbara stands awkwardly in the center of the room, fingering the string of pearls around her neck. She's a very slender woman with narrow features and bleached blond hair that could almost pass as a wig, dressed in a stylish suit jacket, pencil skirt, and heels that make her the same height as Jewels. She couldn't look any more out of place in the dump.

"You know a coat of paint could do wonders to the place," she says. "My son-in-law's a contractor. I could get you a good deal on fixing that hole."

Jewels clutches my arm, eyeing the place like it's about to explode. "Unless your son-in-law's in the business of performing miracles, I think we'll pass."

"Sweetheart, with the price range you asked me to work with, this is what you're going to get." She holds her hands out to her side. "I'm sorry, but this is Manhattan."

"It's okay," I tell her. "Thanks for your time."

We follow her down the three flights of stairs and back outside where two police officers have joined the crowd surrounding the homeless men. One of the homeless men is down on his knees, sobbing, and the other is being detained by one of the officers.

Barbara pulls a business card from her designer handbag and hands it to me. "If you change your mind about any of the places we saw today, give me a call. You seem like a sweet girl. I wish you luck in finding somewhere nicer than this." She casually strolls away past the escalating drama like she's seen it all before.

My phone buzzes with another text from Theo. He's been keeping tabs on us all day, wondering how the apartment hunting pans out. I'm hesitant to tell him just how bad the places were since he was nice enough to send a realtor my way.

"I'm sorry we didn't find anything," Jewels tells me. "Looks like you'll just have to stay with us until you can afford a nicer place." She eyes the police officers, grabbing my arm. "Let's get a taxi and get the hell out of here before we're pillaged or murdered."

"Wait," I say, pulling her back to me. "I'm not staying with you guys. After everything you've been through, you deserve time alone. I know how excited you were to share a place with Adam. And I need to be on my own instead of relying on my bestie to hold my hand. Besides, I found another option."

She draws her eyebrows together. "What? When?"

"Erik offered me his spare room."

"He *what*?" Her eyes light with disbelief. "I hope

you're not seriously considering staying with him! It'd make more sense to stay with us!"

"Would you chill? He's got a *really* nice place, Jewels. He said I could stay free of charge if I clean for him. I guess his cleaning lady quit or something."

Jewels folds her arms with one of her deep, teacher-like frowns. "How do you know he's got a nice place?"

Knowing she's going to be even more livid, I bite my lip. "I went there with Chloe."

The frown dissolves. "Why didn't you tell me?" Now she just looks hurt that I wouldn't trust her with my secret.

"Because I figured you'd freak out like this. I'm sorry, Jewels. I just wanted to give him a chance and check the place out before I made any kind of a decision. His offer seemed too good to be true."

"That's because it is! He's probably expecting you to repay him with sexual favors!"

"Wow. You think I'd agree to do something like that?" I snap with a huff.

"I think it's something *he* would expect! He's not someone you want to get involved with!"

"I don't plan on getting *involved* with him, I just want to live in his apartment." I flinch as the half-lie falls from my lips. "Besides, what do you really know about Erik other than what Adam says? I've probably spent more time with him than you have. He's a little on the arrogant side, but if he's truly the big asshole like you keep saying he is, why would he offer me his spare room?"

"I don't know, Kel. Maybe because he wants to have sex with you?"

I laugh in a hollow sound. "You really think that little of me, huh?"

"Not *you, him!*" Her face turns a dark scarlet, something I rarely see. "God, quit doing that! Don't you remember that I threatened to punch you next time you thought something like that? I *don't* think you're the sex addict you see yourself as. I'm more concerned with what will happen if you move in with Erik!"

Some of the crowd gathered down the street has started to take interest in our conversation, and they're not the type we want attention from. I wrap my hand around Jewels's wrist and lean in. "I appreciate your concern, really. I know you're just worried about me, but I can handle myself. I'm not signing any kind of contract or anything. If it doesn't work out, I'll move back in with you."

Jewels lets out a soft sigh. "I just don't want to see you get hurt."

"I won't. Besides, last night Theo and I entertained the idea of dating." I release her wrist and smile. Suddenly, I realize how much I want this thing with Theo to happen. If I live with Erik, it'll be with the original understanding that we won't have sex. "I'm not going to do anything to mess that up."

"Really?" She beams back at me. "Oh my god, nothing would make me happier than to have my two besties hook up! Wait until I tell Adam!"

"*Please* don't make a big deal out of it. We decided to take things slow. I'm done having sexual romps with random guys. If I'm going to pursue this thing with Theo, I'm going to do it right. I can't even remember the last time I went on a *real* date."

"I'm so happy for you!" She bursts forward to wrap her arms around me. "I hope you're ready for this. I have a feeling nothing could top the kind of dates Theo will plan."

After we return to the brownstone, I sneak out to the backyard to call Erik while Jewels is in the bathroom. I mentally brace myself. *I can do this.*

He answers on the second ring. "It's getting late. I expected you here by now." His tone is light and playful.

"I'm only moving in with you on one condition," I say, taking a deep breath. "We are *not* having sex ever again."

There's a delayed moment of silence. Then, "I was under the impression that you were enjoying yourself last night."

With the deep roll of his voice, I'm reminded just how much I *did* enjoy myself. The memory of his probing tongue and the way he pulled on my nipples makes me throb between my legs all over again. Damn it, why did he have to be so good?

"I did. I'm not going to lie, it was incredibly hot. But I don't need the added complication of random sex in my life. I need to focus on finding a job, and a decent place I can afford on my own or with a roommate. So the only way I'll stay with you is if you promise there won't be any sex involved. I mean it, Erik."

"I promise there won't be any sex involved unless you come crawling back to me on all fours and beg for it. Is that good enough?"

The vision of myself crawling to him makes me immensely horny all over again. I normally wouldn't think I'm the type to enjoy guys telling me what to do, but there's something about the way Erik is always so demanding that I'm unable to resist. I have to swallow before I can find my voice.

"You won't have to worry about that happening." As I say the words, I can hear the uncertainty in my voice.

In the end I agree to let Jewels take me to Erik's, mostly because it's the first time I'll have seen him since we had sex and I'm nervous as hell. We order carry out with Adam before heading down to the subway. He takes the news much better than Jewels did, but he's a little too quiet until it's time to say goodbye.

"Be careful," he whispers during our parting embrace. "He's the master of manipulation."

"Thanks for everything," I answer, pretending his words don't worry me. "I'll come visit after your next procedure."

He pulls away, his eyes downcast. I can't tell if he's disappointed or worried.

I don't know how I'll react to seeing Erik again until he opens the door to his apartment, grinning in that cocky way that's become so familiar when he notices Jewels at my side. "I wasn't aware you were bringing help to clean. You should know I won't pay extra."

My body still responds to him, though his dick-like attitude helps cool me off just fine. I brush past him with my suitcase in tow. "You're hilarious."

Jewels steps in beside me in the center of the living room, her eyes alight as she takes everything in. "Wow. How long have you lived here?"

"Since a month after I graduated high school," Erik answers her cooly. He stands with his feet firmly planted in the kitchen like he's afraid to get too close to us. "I'm so surprised to hear my brother doesn't tell you much about me."

Jewels doesn't answer. She's tight-lipped as she continues to study the place. Excitement reflects in her gaze when she turns to me. "And here I thought I had the coolest place in the city," she whispers.

"I know, right?" I whisper back.

"I assume I'll be seeing a lot of you," Erik says, his steely gaze locked on Jewels. "Let Adam know he's welcome to join you, if it doesn't pain him too much to be around me."

Jewels flashes him a tight smile, making me feel awkward as hell. "I'll do that."

Erik reaches for a duffle bag on the kitchen counter. "I'm heading to the gym." His expression becomes authoritative when he locks eyes with me. "Your key is on the nightstand in your bedroom. I assume you're capable of finding your way around, figuring out how things work. You'll find the supplies you need to clean under the kitchen sink, and a few in my bedroom closet. I expect the place to shine by the time I get back." He faces Jewels. "Don't forget what I said."

Then he slips out of the apartment, leaving Jewels to gape after him. "Is he for real?"

"Pretty sure."

"At least I don't have to worry about you falling for him." She rolls her eyes to the ceiling. "What an *asshole*. I can't believe he expects you to clean this late! Seriously, I'm staying to help. It's ridiculous."

"You're not staying. You have to be up early for your first class tomorrow," I insist, shaking my head. A part of me is extremely jealous that she's continuing school without a break. Hopefully I can get my shit together so I'll only miss one semester. "And I don't want you running around in the subway by yourself in the middle of the night."

She waves her hand through the air, scoffing. "Adam already insisted that I take a taxi back. It's all good."

"Still. I'll get it done. Come check out my room before you leave."

Chills seep up my spine when I open the door to Erik's room to give Jewels a peek. The memory of us making out on his bed is too fresh to deal with. I'll have to be quick about cleaning in here.

"A neat freak, I should've guessed," she comments with another roll of her eyes.

We continue on to my room where I set the suitcase next to the bed. Jewels and I flop onto our backs on the mattress in unison, laughing as we stare up at the high ceiling.

Jewels clicks her tongue. "Really, I can't understand why you wanted to stay here. This place is horrendous. You would've been better off with the rat-infested place in Chinatown."

I poke her in the arm. "It's okay to be jealous."

"Who would've guessed a year ago these two Wisconsin chicks would be living in *New fucking York*? Doesn't it blow your mind when you think about it?"

I turn my head to face her. "I'm sorry I dropped the news on you the way I did. I should've told you right away. It's just after Adam's surgery and every-thing, I didn't want to burden you with my problems."

"Your problems are *not* a burden. You know you can always tell me anything, right?"

"Yeah, and I will. Eventually." I offer her a weak smile. "Once I'm ready to come to term with things at my own speed."

Jewels doesn't stay much longer. By the time we say goodnight, I've convinced myself everything is going to work out the way it's supposed to. She's only gone a few minutes before Theo calls. I close my eyes, realizing I have yet to tell him I'm living with another guy.

"Hey, Cavenaugh."

"Hey," I answer, curling up on my bed. "How was your day?"

"Shitty. I didn't get to see you." His warm chuckles make my toes tingle. "You busy? Maybe I can stop over."

"Actually, I'm just getting ready to clean my new apartment."

"You found a place? *That* was fast. I thought the apartments you looked at today weren't going to work out."

"It's not something we saw today." Closing my eyes, I brace myself. "Adam's brother offered me his spare room until I find something I can afford."

He's quiet for a beat, probably trying to decide

how he feels about me living with another guy, especially if he's heard Adam speak ill of his little brother. "Is it nearby?"

"It's on the Upper West side, near Central Park."

"Great neighborhood." He's quiet again. "Maybe I should've offered my guest room to you. I guess I figured you were trying to find a place on your own."

"I was, but it turns out there's nothing decent in my budget. And I probably would've turned you down anyway. Living together would've just complicated this thing between us, and I don't want to screw it up. But I hope you'll come hang out here soon. This place is pretty amazing."

"So there's no need for me to be jealous of this guy you're living with?"

"Absolutely not," I say too quickly. Lying to Theo feels all kinds of wrong, but I can't have him worrying if we're going to start dating. "The guy's a major prick."

"Good to know."

We engage in small talk for a bit longer before I tell him I have to go. I don't know how long I have before Erik returns.

"Sweet dreams, Cavenaugh," Theo tells me, his voice soft. "I'll see you soon."

With my heart fluttering from our conversation, I quickly start cleaning. Up close the bathroom isn't in the sparkling condition I first thought. The stone in the shower is cracked, and the toilet doesn't sit squarely. At least Erik seems to hit the toilet and doesn't leave a mess on the floor.

I finish in there before heading to his bedroom for the rest of the cleaning products. His closet is like a small room in itself, lined with multiple rows of hanging clothes, dozens of shoe racks, and a hand full of cupboards. It's every girl's dream closet.

The way his clothes are arranged by season and color, Erik appears to be a total neat freak like Jewels suggested. If I weren't so worried that he'd kick me out, I'd mess things up just to ruffle his feathers.

I start opening cupboards in search of what I'll need. Some are filled with meticulously folded clothes, others random office supplies, picture albums, DVDs, just about everything. I didn't see any closets in the rest of the loft, so this must be the only place for general storage. Curious to know Erik a little better, I run my finger across the DVDs and read the titles. A majority of them have the most outrageous titles. It takes me a moment to realize they're *porn*.

"What a *perv*," I say, rolling my eyes.

Moving on to the next cupboard, I gasp when I find furry handcuffs, whips, and an assortment of other sex toys. I take in each object with bewilderment, wondering how many times he's used them and on how many different women. Some are still in their package, as if he's waiting to use them on a random hook up.

Visions of Erik tying me up to his bed and doing things to me with the toys slam into me without the slightest warning. I picture his smooth, naked body perched over me, whip in hand as he—

Slamming the cupboard shut, I stumble away.

It's going to take a tremendous amount of willpower to pretend I didn't stumble across Erik's fetishes.

Chapter Seven

I STIR with the rich smell of bacon drifting through the air. I finished cleaning the loft after midnight, but Erik still wasn't home. Obviously he did more than go to the gym, though I had to remind myself it really isn't any of my business what he was doing. Considering our rather unique arrangement, I get the feeling it will be a whole new experience having Erik as my roommate rather than Jewels.

Crawling from the bed, I stretch my sore muscles. I'm unusually stiff from washing the massive wooden floors on my hands and knees. I quickly throw a bra underneath my tank top and run a brush through my hair before stumbling out to the kitchen.

Erik stands at the stove, shirtless. The toned muscles in his shoulders flex and turn with each movement he makes. I remember running my hands along the deep curve of his back, down to the smooth patch of skin just above his taut ass. I grumble under my breath when my hormones react to the pleasurable sight.

"Good morning," he says without turning around.

"Morning." I bite down on my lips when I realize I'm about to comment that he was out late. *Not my business.* I settle into one of the stools at the island. "Any recommendations on where to get groceries?"

He turns around with a plate of bacon and eggs in hand. "Two blocks south of here there's a mom and pop store that should have everything you need." He sets the plate in front of me, meeting my gaze for the first time.

I swallow down a sudden surge of excitement. "You don't have to cook for me."

"I know. So say thank you, and eat it." He smirks before turning back to the stove.

"Thank you." I take a bite of the eggs, cursing to myself. He's even a pretty decent cook. "You have class today?" I brace myself, hoping the question doesn't come off as too nosy. I'm simply trying to think of polite conversation. It still feels awkward considering he was inside of me less than 48 hours ago.

"Not until eleven." He motions to the other end of the island with the spatula. "I set the want ads out so you could start looking for a job. You can take the subway virtually anywhere in the city, so apply for anything that sounds interesting."

"Thanks." I'm surprisingly touched that he's being so helpful, even though he *is* acting a little cordial, all things considered.

"I was pleased with the way the apartment looked last night. Do that once each week, and you'll earn your keep." His steely blue eyes latch onto me. "Any problems finding what you needed?"

The tantalizing way he's looking at me, its obvious he knows I came across his stash, and it pleases him. I almost choke on a mouthful of eggs, but catch myself before he can detect that his words jolted me. "Your closet's huge, but it was easy enough."

"If you ever find anything in there you want to borrow, all you have to do is ask." He winks before shoveling a fork filled with eggs in his mouth.

Fuck me. This is going to be much harder than I thought.

The day's filled with calls to potential employers, most of which have already filled the position or require a four year education. Frustrated, I visit the grocery store, then spend a few hours trying to make the plain bedroom feel more like *mine*. I eventually give in and flip the TV on, mindlessly scrolling through the channels and eating carrot sticks until I fall asleep.

I start with the sound of the front door slamming against the wall. High-pitched giggles pierce the air. I scoot up from the couch to see Erik embracing a rather curvy blonde sporting a strip of white fabric that doesn't leave one to wonder what she would look like completely naked. Although she's wearing a bit too much makeup, her blond hair is long and silky, spilling across her large breasts, and her skin's a beautiful shade of olive. She's gorgeous, and *way* too old for Erik.

They don't seem to notice me watching from the couch as Erik lifts her by her impossibly small waist to perch on the edge of the island. Blondie wraps her legs around him, her bright red heels and matching manicured fingers moving around behind his back as they begin to make out. I can't see her face behind Erik, but I can hear her heavy breaths and see her long, slender legs locking around him like he's a fly caught in her web.

I become mesmerized by the way they rock together as they kiss—*dry humping* as my sister Megan would call it—their mouths every bit as insatiable as their wandering hands. About the time Blondie removes Erik's shirt and begins to trace his smooth chest with her tongue, I decide I need to bolt. Still, I can't move other than to grab a pillow and hold it in my heated lap. If I get up now, they'll know exactly what kind of pervert I was to watch them this long without saying anything. My other option is to pretend I was sleeping, though I doubt they'll fall for the lie.

The woman's long fingernails disappear beneath the waistline of Erik's jeans, grabbing onto his ass while he reaches down to open a drawer at his side. I duck my head behind the safety of the couch when her face suddenly becomes visible, though her eyes are shut as Erik runs his mouth up the side of her neck.

A few long, drawn-out moments later, Blondie screams with pleasure. When I gather the courage to look again, Erik's looking down, watching himself slam into her as she rides him.

"You like that?" he asks between huffing breaths.

"God, yes. You're fucking amazing," Blondie answers, panting.

Clutching the pillow in my hands, I'm hit with an unexpected, raging surge of jealousy.

That could be me if I would just give in.

Unable to bear watching them any longer, I lay back on the couch and cover the pillow over my head, drowning out their noises of bliss as I try to reason with myself. Just because I may have gotten a touch turned on watching Erik get it on with another woman doesn't mean *I* want to have sex with him. He's no good for me. If I'm going to continue being his roommate, nothing else will ever happen between us. It can't.

Blondie makes one last screech that probably woke anyone in the apartment building who isn't used to Erik's trysts. Erik grunts loudly, and the slapping sounds stop. Once it seems safe to peek again, Blondie's slithering into her dress with a wide smile as Erik zips up his pants. She pulls him in for one last, sultry kiss. Her lips are still lingering in the space between them when she says, "I had fun tonight. Maybe next time we can convince your roommate to actually *join in* instead of just watching."

Blondie turns to wink at me before grabbing her purse and waltzing out the door. By the time Erik regards me with one of his grins that lets the world know he's completely full of himself, I'm seriously paralyzed to the couch, staring at him in horror.

Erik's dark laughter follows him to his bedroom.

By the next day, I'm convinced Erik asked me to move in with him as some kind of sick game to see how long it will take to break me, before I agree to have sex with him again. I wait until I know he's gone to classes before sneaking out to the kitchen, wanting to avoid the awkward questions and explanations that will be coming next time we're face to face.

But he's waiting for me in the kitchen with a plate of his delicious eggs, shirtless once again.

I stop in place, the temperature of my face spiking through the roof.

He raises one dark brow. "Did you sleep well?"

"Aren't you supposed to be in class?" I snap, refusing to step any farther.

"Not today." When he realizes I'm not going to accept the plate, he sets it down with a devilish grin. "Look. If you're embarrassed over what happened last night, don't be. If you had only said something, Maura and I would've been more than happy to have you play along."

"We've been through this. I already told you that I'm not having sex with you again, Erik. If you keep harassing me, this isn't going to work."

"You never said anything about having sex with *others*. Maura would've been more than happy to exclude me. She's done it before."

It dawns on me just how many women Erik has probably slept with before our romp in the alley. Suddenly I feel like the stereotypical notch in the bedpost. How did I get myself into this situation? I cover my face with my hands, moaning, and head back to my room.

The remainder of the week I keep myself as busy as possible with my never-ending job search. My friends are all too busy with work and school to stop over, which is totally understandable, so I test my limits on how far I can wander from the apartment on my own. I become pretty skilled at figuring out the subway system thanks to an app Jewels recommended. It's amazing how many things there are to see around the city without spending a dime.

I finally score an interview with a deli down the street late Thursday afternoon, but can only understand every other word the owner speaks in a thick Russian accent and have to withdraw my application. Otherwise the job hunting continues to look pretty bleak, even after I join a few websites that boast available opportunities in the city.

Whenever I know Erik's going to be home, I either find an excuse to leave the apartment or hide out in my bedroom. It's not ideal, and I can see how much it amuses Erik whenever we *do* run into each other. Yet I begin to feel like the arrangement may actually work.

Friday night I have plans to attend the opening of a new club in the Meatpacking District with Chloe and Jewels, sans any guys. Theo had plans to take his sister to the upper part of the state to celebrate her birthday, and Adam decides he doesn't want to be the only testosterone among the group. I'm finishing up the final touches of eyeliner when there's a knock at my door.

"Yeah?" I call out.

The door creaks open. Erik takes my low cut dress in with a smoldering gaze. "You look good enough to eat. Hot date?"

"Yep," I say, turning from him to add lip gloss. Avoiding his sultry looks seems to be the key to preventing myself from giving in. Because hearing his "eating" comment just adds sparks to my belly.

He steps into my room, resting his elbow on my dresser, watching me. "Is it your plan to completely ignore me the entire time you're living here?"

I sigh deeply. He's like a child, always looking for attention. "Only as long as you continue to make sexual innuendoes. Otherwise, it's actually possible for us to be *friends*."

"In that case, as *friends*, would it be inappropriate for me to ask that you accompany me to a Broadway show tomorrow night? It's a requirement for one of my general credits. I'd go alone, but then I'd have to spend the night warding off pesky advances."

"I can see how that would be bothersome." I glance back at him, smirking. "What. Maura's busy?"

"She's just someone I occasionally hook up with. Broadway shows aren't her style anyway. Besides, she'd be too much of a distraction."

I fluff my hair as I consider his offer. Chloe has a gig in Jersey, and Jewels wants to spend the night in with Adam. With Theo out of town, I really don't have any other options. Plus I really do want to take in a show on Broadway. It seems to be one of those things in New York that everyone has to experience at least once. "How much are the tickets?"

"I've got it." He heads back toward the doorway. "Be ready to go by five. We're going to dinner first."

He's out of the room by the time I realize, in a round-about way, I inadvertently just agreed to a date without even saying yes.

Saturday morning I sleep off a brutal hangover before heading out in search of a simple dress for the show with Erik. I read online that people wear a wide variety of fashion to these things, but among the few items I packed, none of them seem appropriate. I find a sleeveless dress on a clearance rack with a high neckline and knee-length hem that's fashionable while covering enough to keep Erik from gawking.

I'm ready to go a few minutes before five and find Erik in the kitchen, dressed in a blazer and cuffed shorts with a pair of slip-ons. Although still maddeningly attractive, he looks like he's about to sail out on a yacht.

He studies me with his head cocked. "So not what I pictured you wearing, but you look passable."

I roll my eyes. "Thanks. Let's do this thing."

The private car waiting outside takes us to a darkly lit restaurant near Times Square where a delightful aroma triggers a grumble in my stomach.

The host wears a crisp suit and treats Erik like he's VIP from the minute we arrive, rushing us past those waiting to a small table veiled by dark drapes, fussing over us until he's sure Erik is pleased.

We're left alone with a wine menu and the sound of violin music beneath a ceiling filled with ornate chandeliers. Erik peruses the lists of wines, smirking.

I glare around the intimate area, put off by the upscale feel and the fact that we're segregated from the others in the restaurant. Everything here is going to cost a small fortune. "You *know* this is not a date, right?"

"Of course. We're here as friends." His eyes flicker to mine for a brief moment. "Dates aren't something I indulge in."

A waitress appears in a beautiful black dress to take our wine order and bring us full menus. Erik orders a bottle of pinot while I look through my dinner options. The cheapest meal I can find is a salad for $25.

"Good thing you don't make a habit of dating." I say once the waitress has left. "You couldn't have found somewhere cheaper to take me?"

"Having wealthy grandparents gave me the option to dine at only the finest restaurants." He shrugs with a smirk. "Would you rather I take you to McDonalds? You seem slightly overdressed for fast food."

Rolling my eyes, I look back to the menu. "It's just not the lifestyle I'm used to."

"Consider it a cleaning bonus. You take care of me, I'll take care of you."

I squirm in my seat, warning myself not to take the meaning of his words too far. I end up ordering steak and shrimp, Erik the lamb. After my first glass of wine, I finally begin to relax. Erik doesn't seem as flirty as usual, so it's easier to have conversations in which I can trust myself to behave.

"Why'd you pick New York?" I ask him while we're waiting for our meal.

"Same as you." He swirls his glass of wine by its stem, staring down into the liquid. "I wanted to get away. I never imagined my brother would end up out here. He hadn't ever left the Midwest until he met Jewels. The world never seems to be a big enough place."

"Whatever happened between you and Adam must've really pissed him off." I sip my wine, waiting for him to break down and confess.

His stoic expression doesn't change. "Everyone has something in their past they'd like to go back and change. But since that's not possible, you have to move forward. That's what you're trying to do by living here, isn't it?"

"I guess. Maybe it would help if you let up on Jewels and Adam a little. You come off as being arrogant. Not everyone can deal with that type of personality."

He looks up, meeting my gaze. "You seem to handle me without any difficulties."

My cheeks grow warm beneath his baby blues. If only there was a way for me to stop physically responding to him. "I'm not exactly loved by all either. I tend to call things as I see them."

"It's part of the reason you're attracted to me. People like us have to stick together."

I bring my curled hair around one shoulder, giving my shaking hands something to do. "It doesn't mean we should have casual sex, if that's where you're going with this."

"I'm not going to lie to you." He leans forward, closing the space between us. "You stir something primal in me. I really enjoyed taking you in that alley. I'd love for it to happen again."

Leaning back in my chair, I take another drink of wine, pushing back the pleasurable memories of our night together. "Except that I'm moving forward, as you said. So it can't happen again. It *won't*."

The waitress approaches with our food, breaking the uncomfortable flow. I pay for our meal when we're done, letting Erik know that I'm going to start paying him *something* for rent. It's the only way I know how to prevent myself from feeling like a kept woman.

The rest of the night is relatively harmless. He doesn't make any advances during *The Book of Mormon*, and I get so caught up in the production that I almost forget he's at my side. By the time we return to our apartment, the vibe between us feels less like a date and more like a couple of friends hanging out. Thankfully there isn't an awkward moment where we have to say goodnight, or think of what to say to each other next. Erik heads for his room. I change into my pajamas before slipping into the bathroom.

As I'm finishing brushing my teeth, however, Erik appears in the doorway without a stitch of clothing, his magnificent body on display. I drop my toothbrush in the sink and consume every succulent inch of him in with my eyes, my heart lodged in my throat.

"Just so we're clear, I'm used to getting what I want." With his eyebrows raised, smirks. "And I *really* want to fuck you."

He advances toward me in the flash of an eye. I open my mouth to say his name or tell him to stop, I'm not sure which. But he covers my lips in a seething hot kiss and his hands are suddenly everywhere, eagerly groping and kneading my flesh. I stand frozen in place with my hands at my sides, telling myself to back away, but his massive hard on pushes against my stomach and I can't think. I fall apart with memories of our tryst in the alley and moan into his mouth, twinning my hands through the thick of his hair.

We don't stop kissing as Erik lifts me to sit on the sink, then reaches down to one of the drawers. I hear the dull sound of foil ripping. He stops to roll a rubber onto himself, watching me the entire time with a blazing determination. I'm breathless, driven by nothing more than my overwhelming need to have him inside me.

It's like I'm literally on fire when his talented lips return to mine. He's quick to yank down my shorts and underwear in one movement, ripping something in the process. There's no time to think, no time to process what I'm doing. He sinks into me easily, biting my lip and pulling on my pierced nipple. Stars of lechery and delightful pain flash before my eyes.

"Say my name," he commands, his breath hot against my ear. "I want to hear you fucking scream it."

I comply, digging my fingernails into his warm skin. He sinks deeper and deeper into me with each thrust, his steely stare unrelenting. I move my hands down to grip his tight ass, lost in a mix of his tantalizing smell, the taste of toothpaste, the raw sounds of our skin slapping together, and the delightful pang as he pushes into me. My head spins and spins like I'm stuck on a sinister carnival ride.

By the time he climaxes, moaning loudly with one final trust, the cloud of desire passes and the heavy realization of what just happened slams into me with the force of a runaway truck. I don't move when Erik kisses me one final time, his tongue brushing against mine as he gropes my breasts. He sucks on my bottom lip and pulls out of me with a pleased smirk crossing his lips. "It's like I said. I get what I want."

"*Hole. E. Shit,*" I whisper to myself after he's left the bathroom.

What have I done?

Chapter Eight

THE NEXT COUPLE of days are long and stressful as I try to battle the guilt of giving in to my burning needs with Erik *again*. At least he's conveniently away from the apartment most of the time. I have no idea how to interact with him when he actually is around, so I stay locked away in my room. My body craves him despite the misgivings of my mind. Moving out seems to be the only option at this point, but where would I go?

More than ever, I wish I had someone to talk to, maybe help me sort through my dizzying feelings. Growing up with a religious mom, I was told premarital sex is a sin. There weren't any talks of safe sex or waiting for love. I was never told how to deal with a guy afterwards if you *do* give in to your desires. Last year I messed around with Matt on a regular basis, but we were good friends, so hanging out when we weren't having sex felt natural. This back and forth with Erik has worn on my nerves.

Theo calls every night. Instead of answering his calls, I send a text out in the mornings with some lame excuse. I can't talk to him any more than I can look at myself in the mirror.

When Chloe calls one morning to see if I want to hang out, I jump at the chance to set my mind on something else and get the hell out of the apartment. We end up shopping for the things I wish I would've packed from home. As much as I want desperately to confide in Chloe, I worry what she'll think of me sleeping with Erik—especially after she made a comment about him letting me stay with him in exchange for sex. What if that's really what's going on, but I'm just too daft to acknowledge it?

Once we return to the apartment, Chloe throws her armload of bags on the island, huffing with the movement. "This is a *lot* of stuff. I can't imagine starting over like this. Once we get everything unloaded, I can take you to a few of the cheap knock off stores. I would think you're going to run out of new things to wear before too long."

"Thanks," I say, pretending not to be so fearful that Erik could walk through the door at any moment. "Eventually I hope to have my things from home shipped out, but I could use a few more outfits in the meantime."

She shimmies up to sit on to the countertop,

her dark eyes scanning the loft as she swings her feet. I'm thrown off for a moment when I remember the blonde having sex with Erik in the very same spot. "Where's prince charming? Off polishing his fangs? That guy's something else. Part of me couldn't believe you actually took him up on his offer. I mean I get it, this place is amaze-balls, but the attitude...ugh, I don't know. Either you're a lot tougher skinned than I am, or that shit's just an acquired taste that gets some getting used to."

"He had classes or something. I guess he won't be back until late tonight."

Chloe's eyes grow wide with excitement. "Holy shit, I know exactly what you need to do. Let's invite some peeps over for dinner and cocktails, have a little party! It's not every day you land a place this stellar. If you're going to be a real New Yorker, you have to learn to entertain the shit out of people on a whim. We could get some sushi from Chinatown and grab a few bottles of booze from the liquor store on our way back."

I'm instantly intrigued with the idea. Remembering Erik's short list of rules, I decide having a few people over wouldn't violate anything. Having friends over would help relieve some of the tension as well. "It would be a *little* party. You're one of five people I know, Erik included, and Jewels has to work tonight."

Chloe counts her fingers. "Wait. Who's the fifth person?"

"Have you met Theo? Jewels and Adam's friend?"

"*Oh yeah*. That man is one sexy piece of meat, I tell you. Not my type—I like my men to be able to rock a guitar—but I mean, have you seen his massive arms? Those gorgeous eyes, they draw you in with a 'come hither' vibe. I guess he doesn't have a girlfriend, which is a complete travesty. The guy's the complete package."

"He wants to take me on a date." *And I've probably fucked up any chance of us actually being together by continuing to play these twisted games with Erik.*

"Holy shit!" She claps her hands excitedly. "What are you waiting for? Call that hot man up and invite him over already! We'll find you a new outfit to wow the pants off him. It'll be so fucking fun!"

Laughing, I start texting everyone about our impromptu shindig. Even though it will be hard to face him at first with my dirty little secret hanging over my shoulder, seeing Theo again might be exactly what it's going to take to clear my head.

Adam, Jewels, James, Chloe and the two guys from her band—Beckett and Landon—mill around with hip music floating through the air. Dressed in the latest fashion from a boutique near Chelsea, watching my friends in my apartment, I feel incredibly mature and put together. For the first time since leaving home, I finally feel like I was meant to be here, even if it *is* someone else's apartment. Someone who I still need to get away from as soon as financially possible.

Jewels sneaks up to my side with a glass of white wine in hand. "See, this is exactly why I had to switch my shift for this party. You're freaking *glowing*, Kel. I haven' seen you this happy in a long time."

I bring my attention back to the new plate of sushi I was trying to arrange artfully. "Yeah, except Theo still isn't here. Do you think I should call him?"

"Don't over think it. He's coming, I promise. He probably just got held up having to comfort one of the starlets he's been working with. You know how those gorgeous actresses like to get attention, feel wanted."

"You always know what to say to make me feel better," I deadpan, shooting her a dull look.

Her full lips pull back in a grin. "What else are best friends for?"

"Taking this tray over to the living area, and *looking real pretty*." I push the tray into her hands and give her a mocking smile. "Maybe throw a little of that old cheerleader attitude of yours in to get the guys going."

"We've got spirit, yes we do!" she mocks, wiggling her butt. I slap it before she saunters away.

The doorbell rings, creating a bundle of giddiness and fear in the pit of my gut. I haven't seen Theo since I told him that I moved in with Erik. *Or since you fucked Erik again,* an annoying little voice in my head quickly reminds me.

Swinging the apartment door open, I'm delighted with the sight of a smiling Theo wearing a navy button down and cargo shorts, a bright bouquet of wild flowers in hand.

"Cavenaugh."

I burst forward to hug him, shivering delightfully when his solid arms cradle me, bringing me against his rock hard chest. My lungs fill with his crisp scent of Irish soap and cool aftershave. "I missed you," I say, pulling away. "I'm so glad you're here."

Jewels hollers Theo's name behind us. Chloe and one of the guys holler out a "heyyyy!" after.

"Sorry it took so long for me to get here. Traffic was a beast." Theo slips his hand into mine and squeezes, flashing me one of his most gorgeous smiles. "I've been waiting to see you all week."

I tug him inside and shut the door. "What can I get you to drink?"

"I would venture to guess you have Jameson?" He raises his eyebrows, and I laugh.

Taking the flowers, I drop his hand and head for

the collection of liquor on the island. I fill a glass with ice and Jameson, then hand it to Theo. He's distracted, his eyes darting around the spacious loft. I can't quite read him when his eyebrows draw down as the rest of his expression is still light, curious. "Damn, this place is something else. How much is your rent?"

"Um...nothing yet, though I told him I expect to start paying him *something*. For now I just have to clean for him once a week." I stop to swallow hard, realizing how ridiculous it must sound that I'm staying in a place this amazing without paying a dime. "He's only letting me stay until I can afford a place on my own."

Theo turns to me with a sudden, unexpected fire in his eyes. "Does he expect you to have sex with him?"

The question throws me for such a loop that I have to take a moment to catch my breath. "Of course not!" I yell. Jewels stops dancing with Adam to look my way, her brow furrowed.

So technically I am lying, but I *had* sex with Erik, past tense. And when I look into the intriguing eyes of this gorgeous man, I suddenly want to be his girl-friend more than anything. I may have messed up before now, but I vow I won't let it happen again. I don't want to worry about the complicated bullshit that comes with Erik, even if sex with him is hotter than hell.

I want Theo. I can see myself truly happy with him.

Running his hand over his head and down the back of his neck, Theo looks down to the floor. "Shit. That was out of line." His green eyes flicker back on me. "My last girlfriend was sleeping around with guys to get what she wanted. I guess it's made me insensitive. I'm sorry for being an ass."

"It probably wasn't too out of line," I concede, setting my hand on his bulging bicep. "The arrangement *is* a little far-fetched. But I promise, I'm not going to have sex with Erik, so there's nothing for you to worry about."

Theo's bright smile returns. He squeezes my elbow. "Glad to hear it."

Jewels and Adam are suddenly at our side. While Adam and Theo exchange some kind of manly hand-shake/slap combination and launch into a conversation on an upcoming movie premiere, Jewels stares me down with concern, silently asking if I'm okay. I pass her a subtle nod, smiling.

"About time you showed up, big guy," Jewels tells Theo, lightly punching his arm. "Kel thought she was going to have to take me up on the offer to hire a room full of strippers to properly welcome her."

"Glad I could be accommodating," Theo answers with a deep laugh. My stomach stirs excitedly with the sound of it.

"Very funny," I say, taking a sip of my drink.

Jewels stabs her thumb over her shoulder where the rest of the guests bounce around to a hip hop tune. "Why are we standing here when there's sushi and dancing over in *that* section of the apartment?" She takes me by the hand to lead me away, doing a little jig with her feet. She glances back at Theo. "If you want to hang with her, you're going to have to show her your moves."

I shoot Theo a suggestive smile over my shoulder before we join the others, falling into rhythm of the beat. Chloe squeals delightfully, and knocks into me with her hips. Jewels steps in on Chloe's other side, sandwiching her between us. We become a tangled mess of arms and legs, grinding and swaying to the explosive beat.

Soon I feel large hands slipping over my hips, and feel Theo's excitement against my back as he joins in. For a minute I'm jolted, remembering how Erik did the same thing not too long ago. Telling myself this isn't the same, I bring my hands up over my head to wrap around his neck, bringing him close while we sway in sync.

"You're so damn sexy, Cavenaugh," he whispers, his breath hot against my ear.

His hands run up and down my sides, igniting every last of my nerves. Eager to feel more of his wandering hands, my underwear becomes wet. I close my eyes, enjoying his hard body pressed against me, his breath blazing hot against my neck.

Dancing with a guy has always had the effect of an aphrodisiac on me, which always seems to be what gets me in trouble. *Damn*, I really want to kiss the hell out of him.

Realizing this is exactly how things escalated so quickly with Erik, I back away. I can't let things progress with Theo too far, this fast, or it'll just end up another worthless fling. If he gets what he wants from me, he'll likely grow bored and move on. When I turn around in Theo's arms, it's clear by the turned on look in his eyes that he thinks I'm about to kiss him.

I give his chest a small push, distancing us. "Bathroom break."

His hooded gaze breaks and he tips his head in understanding with a little grin. I half stumble away from my friends, drunk on hormones. I pass the bathroom, however, and head straight for Erik's room, locking the door behind me.

The air's cooler in the large bedroom, and Erik's musky scent lingers. Everything is in the exact same place as it was when I last cleaned, as if he wasn't even in here the past week. I pace in front of the large windows, my vision hazy as I look out to the sparkling city lights below. What in the hell possessed me to come in *here*, and not my own room?

My eyes flicker over to Erik's closet. I cross the room in long, quick strides, flinging the doors open.

My heart pounds against my ribcage as I reach for the cabinet I know to have Erik's naughty bits. I find the vibrator I saw earlier, still in its package, and don't even hesitate when I rip it free. I'll replace it with a new one before he realizes it's missing.

It's more important that I find a way to stop these urges if I'm going to be around Theo all night without losing control. I shut the door to the closet, muffling the sound as I turn the switch on, finding my sweet release.

My friends are still sweating it out in the living room when I return ten minutes later. Theo and Jewels are hamming it up together, doing the old sprinkler and reeling in a fish moves to elicit laughs from the others crowded around them, clapping in encouragement.

Adam watches from the island, sipping on a bottle of water.

"Hey," I say, slipping into the stool next to him.

"Hey," he answers, turning to me with a bright smile. Then he squints. "Are you okay?"

Holy shit, I forgot I'd be flushed from my self-induced orgasm. Admittedly, I feel a little dirty knowing what I did considering there was a room filled with guests twenty feet away. "Just warm from dancing."

Adam turns back to peer at the giant windows

framing the living room. "My brother certainly knows how to pick 'em. This place is unreal."

"Funny, that's almost exactly what Jewels told me when she first saw the brownstone you bought for her. Guess the Murphy brothers have impeccable taste." I reach for my drink and run my fingers along the rough texture of the glass. "You know, you should come over sometime when he's here. I think Erik wants the two of you to hang out."

Adam's jaw flexes. "That's not likely to happen."

"Adam, I seriously think he's trying. Maybe it's time you give the poor guy a chance."

"*Poor guy?*" He turns to me, his gaze dark. "Has he told you the reason why we don't get along?"

An uneasy feeling swirls through my gut. As much as I want to hear it, I'm still afraid to hear the truth. "No. He won't talk about it."

"You know how I was sick most of the time as a kid? Erik was pretty resentful of all the attention I got from our parents. I can't really say I blamed him. Keeping up with my doctor's appointments and hospital stays took a lot out of them. By the time they were done running around and taking care of me, it didn't leave much time for Erik. He started acting up in school, getting in fights, pulling 'F's in the easiest of classes. He turned into a real pain in the ass for our parents. They didn't really figure out what was happening until he started high school. At that point, our mom chose spending time with him over staying in the hospital at my side. But that wasn't enough for Erik. He acted out even more. It started with pot and booze, then turned into random sex with older girls, sometimes even women out of high school. He was given a driving infraction his sophomore year when a cop pulled him over for swerving over the center line. He passed the sobriety test, though. Turns out he was swerving because he was having sex with a senior girl while driving down the road.

"Our parents threatened him with everything they could think of—boarding school, military camp, detention centers—but it didn't stop him. He was out of control. I decided it was up to me to fix it, make things right. As soon as I was released from my latest stay in the hospital, I went up to his room to confront him and caught him doing a line of coke. He was loaded out of his mind, and came after me with our dad's gun."

"*Jesus*," I hiss, my eyes wide.

"I wrestled him down, he fired the gun. The bullet landed in one of his pillows, missing my head by a few inches. He became hysterical, begged me not to tell our parents what happened, or that he was using cocaine. After that night he promised to sober up, get his life back on track. I felt sorry for him, knowing half his struggles were because of me, so I agreed to it. He turned his life around just like he promised, stopped using drugs and made the honor roll, but he still played it up to our parents that he was the one worthy of their attention. They spoiled the hell out of him, buying him new cars, sending him on trips to Europe, throwing money at him like he was some kind of king. He never apologized for trying to kill me. Instead he always had this righteous smirk whenever he looked at me, as if he was gloating for never being reprimanded."

"Oh god," I say, heaving a deep sigh. "I had no idea."

He looks from our friends back to me. "I figure you deserve to know who you agreed to live with. I haven't even told Jewels what happened yet."

There's a big difference between simply being a jerk and actually being mental enough to almost *murder* your sibling. All at once I'm angry that Adam didn't tell me sooner. I'm also fearful that I'm living with someone menacing. "This was probably something that would've been helpful to know *before* I moved in with an attempted murderer."

"Considering you told me just as you were leaving to move in with him, I didn't have much notice to work with. Besides, I don't think he's physically dangerous now that he's staying off drugs." Rubbing at the back of his neck, he glances at Jewels. "I'll probably tell her now. I don't want you to have to keep that kind of secret from her. She's probably going to freak, maybe even beg you to move out. I'm not going to tell you what you can or can't do, but you need to be extremely careful around him. Erik knows exactly which buttons to push to manipulate people into getting what he wants. If you get hurt by him, I can't help but think it'd all be on me."

I bite my lip, watching as Theo and the others quit dancing when the song ends. They talk animatedly, laughing and carrying on. Theo's gaze catches with mine, and his smile grows.

One thing's clear in this moment: time to find a new roommate.

Chapter Nine

MY HOUSEWARMING PARTY is still going strong at eleven. I keep thinking I should kick everyone out before Erik shows up, but since I'm going to move out soon anyway, I just enjoy the night. We dance, and drink, and devour every last piece of sushi. I'm more relaxed around Theo, letting him move against me without it feeling dirty. He whispers sweet words into my ear, and touches me with unassuming reserve. I can't believe how lucky I am to find such an amazing guy.

Being with Theo feels *right*. I'm able to be myself around him like he's an old friend. He's fun, and gorgeous, and lights up when he's around me in a way that gets my heart fluttering. I just hope I can get my shit together so we can give our relationship an honest try.

It's after midnight when Chloe, Beckett and Landon announce they're leaving. Soon Adam and Jewels follow suit. After we say our goodbyes to James, I take Theo by the hand. "I haven't given you an official tour."

He follows me back to peek inside Erik's room. I flush when I think of all the toys accessible to us. I've never tried the kind of sex that involves whips and handcuffs, though something tells me it'd be thrilling to try with Theo.

Theo squeezes my hand. "Now that's a stellar view."

I drag him across the hallway to my bedroom. He drops my hand to step inside, his eyes flickering around the minimal contents.

"Yeah, I know it's boring. I'm waiting to muster the courage to ask my parents ship my things from home."

Theo shrugs. "I could arrange for movers to do it for you. They'd just need your parents' permission to pack up your things."

"Thanks, but I can about imagine my mom's face when a bunch of strangers waltz in to take my things away. I better handle it myself." I cross my arms, fighting back the urge to tackle Theo to the bed. "I've been dying to tell you all night that I'm ready to try this dating thing with you."

His face cracks with a bright smile. "About damn

time!" He rushes to my side, wrapping his arms around me and literally sweeping me off my feet. "When can I take you out?"

I'm giggling as he sets me back down. "That'll depend on whatever schedule I'll have *if* I ever find a job. I'm having a hard time finding something decent. Any suggestions?"

"I'm sure I could find you something. The station's always looking for assistants of some kind. The pay isn't the best, but it's probably no less than what you'd get waitressing or working retail."

"Theo!" I scold, covering my face for a moment. "Just because I agreed to go on a date with you doesn't mean you have to take care of all my problems!"

A grin tilts the side of his mouth. "Maybe I *want* to take care of you."

"Thanks, but I'm a big girl and can take care of myself. Besides, you couldn't possibly fix all my problems. *Believe* me."

"I can try." He starts toward me with a smoldering gaze. "Can I start by taking care of your beautiful lips? I wanted to kiss you all night."

I inhale sharply as he hovers just inches away, smelling all kinds of wonderful as he waits for my permission. I've been just as eager to kiss him, but know just how much I have to hold back if things are going to keep under control. The presence of his large, hard body so close to me, his large lips ready for the taking, sends me into a sensual overload.

"Just one kiss," I whisper, unable to take my eyes off his mouth.

He slips one hand behind my head, gently cradling it. His other hand rests on the side of my face. There's a ghost of a smile on his lips when he leans in, his eyes fixed on my lips. My heart races in anticipation.

The moment's interrupted as the front door slams shut.

I hop away from Theo as if electrocuted. "*Shit*. It's probably Erik."

Theo immediately looks dejected, his eyes falling to the floor. He moves past me. "Then I guess I should go."

I grab his arm, stopping him. "Hey, look at me." When he looks up I smile and slip my hand back into his. "We can save the first kiss for our big date. C'mon, I'll walk you out."

My words seem to lighten his mood as he smiles, motioning for me to lead the way.

Erik stands at the sink with his arms crossed, taking the loft in with his eyebrows raised. There isn't much out of place other than some empty trays and glasses. I suddenly see Erik in a whole different light after Adam told me what happened. It would seem Adam's crude names for his brother were actually quite validated. My stomach turns when I remind myself I had sex with the bastard.

"It appears I missed a party."

"I hope you don't mind," I say, my tone light. "I just had a few friends over. Erik, you remember Adam's friend, Theo?"

Erik tips his head at Theo with dull eyes. "Of course." He looks back at me. "I expect this mess to be gone by morning."

I feel Theo stiffen beside me, pulling in a breath to say something. I quickly squeeze his hand. "Yeah, of course. I wouldn't dream of leaving the apartment this way. I was just getting ready to walk Theo out first."

"Nice seeing you again. Take care," Erik tells Theo without any emotion to his voice.

"You'll be seeing me around," Theo returns in the same tone. Once at the door, he tells me, "I'll call you tomorrow when I have information on any job leads."

I wrap my arms around him. As much as I'd love to properly wish him goodnight, I don't want our first kiss to be in Erik's line of sight. "I'm so glad you came," I whisper.

Theo pulls me in closer, rubbing my back. "I'll be waiting for your call to set up our date." He releases me with a kiss to my forehead. After starting down the hallway he stops, throwing a glowing grin over his shoulder. My insides turn to mush.

Erik stands in the same place in the kitchen, watching me walk back inside. "I sure hope you weren't back in your bedroom, violating one of the few restrictions I placed on you." He smirks, though his eyes remain dull. "I'd hate to take some kind of... action."

An instantaneous erotic surge hits me as I picture Erik coming after me with the leather whip I found in his closet. From the sudden spark to his gaze, I realize he has every intention of fulfilling the fantasy.

Digging my nails into my palms, I remind myself of Adam's confession. And then there's *Theo*.

"*Take action*?" I scoff, frowning. "I'm not a *child*. In fact, I'm *older* than you. Not that it's any of your business, but no, I was *not* back in my room violating your twisted rule. Theo and I actually agreed to start *dating*. You know, the thing you do when you want to get to know someone better, instead of just wanting to get in their pants."

Eyebrows raised, he smirks like he doesn't believe a word I just said. "You wanted in *my* pants as much as I wanted in yours. *Both* times."

"And both times it was a mistake."

"Is that why you've been hiding out in your room these past few days? You've decided it was a mistake to be with me?"

"Yes, it was. It never should've happened. The two of us together is far too complicated. It's over."

He chuckles loudly. "That's what you said after

the first time we were together. Admit it, Kelly, you're never going to be able to say 'no' to me."

"I'm saying it now." I march over the island and begin clearing the dirty dishes. "And from now on, my personal life isn't any of your business. I appreciate the opportunity to let me stay here, but we're nothing more than roommates until I can find somewhere else. With any luck I'll be out of here by the end of the week."

"I didn't realize you were in such a hurry to vacate." He moves in closer until I can feel the heat of his body against mine. My body reacts to him in ways that enrage my mind. "What changed your mind?"

I reel on him, suddenly livid. "You did! I can't stay here when you're always coming onto me like this!" I toss the dish-rag back into the sink. "You know what, fuck this. I'll finish up once you've gone to bed. *Goodnight*, Erik." I shove him with all my strength before storming from the room.

Erik's gone in the morning. I was up pretty late, tidying the place to meet his standards, and slept in longer than planned. I check my phone to find a message from Theo, telling me to put on something nice, and that he's sending a car for me at noon. I shower and curl my hair before rummaging through my recent purchases with Chloe. I'm thankful for her fashion advice, knowing whatever I would've picked out back home wouldn't work as well for New York. I settle on black leggings and a silky white tunic, dressing them up with a long, silver chain and dangling earrings.

I'm ready and down in the lobby just minutes before the doorman tells me my ride has arrived. It's thrilling to ride all alone in the back of the black sedan, the rich smell of the leather seats filling me. Of all the traits I adore in Theo, I sometimes forget about the perks that would come with his prestigious career. A girl could get used to this lifestyle.

Charles, the sweet driver of the town car who recently moved to the city from Great Britain so he could get to know his new grandson, chats animatedly with me on the ride. He seems agile for someone nearing 90. My racing thoughts take me away from the view outside, and we're pulling up to a curb in no time.

A gray-haired man in a suit rushes to the car, opening my door. "Good afternoon, Miss Cavenaugh." His eyes crinkle with a bright smile. "I was asked to bring you up to see Mister Roberts."

"Thank you," I say, a little put off by the formality. I suddenly feel really small-town for this kind of thing and wish Jewels was along to lighten the mood.

I follow the man inside the tall, tan skyscraper with gold-trimmed doors, and through the bright lobby. A beautiful woman sitting behind the receptionist's desk, wearing a billowing blouse and cradling a phone to her ear, greets me with a bright smile and nods. We continue on to a set of elevators. The man presses a button and holds his arm out, waiting for me to enter first. He enters behind me and presses a button. We stand in silence as a horribly redone instrumental of a Bruno Mars song rings overhead.

We reach the tenth floor and the man again waits for me to go first. The reception area, a stark white, is brightly lit like the lobby downstairs. A super Betty with darkly painted eyes and dark hair styled like a pin up girl from the 50s sits tall behind a plain white desk. She wears a tight-fitting red shirt cut low enough to show off her obviously surgically enhanced breasts. As we approach, she watches me carefully. I'm lit with jealousy to know that Theo works with such an attractive woman.

"Hey, William," she greets my companion. "Who do you have here?"

"Raquel, this is Miss Cavenaugh. She's here to see Mister Roberts."

Raquel presses her lips together and nods, reaching for the phone. She studies me from head to toe as she speaks. "You have a *visitor*."

Yeah, I'd love to wrestle the snooty bitch down to the ground. Then again, I'd probably be resentful too if I had an incredibly hot boss who apparently doesn't have time for his secretaries outside of the office. I flash her my best smile while we wait for Theo to emerge from the set of etched doors on her right.

Wearing a designer gray suit and bright blue tie, Theo looks so amazing that I nearly forget where we are and jump into his arms. He lights up like the New York skyline when he takes me in. "Cavenaugh, I'm glad you're here."

Raquel makes a deep throated noise before looking away to her computer.

I step forward, not sure how I'm supposed to greet him, considering he's at work. He wraps me in his massive arms before I can put too much thought into it. I catch him sniffing my hair before he breaks the contact. "Did you eat yet?"

I shake my head.

"Good. I ordered us carryout." He takes my hand and turns to the front desk. "Raquel, go ahead and have them bring our food back when it arrives. We'll be in my office."

Raquel gives him a bright smile. "Sure thing, Theo." I catch her shooting me a dark glare before I follow Theo through the etched doors.

Pictures of celebrities on location line the brightly lit hallway. I stop in my tracks to gape at a picture, just about pulling Theo over. "Holy shit! That's Norman Fucking Reedus!"

Theo dwarfs my favorite actor in the picture,

their arms looped around each other's necks. They're both wearing sunglasses, and it looks like Norman's in costume for *The Walking Dead*. They both have deep grins on their face as they flash the camera the middle finger.

"Another Dixon Vixen. I should've guessed." Theo chuckles at my side. "Maybe I can arrange for you to meet him sometime when he's in the city."

Dazed by Theo's connections, I let him pull me away, but still take my time studying the other pictures as we pass them by. I can't imagine a life where working with famous actors and actresses is no different than having coworkers at an ordinary office. Theo ducks into another set of double doors at the end of the hallway. We enter a large office with fluffy white carpet and a line of shelves holding various awards and memorabilia.

"This is where the magic happens," he tells me, dropping my hand. He pulls out a black leather chair facing a black desk with a glass top. "Have a seat."

As Theo settles in the chair behind the desk, I take in the phenomenal view of the city through the floor-to-ceiling windows. I swear I can see all of Manhattan in its glory. It's the kind of set up you'd see in the movies, not in real life. It's laughable how out of my element I've become.

"What's so funny?" Theo asks.

I bring my focus back to him, hiding my smile behind my hand. He's leaning back in the chair with his hands resting at his sides, smirking. Although I'm totally out of *my* element, he's completely in *his*. He owns the room with confidence, making him even hotter. Letting him take me right here, right now, with such a killer view beside us would be off the hook.

"It's just a bit...surreal. I knew you were a big Kahuna, but I never thought I'd find myself hanging with someone like you in a place with a killer view like this." I sit taller, suddenly nervous. "I'm starting to think you're out of my league."

"Nah, I'm just a kid from the Bronx who served our country. Guys as young as me don't usually get this lucky without at least going to college. I fell into this job because of my father." His mouth turns up with the sexiest of smiles. "I'm in no different of a league than you, Cavenaugh."

My heart races. I love it when he calls me by my last name. No guy before him has done it. It also makes me feel like less of a sex object, and more like an actual person he's genuinely interested in getting to know.

"Who's your father?"

"The name probably won't mean anything to you, but he's a big name in the industry. People in this line of work tend to bend over backwards for him."

"Still, this is all pretty impressive."

"Just wait until our date," he teases, winking.

I pat the arms of the chair as I look around the

room. "So. Did you bring me here just so you could show off?" I meet his gaze again. "Seeing you sitting in front of a view like that is making it very difficult to keep my hands to myself. It's...impressive."

He chuckles, though the look in his eye is quite serious, as if he doesn't want to keep his hands to himself either. "I brought you here because I found you a potential job." There's a knock on the door. "Come on in!" he calls out, reaching for his wallet from his jacket pocket.

A tall kid enters, as willowy as a new tree, his neck and face peppered in acne. He sets a brown paper bag on the desk. "Hey, Theo."

"Josiah, my man!" Theo rises to slap the kid's hand, giving him a sincere smile. "I figured you'd be back in school by now. Did you find yourself a girl-friend this summer?"

"Not yet. School doesn't start for another week." Josiah's bulging eyes flip between me and Theo. He leans in to whisper, "Should I know her?"

Theo laughs brightly, cupping the kid on the shoulder. "Not yet, but maybe one day. She's someone I'm courting."

I snort under my breath at Theo's outdated term. "I'm Kelly."

Josiah throws me an awkward wave. "Hey, Kelly. *Really* nice to meet you."

Theo claps the kid on the shoulder before passing him a $100 bill. "Yeah, yeah. Keep the change and go find yourself a girl to treat nice before the summer's over. Maybe take her out to the movies, or buy her dinner."

"Whoa, I can't take this much money, Theo!"

"Consider it a bonus for all the times I've made you come all the way across the city."

"Wow, thanks!" Josiah chirps, taking the money with a bright smile. "You two have a great day!"

"Bye, Josiah," I call after him. "It was nice meeting you too!"

Theo digs into the bag, releasing the fragrant aroma of pasta. My stomach growls in anticipation. "Are you ready for the best pasta in the city? I ordered manicotti for both of us. Hope you don't mind."

"Are you kidding me?" I rub my hands together when he sets one of the containers in front of me. The gooey mess of noodles and cheeses looks divine. "Manicotti's my *favorite.*"

Theo grins proudly. "I know. I asked Jewels."

I pull in a small breath, surprised by the sweet gesture.

He moves over to a small refrigerator underneath the wall of awards. "Soda or water?"

"Water." I wait for him to return with two bottles of water before digging in along with him. The variety of cheeses and herbs explode inside my mouth. I let out a long, throaty moan.

Theo draws his eyebrows down, smirking. "How

do you expect me to keep acting like a gentlemen when you make noises like that?"

"Sorry, but I just had a mouthgasm," I say, closing my eyes and licking my lips. "I have a feeling I'm going to gain a lot of weight with all this sensational food at my disposal."

"Now you know why I'm always running. Gotta stay in shape if I'm going to eat like this." He takes a bite. "Jewels mentioned you're a runner too. If you're interested, we could meet up in Central Park sometime."

"I'd *love* that. I haven't ran in over a week, and my legs are getting restless."

He wipes his face with a napkin, then takes a swig of his water. "Back to why I brought you here...I'm not sure how you're going to feel about this. One of the shows I'm producing is looking for fresh talent. They need a woman to play a witty vixen in a futuristic show. You know, kind of like a dystopian thing. I thought *maybe* you'd be interested in trying out for the part."

I shoot a mouthful of water across my lap. "Oh *god.*" My face turns red as I reach for a napkin and begin patting my leggings down. At least it wasn't pasta I spit.

"You okay?" Theo comes around the desk, intending to help, his brow drawn in concern.

"I'm fine, I got it!" I snap, waving him away. "*Why* would you think I'd want to be an *actress* of all things? I wouldn't know the first thing about it."

He leans back on the desk, arms crossed. Though he's clearly thrown by my reaction, he also seems pleased with himself. "Because you're incredibly sexy, and I'm willing to bet you've got the confidence that would work for it. It wouldn't be the first time someone without acting experience was hired. A job like that could pay the kind of money you need to set you up nicely in this city. You would be able to afford your own place."

"Is that what all of this," I wave my hand between us, "is about? You were looking for someone to fill a part?" A storm brews in the pit of my stomach, threatening to chuck what little manicotti I ate. "Is that why you're trying to impress me with dates and private cars?"

"Of course not." He shakes his head. "I didn't even consider you for the part until today. I promise you, that's now how I work, Cavenaugh. Where's this coming from?"

I stand from the chair to move away from him, feeling as if I'm going to be sick. "Have you considered how that would look? The producer of the show, *courting* or whatever you want to call it, the star? That's why you made that comment to Josiah about one day knowing me, isn't it?"

If my family and everyone back in my hometown got wind of such a scandal, I'd never be able to show my face in Wisconsin again. It'd be the exact image they've created for me—someone who's willing to sleep around to get what they want. It'd be the cherry on top of this big, fucked-up mess I created for myself.

Theo holds the palms of his hands out, as if to calm me. "I'm sorry, I never would've suggested it if I knew the idea would upset you like this. I just want to see that you're taken care of."

"I don't need *you or anyone else* to take care of me," I tell him, sulking for the doors. I'm suddenly pressed to find my breath.

"Wait!" He moves toward me with his brows furrowed. "I don't understand why you're so upset. I thought you'd be excited by the opportunity. I was taking a chance offering an unknown up to the writers of the show, but I really believe you've got what it takes."

The doors to the office open before I get to them. His secretary stands in front of me, her dark eyes wide. We're the same height with her garish red heels. I look down to see she's wearing the shortest skirt in the history of office attire. "Everything okay in here?"

Theo catches up to me, cradling my elbow. "Raquel, it's fine. Go back to your desk."

"It's fine, I'm leaving," I insist, slinking away from his touch. As I pass Raquel, she holds her hands up by her bugged out eyes, smirking. I hear

Theo quietly arguing with her behind me as I make a dash for the elevators.

In the taxi ride back to the apartment, I'm shaking the entire way. How could Theo think offering me such a position would be okay when we've agreed to take things slow? How could he *not* see how awful it would look to everyone else? As much as I refuse to allow myself to cry, there's a giant ball stuck in my chest, threatening to turn me into a blubbering mess.

I stumble from the taxi, anxious to crawl into bed and hide beneath the covers for the rest of the day. I nearly rub my eyes in disbelief with the sight of the striking brunette standing outside the apartment building, shifting her weight and frowning as she taps at her smart phone with a manicured finger. A small line of sweat glistens beneath the thick braid on her forehead that continues down off to one side of her face, stopping midway to her core. Her fashionable, short sundress in a bright print could easily be something out of my closet if it weren't for the fact that she's a size zero and I'm a four. The gladiator-style sandals she wears are the exact same shade of blue as the flowers on her dress, a detail that doesn't surprise me in the least.

Between her $200 sunglasses and the designer handbag hanging from her arm that Mom and Dad gave her last Christmas, she could pass for one of the local socialites I've seen passing through the neighborhood. Though she's only a year and a half older than me, my youngest of four sisters always appears at least a decade more grown up just by the way she carries herself. I guess it's all that grooming they put her through in pageant training.

I balk at her. What in the hell is my sister doing in New York?

Chapter Ten

"GLO?" I call out, not sure if I should run *toward* my sister or *away*.

When she looks up in my direction, her rich brown eyes soften. "Kel, thank God!"

Glori hurries toward me for a spirited hug. I take it, but don't make any movements to return the gesture. She's short enough that her head barely grazes my chin—a curse that she claims stopped her from taking the actual title of pageant beauty queen. I'm actually surprised she isn't wearing 3 inch heels for once to make up for it.

I inhale with resolve, catching her signature scent of gardenias. "What the fuck are you doing here? How'd you know where to find me?"

"Such *language*." She clicks her tongue and backs away, arms crossed. "Mom got your address from Jewels. I guess she got real emotional about it, said she didn't want to rat you out, but she didn't want you to make her mistakes or something like that. I don't know. Mom didn't tell me the whole conversation because I was in a dressing room for a fitting when she called."

"Sounds about right," I mumble to myself. I make a mental note to "thank" Jewels later for giving me a heads up.

A tight-lipped woman with flawless blond hair and a designer track suit walks our way with a handful of leashes, walking a gaggle of Yorkies with little pink bows on their heads. I kneel down to greet them, letting them cover my hands in kisses.

"They're adorable!" I peer up to see the uptight woman smiling. "What are their names? Are they all yours?"

"Sorry," Glori apologizes to the woman on my behalf, "she's been an animal magnet her whole life." She pulls me back up by my arm. "*Focus*, Kel. I'm here, remember?"

The woman brushes past us, throwing Glori a confused look. My sister looks up to the apartment building with a lowered gaze I've seen a million times before. It's something she *wants*. And I've witnessed her stepping in stilettos over her "friends" to get whatever her sights are set on. "I thought maybe she gave Mom the wrong address when the cabbie dropped me here. How can you afford to stay in this neighborhood?"

"I have a roommate." I cross my arms, then quickly uncross them when I realize I'm a mirror image of my big sister. "Seriously, Glo, why are you here?"

She rests her hand on my forearm, her eyes drawn down. "Mom and Dad have been a complete wreck since you took off. Mom goes to the confessional nearly every day. She's worried 'the devil has her baby in his clutches'." She hooks her bright pink fingernails in the air as she quotes our mom.

"It's not like I haven't been talking to her. I *have* called her." I don't mention how rare or painful those calls have been.

"Yeah, well, they feel responsible for driving you out of town."

I push her hand away, feeling the anger rise back up. "Basically, they did. You *all* did."

"Don't be ridiculous. What happened was a big misunderstanding. You left Wisconsin on your own."

Anger boils my blood into lava. I turn to see if our doorman is listening in, but he's busy chatting it up with one of the Wall Street guys who lives a floor down from us.

I turn back to Glori, forcefully taking her elbow in my grip. "I'm not going to talk about this with you right here."

"Let go of me!" Glori snaps, clawing at my hand.

I don't back down, knowing I can take her. "You shouldn't have come."

"I'm not going anywhere until we talk about what happened!"

"Hey!" someone calls out behind us. We both whirl around to see Erik marching our way with his school bag slung over his shoulder, his expression hard. "What's this about?"

My spirits crumble down to the sidewalk. If my sister spreads her poisonous lies to him, it'll all be over. He'll tell everyone, and the secret I wanted to keep back in Wisconsin will have followed me here.

Glori smooths her dress down at her nearly non-existent waist, narrowing her eyes with suspicion. "I don't see how it's any of your business. Who are *you*?"

"I'm her boyfriend," Erik answers swiftly, his hard stare on her unrelenting. "Who are *you*?"

What the *actual fuck*? I bite down on my bottom lip to keep my jaw from dropping.

Glori scoffs like she's onto the farce. "*Boyfriend*? I'm her *sister*. She hasn't mentioned a *boyfriend* to any of us."

Erik reaches down to lace his fingers with mine. "From what I understand, she hasn't really been in communication with any of you, so how would you know about me?"

This time my jaw *does* drop. How does he know I'm not talking to my family? I haven't even told Jewels what happened. And *why* is he pretending to be my boyfriend?

If I weren't so mad at my sister, I'd maybe feel sympathetic the way Erik's eyes bore into her. "I want to know why you're standing outside of our apartment, screaming at my girl."

I'm quiet, still baffled by this new side of Erik. Where is it coming from?

"It's a *family* matter," Glori tells him, raising her chin. "I'm not going to stand on the sidewalk and air our dirty laundry with a stranger."

"I'm not a stranger," Erik insists. "And if you can't treat Kelly with respect, you need to get the hell out of here."

Glori looks Erik up and down, disbelief spreading across her expression. She finally looks back at me. "I don't know what this is about, but you and I need to talk when your guard dog is off duty. I'm not leaving the city until we do." She spins around, marching out into the street, her arm raised for a taxi.

I make it all the way up into our apartment at Erik's side until the pressure everything finally releases. I become a sobbing mess in Erik's arms. His embrace is stiff, making me wonder if he's ever held a girl like this. I've never broke down in a guy's arms, so I don't have a lot of experience in the matter either. I'm exhausted from finally letting myself feel all the emotions that have built up ever since I left home.

"Are you going to tell me what you're blubbering

about?" he asks in a cool tone after a few minutes have passed.

I wipe my face and let out a long sigh. "I just wanted to leave the lies back home." My strained voice crackles.

"Considering your sister's in the city, it seems the cat's out of the bag whether you want to admit it or not."

I look up at him, knowing he's right. I could only avoid the truth for so long before it would bite me in the ass. I close my eyes for a moment, gathering courage.

"When I was a counselor this summer at my family's camp, I'd go down to the local tavern for burgers on Friday nights with my three sisters and the other counselors. We'd usually end up closing the place down. One night my sisters were out of town so I went alone and met this older guy who I was attracted to right away. He was sweet and had a great sense of humor. I was intrigued when he told me he trained horses. The way he kept touching my shoulder and giving me these hot glances, I knew he was into me, too. When he asked if he could see me again, I made the decision to keep him a secret, figuring once my sisters Glori or Megan saw him, there's no *way* I'd have a chance.

"Our first *date* was at the state park a few miles down the road from camp. I guess the fact that he didn't want to meet somewhere public should've been my first warning sign that there was something off, but I just figured he was a nature kind of guy and wanted to take me for a picnic or whatever. Once we met up, we were all over each other like magnets. We ended up having sex right there in a grassy field. We met up a bunch of times after that, always in the same park. Our meeting time kept getting later and later at night. He claimed the strange hours were because he was putting in overtime at the factory he worked in. I was stupid enough to believe him.

"The sex was great, and we were really into each other. I considered him my first *real* boyfriend. If there were other red flags, I didn't catch on to them until one night about a month and a half into our relationship when he showed up wearing a wedding ring. At first he was embarrassed that he forgot to take it off for our meeting, but then he got crazy mad at *me*. Like I had any fucking clue he was *married*. I was crushed because I was falling for him. I told him he was an asshole and I didn't want to ever see him again. I wasn't about to break up someone's marriage.

"But he wouldn't leave me alone. He started coming to see me at camp, begging for another chance. He told me he was going to leave his wife so we could be together. Glori, the sister you met just now, caught him trying to kiss me. I guess she knew the guy. She told the rest of my family about our 'affair.' That's how I found out that not only was he married with two little kids, but his wife was in hospice care with fourth stage melanoma."

Erik make a low, throaty sound, but doesn't say anything.

"I didn't believe my mom when she first told me all the sordid details, so one night I followed him from the bar to his house. I saw her lying in a hospital bed through the bay windows. She was incredibly frail, skeleton-like. I felt like the biggest dirtbag on the planet and spent half an hour puking my guts out. I swear to God, I *never* would've slept with the guy if I knew *any* of those things about him. That's not my style.

"My family accused me of keeping the affair secret, saying I *knew* he was married and I *knew* his wife was dying. They'd never been especially proud of me in the past, but this was taking it too far. One of the counselors who hated me for reasons I'll never understand overheard my sisters talking, and told everyone she knew about the affair. I became the town slut. Turns out the wife was one of the most beloved people around. She was a freaking *kindergarten* teacher. People started either avoiding me or treating me like I was scum of the earth. Hate emails started pouring in, and I eventually had to close my Facebook account. My car was vandalized. Some woman—I guess it was a sister-in-law—physically attacked me at the grocery store.

"I couldn't tell Jewels what was going on because

she was busy dealing with Adam's surgery. I didn't think it was fair to drag her into my mess. When I heard they were moving out here, I jumped at the excuse to get the hell out of town. I threw everything at camp into my suitcase and decided I was leaving for good.

"I've never been ashamed that I like to have sex, because I'm single and guys are always telling me I'm amazing in bed, so why should I hold back? I mean, there's nothing like having a good looking guy look at you in a way that tells you he *wants* you. I'll never get tired of that look. It's good for a girl's ego. But everyone was so quick to judge me after what happened with Brad that it made me stop and realize it's time to reassess my priorities."

Erik's smug smirk is almost comforting for a change. "No judgments here. When we first met and you told me your life was a mess, I knew that look you gave me. I figured you were running from a pretty dark secret."

"I just don't know what to say to my family. I tried to explain my side a hundred times. They won't listen. It's a waste of breath." I run my hands across my face. "I can't believe I'm having this conversation with *you*. I should be telling Jewels."

He spreads his arms across the back of the couch, looking so sure of himself. "You're secretly worried she's going to judge you. I get it."

"Adam told me what happened between you two," I blurt.

He stiffens and looks away, stretching his neck. "Obviously you're not the only one with a dark past. I've done a lot of moronic things myself."

"He says you never apologized."

Erik looks back at me, the cold chill of anger crossing his gaze. "How could I? I was high on coke and tried to *kill* my brother. That's not something you can just apologize for."

"You could start by telling him you're sorry."

"And what if I'm not?"

My blood turns ice cold. I stare at him, waiting for him to take it back.

"My childhood sucked. I was the kid whose parents never came to anything. I was no different than one of the girls in my grade who was in foster care. I was always home alone, because my parents decided the hospital wasn't a place for healthy young boys. I hated my brother for taking them away from me. It's fucked up, I know. I don't expect you to understand."

"You're right, I don't. Not really." I look down to pick at my fingernails. "At least not how you could want your brother dead."

"I don't anymore. I wouldn't mind spending time with him, though, if such a thing is even possible."

"I wish I could tell you that it is, but Adam seems to be holding a pretty big grudge against you." I look at him, shrugging. "I'd say you just need to give him time. The fact that he came over last night, knowing it was possible he'd run into you must count for something."

Erik leans forward, closing the distance between us. "Considering how incredibly wounded we both are by our own families, I'd say we're well suited. Maybe it wasn't nearly a coincidence that we crossed paths."

His smoldering gaze stirs the fire inside of me that won't stay out. A small breath falls across my lips. He reaches out to run his finger down my arm. My breathing hitches, and my body responds to his touch with quivering appeal.

"No, Erik. I can't do this," I whisper.

He brushes his lips under my jawline, tasting me with the flick of his tongue. "Why not?" His finger continues to trail its way across my exposed skin, leaving a blazing trail in its place.

I hold back a moan. My body wants him so badly. I close my eyes and swallow. "When I moved here, I promised myself that I'd be done with flings. I want to actually fall in love for once. You managed to break my resolve in record time."

"Who's to say I'm not capable of love?" he asks, his lips brushing my ear.

Finding my resolve, I push him back with all I've got. "Basically you, ten seconds ago. You said you can't apologize to your brother for trying to *murder* him." I rise from the couch on unsteady feet. "I may be fucked up, but I never purposely tried to hurt anyone. I was right, I should've told Jewels what happened instead of you. This kind act is just another way for you to manipulate me into fucking you again, isn't it? After everything I told you, you're ready to take advantage of me!"

"Always delusional." He leans back, huffing with a roll of his eyes. "If I only wanted a warm body in my bed, I wouldn't have to try so hard with you. I have the numbers of dozens of women who'd beg me to fuck them."

"Then give them a call! These games you like to play with me are psychotic!" I start toward the front door, shaking my head. Then I turn back to him. "Do yourself a favor and get some professional help!"

Pulling a typical Kelly Cavenaugh, I run from my problems.

The untouched glass of Jameson sitting on the worn, wooden bar sweats into a little puddle. Annoying 80s music blasts from the speakers, dulling the conversations of the other patrons in the darkly-lit bar filled with cherry wood and dark green accents. The stench of stale peanuts nearly gags me. Even though it seems the AC in the pub may be on full blast, the ice in my drink has already melted, and I'm sweaty. I'm starting to understand why Chloe is so anxious for fall to arrive. The stifling city air gets old, fast. It's making me physically exhausted on top of being mentally anguished.

Hearing just how messed up Erik is *almost* made me feel better about my own problems, until I remembered that Glori's in the city, ready to convince me to come back home. I can't deal with her, or anyone else from my family. And there's no way in hell I'll return to Wisconsin, no matter how hard she begs. Why should I feel sorry for putting my parents through anything when they weren't willing to give me the benefit of doubt? I should've known that I wouldn't be allowed a fresh start, pretending I'm not the slut everyone thinks I've become. Who am I kidding? I can't even dance with a guy without giving in to him, or at least masturbating. Jewels thinks she knows me. Would she still see me the same way if she knew what I was doing while they were in the next room?

Theo has tried calling several times, and sent half a dozen texts, begging me to talk to him. As much as I want things between us to work out, it still infuriates me that he wanted to "take care of me" without thinking how it would appear to others. And how do I know he wasn't just buttering me up so I could be his golden ticket to a hit show? I know it sounds conceited to think such a thing, but it all seems so suspiciously convenient that I can't help but wonder.

The bartender who looks around my age stops to hover in front of me, setting one hand on the bar, outreaching the other my way. He's stout and considerably nice-looking with dark brown hair, mischievous hazel eyes, and a scruffy beard. The trail end of a colorful tattoo on his bicep peeks out beneath his t-shirt sporting the name of the bar. "Hiya, I'm Mick." Agh, cute *and* an Irish accent.

I take his extended hand. "Kelly."

"How long are ya in the city for, sweetheart?" He releases my hand.

"What? I don't look like a local?" I tease, sitting taller. "I just moved here, actually. Guess I don't exactly fit in yet."

Mick flips a towel over his shoulder, grinning. "The big city attitude will come with time, I suppose. You've got an open kindness to you, like someone from the Midwest."

I let my shoulders slump. So much for fitting in. "It's that obvious?"

"I'd take it as a compliment."

Swirling my glass in my hand, I contemplate sucking the entire thing down, and asking for another. Maybe I could disappear in the comfort of a warm buzz.

"I can't help but notice you look like someone

pissed in your gravy. Would ya like me to get you somethin' else? That whiskey certainly isn't going down easily."

"If you could get a me a new life, that'd be great." I fake a smile. "I seem to have made a considerable mess of the one I already have."

"Everyone's got problems." Chuckling, he motions to the other side of the bar. "Why do ya think this bar's so full on a weekday afternoon? You have to learn to control your life before it controls you. No one else can make you happy. No one else can make the changes that'll make it right. You have to decide what you want, and make it happen. Only *you* can decide your destiny."

"That's some stellar advice." I raise an eyebrow. "Are they teaching philosophy to bartenders now?"

His lips pull back in a bright smile, showing a row of somewhat crooked teeth. "I'm studyin' psychology at college. The bar's a family business, but it isn't for me. I don't want to spend the rest of my life handin' out advice to pretty girls unless I'm gettin' paid."

"Controlling your destiny. Good call."

"Now would you quit your sulkin'? It bothers me to see such a lovely face in pain." He winks before filling a mug with tap beer. "If you're unhappy, do somethin' about it. Take the lead of yer own destiny."

After he leaves to wait on another customer, I

spend a few minutes chewing on his advice before I decide he's right. I text Glori, telling her where she can meet me. I'm done letting others walk all over me. It's time I focused on my future, instead of worrying about the mistakes of my past.

Chapter Eleven

"THIS PLACE IS HORRENDOUS," Glori whispers before hopping into the stool next to me. "Couldn't we have gone somewhere that doesn't smell like old shoes?"

I laugh as she considers placing her purse on the bar, then sets it in her lap instead. "Get over yourself, Glo. It's just a bar."

Mick approaches us with a bright smile. "Ah, there's two of ya! What can I get for *you*, luv?"

Glori looks him up and down, her lips tight. "A rum and coke, *no ice*." She pushes my drink toward him. "And you can take this away. Ice in places like this is worse than drinking toilet water. She'll have the same as me."

Mick looks to me questioningly, and I just shrug. There's no changing my sister at this point. She may be the most gorgeous of all the sisters, but she's always been prim and proper, and a bit of a pain in the ass. At least I can be grateful her uppity attitude didn't rub off on me while we were growing up.

"Comin' right up!" Mick throws me a wink before walking away.

"Everyone in this city is so *crude*," Glori says, rolling her eyes. "Who does he think he is, calling me *luv*?"

"He's just being *nice*." I turn to face her, setting my hand on the back of her chair. "Glo, I'm not going to drag this out any further. What happened between me and Brad is not what you or the rest of the town thinks. I met him that night at the bar, when you were at that bachelorette party in Green Bay. I didn't tell you guys about him because I figured he'd be more attracted to one of you since you were all closer to his age. He didn't wear his wedding band when we were together. If I had known he was married, even without kids or a terminal wife, I *never* would've agreed to see him.

"I refuse to talk to anyone in this family again until you agree to believe me, and apologize for thinking I would stoop so low. Do you have any idea what it's been like for me, having been branded with a scarlet letter? Pretty much all of my high school friends blocked me on Facebook when one of them spread word of what happened. You think it's tough having judges give you low scores at your pageants? You should try having people openly call you crude names for everyone to read online.

"Running out here was an act of self-preservation. No one would listen to me. If I hadn't done it, you probably would've found me in a bathtub with my wrists slit wide open. It fucking *sucks* that no one stood up for me! I can't believe you would all think I'm capable of breaking up a family! I would *never* knowingly hurt someone that way!"

When I stop to take a breath, I notice Glori's lips are quivering, and her eyes are filled with tears. "Are you done?" she asks in a soft voice.

Mick sets our drinks down, glancing between me and Glori. "These are on the house." He backs away, appearing indifferent to our conversation.

Glori's hands wrap around her glass as she looks at the drink for a minute, deep in thought. "At first I believed that you knew Brad was married. The way you kept it a secret...and I saw the two of you looking so intimate at camp. I was ashamed that my little sister was doing something so devious. After awhile I started to really listen the other rumors that started up—that you were latching onto Brad knowing his wife was dying, and that he was loaded, or that you were arranging to have his kids sent away to boarding school so that the two of you could be alone. I knew *those* things at least weren't something you'd do.

Before long, I realized it was *all* a bunch of crap. I

got tired of everyone slinging your name through the mud. I went to see Brad a few days after his wife died. Being the complete sleezeball that he is, he tried to deny it at first. Eventually I convinced him that it was in his best interests to tell me the truth."

I raise my eyebrows, wondering what techniques my pristine sister would convince someone like him. Most of all, I'm surprised that she actually wanted to consider my side of the story. I don't recall a single time when one of my big sisters stood up to someone for my benefit.

"Dad made him confess everything on Facebook. The next day after he did it, there was a for 'sale sign' in his yard. He left town with his kids." Tears slip down her face as she takes my hand. "It was wrong of us not to believe you, Kel. We all were. I'm sorry you had to go through such an awful thing alone. I should've been there for you. If you would've answered my calls the past few days, I would've been able to tell you this sooner."

"This really messed me up, Glo," I say, my own tears breaking free. It's infuriating how I continue to lose control in public. "I think I'm broken."

"No, you're not. You just think you are because you didn't have anyone to support you while this was going on. But you survived, because you're strong." She smiles and reaches up to push my hair behind my ear. It's something our mom always does when she's giving us heartfelt advice. Honestly, it makes me a little homesick. "Come back with me. Everyone knows the truth, and we all want you back home. You've only missed a week of classes. There's still time for you to go back."

"I can't go *back* there!" A humorless laugh falls from my lips. "Just because they know the truth doesn't change the way everyone treated me! Jewels is the only friend who was always there for me, and she's *here*. I'm staying in New York. I've already made some other friends here. Although I've already managed to make a small mess of things with some of them, I think it can still be repaired. But I think...maybe I need to see a psychologist or something."

Glori wipes at her tears, nodding. "I guess I can understand why you wouldn't want to go back. Still, I hate that you'll be so far away from us. Can't you come live somewhere closer? Maybe find a place in Green Bay or Chicago? You'd just be a short train ride away."

"I don't want to go anywhere else. I really like it here," I tell her, finally able to muster a smile. "It's exciting and kinda scary at the same time since I don't know if I'll ever find a job or a better place to live, but I'm ready for a challenge. For once I want to decide my own destiny and not do things based on what other want me to do."

Mick casually throws me a knowing grin over his shoulder.

Glori sighs dramatically at my side. "The whole family is sick over this, Kel. How are we going ever to make it up to you?"

"You could start by convincing mom and dad to pack up my things back home, and ship them out to me." I touch her hand, suddenly grateful that she came all this way to see me. "And while you're here, you could help me pack up my things so I don't have to face my manipulative roommate on my own. I really need a job so I can find a place to live that's in my price range. The apartment I'm staying in is incredible, but the guy you met is *not* my boyfriend. I actually need to get away from him. He's really kind of an asshole and always trying to play games. What you saw today must've been him feeling some misplaced need to pretend on my part."

"Well that's a relief. He was hot, but I didn't see him as your type. Plus he was *rude*." She giggles a tittering laugh before taking a drink. Her phone rings in her purse, playing some obnoxiously snappy pop tune. She slides it out, frowning. "Sweetie, I'll be right back. I have to take this, it's work-related."

I nod, and she slides off her stool, heading for the front door.

Mick saunters over. "I'd be a lyin' git if I said I wasn't listenin' in. Sorry, but it's sometimes hard not to hear everythin' when tendin' bar. Would that be your sister?"

"Yeah. Piece of work, huh? She's decent though.

She flew here from Wisconsin to make things right, and try to convince me to come back home."

"I also happened to hear yer lookin' for a job, and a place to live. Have any bar-tendin' experience?"

I perk up, smiling. "*Some*. I filled in at a local tavern one year over winter break. I'm not really good with knowing my drinks, though. I had to Google a lot of them."

"My sister owns the place, an' she has an openin' for the night shift. They're *terrible* hours, but if yer interested, you could fill out an application." He rubs his short beard. "Tips are pretty decent, especially when the business and college crowds stops in for karaoke or live bands. And there's a room above the bar that's vacant. She usually rents it out to college students. It's not much—crowded, but clean, and she'd maybe give you a deal as an employee. You could help mop floors and such down here in the mornin's."

My pulse skips excitedly. I was convinced I was going to have to put my tail between my legs and move in with Jewels and Adam. "I'd love to see it."

"Atta girl." He smiles, pointing his index finger at me. "That's what I call 'takin' charge of your destiny.' Maybe you can have that new life you asked for after all."

By the time Glori returns to my side, I'm beaming with hope.

Mick's sister, Tess—a portly, friendly woman with

kind eyes—gives us a quick tour of the upstairs where two other renters live, both female college students. There's a common area with a couch and a TV, a small kitchen with the basic appliances, and three bedrooms barely large enough to fit a twin bed. Though it feels a bit cramped, it's still charming in its own way. The dark wooden floors and brightly painted walls give off a positive vibe that I can't shake. It gives Glori the creeps, which only makes me laugh and like it a little more. Things are beginning to look up.

As Glori's only in town for a few days, we immediately return to the apartment so I can pack my things. Luckily, Erik's gone. Since I really don't have much to pack, it doesn't take that long. Still, Glori doesn't shut up about how amazing the place is the entire time we're there. Before we leave I write a note, saying I'm sorry things didn't work out, and that I hope he can find peace with his brother one day.

Jewels sounds both excited and confused when I call to ask if Glori and I can both stay at their place through the weekend. As we enter the brownstone an hour later, she's filled with so much energy that I want to ask if she's been huffing something. She throws her arms around me. "I have my old roomie back!"

"I don't know for how long," I warn, hugging her back.

"You have a lot of explaining to do," she whispers before releasing me.

"Jewels, it's been a while," Glori greets my friend with a smile. "You look great!"

"So do you!" She takes one of my bags. "Guest room is all ready to go for you guys. After I get showered up the three of us can go out for dinner somewhere fun."

"No Adam tonight?" I ask.

"He's going out with *Theo*," she explains in a strange voice, as if using code words that only her and I will understand. Then I realize it must have something to do with me.

I nod sullenly, letting her know I understand. If I'm going to start making things right, I'm going to have to give him a call sooner rather than later.

While we feast on a Mediterranean dinner atop of a building with a killer view overlooking Central Park, I end up unloading every last one of my dark secrets on Jewels. She doesn't say much of anything as I walk her through the events, starting with my relationship with Brad, and ending with me returning to her doorstep a few hours ago. All three of us are crying by the time I'm finished nearly an hour later.

The waitress shows up just as I'm finished talking. "Can I get you—"

"A round of shots," Jewels tells her with a wave of her hand. "Your best tequila. Two for each of us."

The heavy-set woman eyes each of us skeptically, like we're not the type to take shots. "Anything else? Water, maybe?"

"*Just the shots and limes,*" Glori snaps, throwing me off guard. She's usually not much of a drinker, and I can't say that I've ever witnessed her taking a shot. She dabs at her eyes with her linen napkin.

The waitress nods, unsmiling, before leaving us alone.

Jewels sinks back in her chair. "Damn, Kel. I can't believe you didn't call me when any of this happened. I should've known something was up when you disappeared from Facebook. It wasn't like you. Why *did* you keep all of this a secret?"

"Her *family* knew," Glori pipes in, her voice strained. "We knew and we failed her."

"I don't know, Jewels," I tell my friend, even though I do. I take a deep breath. "You watched Adam nearly kill himself before he agreed to have the transplant. Then everything completely flipped around when you two moved out here. You were finally happy. I didn't want to bring you back down again. You've been through enough hell without me pulling you into my drama."

Jewels's eyes fill with a new set of tears. "Sometimes I worry you don't see me as a good enough friend to trust me with these things."

"God, no! That's not it at all!" I reach out to squeeze her hand. "Really, I just wanted to come out here and pretend like it didn't happen. I knew once I told someone about it, I'd be forced to feel all the things I was trying to avoid. I wanted to prove to myself that I wasn't some kind of whore like everyone said. I guess I failed miserably."

Jewels presses her eyes closed. "You're *not* a *whore*." Her wounded gaze flips back to mine. "Why is it when guys have casual sex, they're allowed to brag to their buddies and pat each other on the backs like they're some kind of studs, but when most girls do the same thing, they hide it, thinking they're sluts? It's ridiculous! We live in a world of double standards. What happened with this Brad douchebag wasn't your fault, except that you seem to have a thing for assholes now that I know what exactly happened with you and Erik. How many times do I have to reassure you that you're *not* some kind of sex addict or whore?"

"Maybe it's because I don't believe it." I wipe at another tear. "So many people called me these *awful* names this summer. I think it just reinforced my darkest fears. I'm hoping when I go talk to someone about my problems, they'll help me figure out how to deal with all of it."

"You're going to be okay," Glori promises,

touching my arm. "You're strong enough to make it this far, sweetie. And you've already taken so many steps in the right direction. You moved away from Erik, and you may have already found a job that will keep you occupied so you can't continue to dwell on the past. These are all good things. You have no where else to go from here but up."

I frown, picking at a hangnail on my thumb. "I don't know. Working in a bar doesn't sound like the best place for someone who's trying to avoid having sex with strangers. Maybe I need to keep looking."

Jewels stops me from picking my hand. "From now on, I want you to think of me as your lifeline. Any time you feel like you're going to slip up and disappoint yourself, I want you to call me. I don't care what time of the day it is. This quest of yours for love is admirable, and I want to help you complete it. Whatever it takes."

The waitress sets our shots on the table next to a salt shaker and a bowl filled with limes. Jewels hands her a credit card.

I stare at my friend, chewing on my lip. "Are we going to talk about the thing with Erik? I'm sorry I lied to you."

"Adam told me everything after we returned from your party. I haven't told you that I know because I wanted to give myself time to cool off. When you said you were moving out, it was the best news I've had since Adam told me he was going through with his surgery. I understand that you didn't want me telling you what to do, but I wish you would've listened when I tried to warn you about him. As much as Adam refused to forgive Erik, I knew something horrible must've happened." Her eyes open wide, and she flashes a little smile with a tilt of her head.

I gasp. "Wait! Was that an 'I told you so' look you gave me just now?"

"Shut up and take your shots like a big girl," Jewels grumbles, sprinkling salt on her hand and holding a glass up. I laugh happily, remembering a time when I said the exact same thing to her.

Glori and I lift our glasses. I smile at each of them. "To new beginnings."

"To Kelly's quest," Jewels adds with a wink.

The three of us proceed to get hammered on the roof overlooking the phenomenal view of the twinkling city skyline. We talk and laugh for hours, filling my heart with joy. I feel lighter knowing everything's out in the open, and I no longer have to guard any secrets from my best friend or my sister.

At one point Jewels calls Adam to let him know where we are. We're all surprised when he approaches our table with a casually dressed Theo at his side. I'm overwhelmed with a tornado of emotions.

"*Theo*." I stand and reach for him, wanting to tell him everything once and for all, though my mind is a drunken haze of mismatched words. "I...shit. I have so much to say. I just..."

Hushing me, he cradles me in his large arm. I can't decide if I feel him sniffing my hair, or if it's my imagination this time. "Not tonight, Cavenaugh. I'd rather do this when you're sober. I just want to make sure you make it back in one piece."

Glori rides with Theo and I in the waiting town car while Jewels and Adam wait to grab a taxi. On the ride back, I snuggle into Theo, glad he at least cares enough to see me make it home safely. He smells so good, and I never want to leave the solace of his arms. "You should grow your hair out," I slur at one point, running my fingers over his short hair. "It'd be soooo sexy."

Theo doesn't say a word until he drops us at the brownstone. "When you're feeling up to it, I'll be ready to talk. Just give me a call."

I look into his hazel eyes and want to kiss him all over. Somewhere inside, however, the new and improved Kelly knows it's time to say goodnight. He kisses the top of my head and I leave the taxi with a mere nod.

The three of us aren't ready to call it a night, but Jewels has to work mid-morning, and she hasn't been this drunk in awhile, so she's worried about having a brutal hangover if we keep it up. She wraps her arms around my neck. "I love you, Kelly Cave-naugh. You're my only sister. Don't ever forget that. I'll always have your back."

"And I'll always have yours," I return, kissing her cheek.

"We should get some kind of sister tattoos. Maybe some matching hearts and shit. Not like each other's names, but something that means something to us. I mean once we've both saved up some cash. Those damn things aren't cheap. Wait!" Though she's slurring, her words become more excited like she's just waking up. "I know! Chloe said she could give us good deals if we ever want one, once she has her own booth!"

Laughing, Adam gently pulls Jewels away from me and kisses the top of her head. "Time for bed, babe."

"Oh my god! My sweet Adam! I love you so much!" She leans in to nuzzle him, her eyes closed. Adam smirks at me before leading her to their room. It's so touching to see how much passion they have for each other. Sometimes it's like they've known each other their whole lives the way they interact.

"Good night, love birds!" I call after them, giggling.

As I settle into their guest bed at my sister's side, I'm filled with an inner peace I haven't felt in years. All is right with the world again. I didn't scare Jewels off with the brutal truth. It seems I may have my life on track, though there still may be some struggles along the way. The way Mick carried on before Glori and I left the bar, I'm hopeful that I may have a job and a place to live within the week.

Yet there's still a nagging feeling that keeps me up for hours into the night once I begin to feel the alcohol's grip fade away. Something tells me Theo won't be as accepting of my secrets as Jewels and Glori had been.

Chapter Twelve

THE MINUTE I'M AWAKE, I send Theo a text saying to call, eager to get our meeting over with. Glori and I are on the Staten Island Ferry when he finally returns my call. I show my sister the screen and she claps her hands, squealing in a high pitch. It's the same over-the-top reaction she had when she found a knock off of her favorite perfume earlier in the day. Something is definitely up with my normally placid sister.

"Cavenaugh!" Theo blurts the moment I accept the call. "How's the head?"

"Still there," I answer smartly. "Thanks for taking me home last night."

"I didn't want you to decide to stop at some random bar on the way home."

The ferry horn blasts.

"Where are you?" he asks.

"Looking at the back end of the Statue of Liberty."

I watch Glori pretend to pinch the statute's rear, something we'd do with our sisters when road tripping as kids. Unable to help myself, I cover my phone and laugh. I haven't seen Glori act so carefree in years. Between the shots the night before and the way she's acting, I almost wonder if she's becoming more of a free spirit and leaving her pageant days behind.

"I'm glad you're showing her the city while she's here," Theo tells me. "More than that, I'm glad you agreed to talk to me. It was pure torture when you wouldn't return my calls."

Sighing, I rest my arms on the ferry's railing. "Theo, you know I'm damaged, right?"

"Of course. I remember discussing demons in the closet."

"Well there are multiple *layers* in my closet. We're talking a two-story monstrosity with rotating shelves. It's basically the reason I stormed out of your office yesterday."

I hear him laugh. "I figured it must've been significant if you were willing to leave the manicotti behind."

"That *was* pretty amazing manicotti. I don't even know if I got a chance to thank you for buying me lunch."

"Maybe we can try lunch again?" His tone is tinged with hope.

"You may want to hear what I have to say before you offer that. I've done some pretty shitty things, some of them since I met you."

Glori moves to stand next to me, draping her arm around my shoulders and squeezing. As mad as I once was at her, it feels damn good to suddenly have her support after all this time. I'm going to miss her when she leaves.

"I was in the Corps, remember?" Theo answers. "It takes a lot to scare me."

"You may change your mind after hearing me out."

"That's for me to decide. Can I pick you up tonight?"

I loop my arm around Glori's waist, and rest my head against her shoulder. "I'd rather wait until my sister's gone before we do this. She's only in town until tomorrow night."

"Invite him to come along with us tonight!" Glori whispers.

I press my phone to my chest, frowning at my sister. "Wait, are you sure?" Glori pulls my phone back up to my ear, nodding. "But...Chloe's band plays tonight in Times Square and we're going with Jewels and Adam. I know last time we saw them together it wasn't exactly fun, so if you don't want to join us, I'll totally—"

"I'll be there," he blurts.

My insides light up with excitement.

After a going to the top of the Empire State Building and visiting the giant Macy's store—some of the sights Glori missed on her last trip for a 2-week beauty school—we doll ourselves up with Jewels and hit the subway with Adam. The bar Chloe's band plays in this time isn't some kind of redneck redo like the last place, which comes as a relief since Glori's along. She's having a hard enough time dealing with the "different music" as she calls it.

The crowd gathered seems to be tourists in the mood for unrestrained fun. Laser lights flash across the black and white floor, while the rest of the long, narrow bar is barely lit with glowing blue lights. The acidic smell of artificial fog is thick. The name "Retro Revenge" seems appropriate.

Seeing Chloe and the guys rock the stage is a different experience now that I know Landon and Beckett from the party at "my" place the other night. I stand with my sister and friends at the front of the stage to cheer for the band, keeping the dancing on the down low for my benefit. Jewels didn't tell Adam the truth as to *why* we weren't doing the usual bump and grind, instead telling him that kind of dancing wasn't Glori's thing. In all honesty, my sister would've sat on the sidelines and watched us anyway. I feel the bond between us strengthening after our heart-to-heart.

A few songs into The Blood Legion's first set, I feel a large hand press to my lower back. "Hey!" Theo greets me in his deep tone.

Turning to him, I feel a surge of excitement when our eyes meet. I take a moment to appreciate his gorgeous features. Even if he decides I'm not worth pursing after I tell him everything, I'll always remember how his dark brows and sparkling eyes did things to my gut that I can't explain in words.

I lean in to hug him. His arms wrap around me like they're meant to be there. We stand holding each other for a minute longer than considered kosher. This time I *know* I can feel him breathing in the smell of my shampoo before he backs off. "Want something to drink?"

"I'm good," I decide, throwing him an appreciative smile. Jewels and Glori decided it would be best if I avoid booze while around Theo so I can be in complete control.

Other than the hug, Theo and I hardly touch for the rest of the night. I do my best to keep an invisible line between us, knowing it will only be a challenge to keep my hormones in check the way I keep swaying to Chloe's guitar riffs and throaty melody. He respects it, sticking to Adam's side. The band's done at midnight. Chloe, Landon, and Beckett join us for drinks after they pack up their gear. We all gather around a table beneath the blaring 80s rock playing from the bar's speakers.

"Glad you could catch the whole show this time!" Chloe teases, pushing on my shoulder. Her eyes flip over to my sister. "What'd *you* think? You really don't seem the type to like our music. It's okay to be honest. You won't offend me, I assure you. We have a pretty decent following even though we don't necessarily appeal to the masses."

"It was great!" Glori answers with a surprising amount of enthusiasm. "You sound a lot like a band I've heard on Spotify!"

Everyone at the table stares at her, waiting for her to say she's joking. Her smile fades a little. "What?"

I clear my throat, drawing everyone's attention away from my poor sister. While it seems she's attempting to change, I don't think she's quite comfortable with her new self. "So, Chloe, when do you guys play again?"

"Not until next Thursday. I have to work at the shop Monday and Tuesday, but I have Wednesday off if you still want me to come by and help you find discount places to spice up your room."

"About that..." I pivot in my seat to face Theo. "I moved out of the apartment. Erik was too controlling. I'm back with Jewels and Adam until something else comes along. I think I found a reasonable place, but they're waiting for the background check to go through before I get the final word." I glance back to

Chloe. "I wanted to let everyone know right away so you didn't show up at Erik's door, looking for me."

Beckett slaps the table. "Damn, that was such a *killer* loft!"

Chloe reaches back to press her hand to his mouth. Sometimes they act like they're a couple rather than just bandmates. "Just an excuse for another party, right? This time we can invite some of your neighbors so you can get to know them a little better. No better way to start off on the right foot."

"The place I'm looking at is *way* too small for a party," I shake my head. "But it's over a great Irish pub. If everything goes the way I hope, I'll be working there too. We could probably throw a party down there instead."

When I glance at Theo, he's completely unmoving, the corners of his eyes creased like he's somewhere far away with his thoughts. My throat tightens. What is he thinking?

"What's the name of the place?" Chloe asks. "If we haven't played there before, maybe you could get us in for a gig."

Sucking in my breath, I turn back to her. "It's Flanagan's, near Riverside Park."

Chloe cocks her head, rolling her eyes to one side. "Never heard of it."

Beckett elbows her in the ribs. "Yeah you have. We've played there." When the other two stare blankly back at him, he raises his hands. "Remember

Tess and her brother Mick? They were the ones that paid us extra to play another hour on Mick's twenty-first birthday last year. Goofy Irish guy? Squarish woman that smelled like goat cheese?"

"Oh yeah!" Chloe perks up. "That Mick guy is *adorable*. He tried to serenade his girlfriend when we were finished, but she was so embarrassed she ran out of there like her fucking hair was on fire! Poor guy. He was a real trooper though. Just laughed it off like it was the most natural reaction in the world, and bought the entire bar a round of shots. He was the cutest damn thing, I swear."

Beckett rolls his eyes, like her story makes him sick. I laugh with the vision of Mick doing such a thing. He's seems like such a positive guy that I imagine he took his girlfriend's rejection with a grain of salt.

"Can I talk to you for a second somewhere private?" Theo whispers, touching the back of my arm.

I nod before telling the others we'll be back. My sister and Jewels each flash me a look of restrained concern, so I wink and give them a small nod to let them know it's okay. I'm not about to let Theo take me somewhere *private*, and the no-dancing or alcohol rule seems to have cut back on my attraction to Theo —a *little*, anyway. While he steers me through the crowd and out the front door, my skin still twinges delightfully from his touch.

"Are you okay?" he asks once we're somewhat alone with the smokers. He looms from a few inches away, the distraught look in his eye making me believe he wants to hold onto me. The enchanting pull I've always had for him has become stronger, scrambling my coherent thoughts.

"Huh? I mean...*yeah*. I'm fine." I draw my eyebrows down. "Why are you asking?"

"I just think it's strange that so much has changed in forty-eight hours considering the other night you were excited about the loft apartment. What made you so suddenly move back in with Jewels?" He presses his fingertips to my elbow with someone dark passing through his gaze. "Did Erik do something to make you uncomfortable?"

"No. I mean, kind of, but not in the way you think. He's part of the truth I have to tell you." I bring my hands up to my face, inhaling the cloud of smoke around us. "I wasn't planning to do this tonight."

Theo jams his hands into his pockets, looking to the street still bustling behind us despite the late hour. His clenched jaw flexes. "Did you have sex with him?"

"Yes," I squeak in an unrecognizable voice.

He hardly looks back at me for a full second before looking away again. "When?"

"Theo—" I bring my hand to his chest, but he stops me, grabbing my wrist.

His hazel eyes darken. *"When?"*

The thing about having casual sex is you have to be able to own up to it without feeling dirty. I've always been able to do that in the past, and normally it wouldn't be a problem, except that I have to admit that I was having casual sex with someone else between the time Theo bought me a drink and took me back to Jewels and Adam's place, and then again just hours before I agreed to go on a date with Theo.

"I can't." I shake my head, breaking a teetering tear free. "I'm not ready to do this. I'm sorry."

His clenched jaw jumps again. "When I asked you out on a date, I thought it meant you were ready to give us a shot and took it as a cue that you were done messing around with other people." He releases my wrist, fuming. "I know we never discussed being exclusive, but you told me I didn't have to worry about you having sex with that guy. In other words, you lied to me."

I look down with a burst of shame. "I didn't lie. It happened before I told you that."

"So you moved in with him *after* you slept together? Are you fucking kidding me?" His sharp words cut through the night, causing a group of girls behind us to giggle.

"It's complicated," I say quietly, looking up with tears spilling from my eyes.

Theo moves closer, bringing his hands up to

cradle my jaw. I gulp down a surprised cry. His touch feels so damn good.

"I'm going to be honest with you, Cavenaugh. The day Jewels introduced us, I was like some love sick school boy for *days*. I couldn't wait for a chance to see you again. Most of the women I meet have become hardened by big city life. You've got the same confidence and sexiness, only there's something soft underneath. It makes me want to protect you, make sure you're taken care of." His thumbs stroke the sides of my face. "I can't be with you the way I want if you're lying to me. It's like I told my last girlfriend—I can handle infidelity to a degree. What I can't tolerate is straight up deceit. If you can't be truthful with me, then I can't be with you."

Then he leans in, at first gentle when he presses his thick, soft lips to mine. I gasp, making way for his whiskey-flavored tongue to slip inside and massage mine with a much harder, much more desperate fervor, like he's trying to make up for the time since the mere kiss in Erik's apartment. Still unable to process the kiss despite his contradictory words, I don't move my hands, though my tongue and lips eagerly respond with all the passion I've been holding back.

Each moment when it seems it couldn't become any more amazing, Theo ups the intensity of the kiss. His fingertips slip underneath the back of my shirt to stroke my bare skin, soft and slow. I want those fingertips all over me, kneading my breasts and releasing the warm ache between my legs.

Remembering that we're standing on a public street in Times Square, and there's no way we could take this any further even if we weren't, I break the seal of lips, bringing my fingers up to test the swollen state of my mouth. My eyes snap onto his. "What—"

"I've been dying to do that for weeks. I wanted to see what our first kiss would've been like." With an abrupt coolness that stings like a sharp blade to my chest, he takes a step back, his gaze dark. "I guess it's ironic that it was also our last."

He leaves me standing all alone outside the bar.

Chapter Thirteen

RATHER THAN SENDING my belongings in the mail, my parents bring them with on a surprise visit a week later. Our reunion is bittersweet, filled with tears and apologies on both ends. They both seem so different. There's a bit of gray mixed in with my dad's chestnut hair, and the way his cheeks cave in slightly I wonder how much weight he's lost since the beginning of summer. My mom's dark hair is done up in a chignon, pulling the wrinkles back around her dark brown eyes. They're barely in their forties, but they suddenly look *old*. I briefly consider their advanced aging could've brought on by my reckless decision to move away.

They're only able to stay for two days as they need to finish closing the camp down for the season. Still, the emotional toll their brief visit takes on me is remarkable. I already feel hallowed out after

Theo's emotional goodbye, and there are days I'm only able to survive on auto pilot mode, smiling even though I don't feel the slightest spark of happiness. Before my parents leave, we find a psychologist who the three of us not only agree on, but who can fit me in within a few days despite her tight schedule.

I'm nervous as hell during my first appointment with the psychologist. Her office is considerably modern, the furnishings looking like something straight off an IKEA showroom, and it smells like freshly cut flowers. Jean Ritter, MS, LPCC, a very slender woman around 45 or so with short, dark hair and friendly brown eyes, watches me from one of the leather armchairs. She's casually dressed in a soft tunic and capris with a ton of bright jewelry. My eyes keep skimming down to her flashy heels that totally make her ensemble and most definitely came from a high-end designer.

After we run through the niceties in which I give her a background on where I grew up, what I have for a family, where I went to school, and other things that feel mundane and less important all things considered, Jean gives me a genuine, bright smile. "Why don't we address the reason you're here? Your mother told my assistant that it was your idea to see a therapist." Her soft voice holds the hint of a southern accent.

I nod, my eyes flashing back down to her shoes. "I'm fucked up."

"Well, that's a relief. I guess my job here is done. Where would you like me to send your prescription?"

My eyes snap onto hers. She laughs merrily, tipping her head down and looking years younger than I originally guessed her to be. "Let's drop the labels and assumptions for a minute. If you were so 'fucked up' as you say, then you wouldn't have decided to come see me on your own. What happened that made you see yourself this way?"

I look to my lap and pick at a hangnail on my ring finger. "I don't seem to have any self-control when it comes to sex. I used to think there wasn't anything wrong with random hook ups. Guys do it all the time and no one bats an eye. But I changed my mind this summer when I unknowingly slept with a married man who had a terminally ill wife."

Jean regards me with interest. "This man didn't tell you he was married?"

"No, but I should've guessed there was something wrong the way he always wanted to meet me somewhere private. Maybe a part of me suspected and that's why I started to believe there's something wrong with me. My entire family knew he was married, though, and they just assumed I knew it too. Once word got out, I became the town jezebel. I got so tired of everyone hating on me that I packed my bags and came out here. I couldn't take it anymore. I have a history of running away when things get rough. It's what I do best."

"How did you feel when you discovered he was married?"

"Pissed. And sick. I actually threw up. That's not something I would knowingly do—sleep with a married man. When my friends and family believed the rumors that I knew all along, I just wanted to disappear. I wanted to…check out."

"You mean kill yourself?"

I think back to the night my mom told me to get out of her house. I begged her to listen to me with tears streaming down my face, my throat raw from screaming. My sister Megan was the only other one around, and she just watched on with her arms crossed, judging me in a way that felt foreign, as if I was in someone else's body. For one very dark, lonely moment, I wished I was dead. Then anger took over, and I never had that thought again.

"I never would've actually killed myself, no," I say, fighting back a burst of tears. "But there were times I wished fate would take over and make that decision for me."

Jean watches with an open expression, more curious than anything. "And this is why you think you're fucked up? Because you found out you slept with a married man who lied to you?"

"No, it's more complicated than that. I came to

New York to start over. I wanted to erase the labels everyone back home had given me. I wanted to prove to myself that I wasn't a whore, or a slut like they said. When I got here, my friend Jewels introduced me to this *really* great guy—Theo. Even though I thought it was a bad idea to start another relationship so soon, I wanted things to work out between us...I still do. But then I met Erik, her boyfriend's brother, and hooked up with him twice even though I swore to myself that I wouldn't. He's even more messed up than I am—he once tried to kill his brother. And he made it clear he's not interested in an actual relationship, just sex. Still, it's like I couldn't control myself around him. Having sex with Erik completely fucked everything up with Theo. He hates me now, and I can't blame him. I don't know why I slept with Erik when Theo's the one I really want. And I was so insistent with Theo that we take things slow. I wonder...I mean sometimes I think maybe I'm addicted to sex."

"I see. Tell me, Kelly, do you think about sex often?"

"Not unless I'm around Theo or Erik."

"What about pornography? Do you watch movies, buy magazines, or look at sexual images online?"

I laugh, wiping at my eyes. "I watched a porn flick once with a guy in high school. It was the dumbest thing I've ever seen–the acting was terrible. But I've never bought a 'dirty' magazine. And, um, does looking at hot guys on Pinterest count as 'sexual images?'"

"There wouldn't be enough therapists in the world if it did." She winks and crosses her arms. "What about masturbation?"

"Yeah…maybe a few dozen times or so since high school."

"Have you had more than one sexual partner at a time?"

My eyes grow wide. "You mean like a threesome?"

"That, or just having relations with two men over the same time period."

"No threesomes. I was out with Theo the first time I had sex with Erik behind the bar. We weren't officially dating yet, though. We were just hanging with my friend Jewels and her boyfriend. Does that count?"

"Behind the bar?"

"In the alley."

Jean stops to write something on her little notepad for the first time since I came in the room. "Do you have sex in public often?"

"No way. It was my first time. What are you writing? Did I flunk some kind of sex test?"

"There aren't any tests, Kelly. There *are* warning signs, things that would make me believe that you are, in fact, addicted. The impulsive sex does seem disconcerting, though it doesn't seem the idea of sex has interrupted your daily life." She leans back in her chair, studying me. "Tell me about the time you lost your virginity."

My chest grows tight, and the tears finally break free. "It's not something I'm proud of."

Jean hands me a box of tissues. "I'm not here to judge, Kelly. I want to help you understand your actions. I want to help you feel better about yourself, and get you back on the right track."

"Okay." I take a long, stuttering breath and wipe at my tears with a tissue. "It was the summer before my junior year of high school. I went with a big group of friends to the house of some guy we knew who was home from college. There was a shit-ton of booze. I had only met the guy throwing the party a few times before. He was nice and everything, but I wasn't attracted to him. At all. Me and my friends were acting like a bunch of idiots, doing a ton of shots and drinking everything in sight. I blacked out some time in the night. The next thing I remember is waking up in bed next to the guy who threw the party. We were both naked. I knew we had sex right away because there was a dull pain between my legs. I was mortified. I always thought I'd lose my virginity to a boyfriend, and not during some random one night stand thing when I couldn't even remember doing it."

"What did this older man have to say?"

"I don't really remember. It was like I was stuck

in some kind of nightmare. I think he said some-thing about having a good time. I got the hell out of there and went out of my way to avoid having to see him ever again. I was so fucking embarrassed."

"Did you tell your parents what happened?"

I laugh loudly. "Are you kidding me? My mom probably would've taken me in for an exorcism if I did. My sister, Sarah, took me to the clinic for birth control when I told her I was having sex my senior year. My mom didn't know I was having sex until she found out about the married guy. I didn't think she'd ever speak to me again up until they came out a few days ago. I don't know what changed, but she kept going on about how sorry she was that she didn't believe me when I swore I didn't know there was a sick wife."

"Did you tell Sarah or any of your other sisters how you lost your virginity?"

"I didn't tell anyone. The only ones who knew were my friends there that night. Half of them were too messed up to really know what happened."

"When was the next time you had sex?"

"A few weeks later. I knew the next guy, though. We had been going to school together since elemen-tary. He was one of the most popular guys in our grade and all the girls were dying to hook up with him."

"Was he your boyfriend?" Jean asks, crossing her legs and tilting her head.

"No. I haven't really had a lot of boyfriends, and I've never been in love. I want to, though. It's one of the reasons I want to stop having meaningless sex with random guys. I want to make myself wait until I'm in love for once...if that's possible."

"Why do you think you kept having 'meaningless sex' after the night you lost your virginity?"

"The first time it was because I wanted to experience it when I wasn't blacked out. The classmate I slept with had been with a lot of girls and really knew what he was doing. I loved it. We hooked up again once during our senior year. Other than that, I would sleep with guys I met at parties and concerts. At one point it was my goal to find the hottest guy in the room and sleep with him. Once I started college I was comfortable having sex for fun without the complication of a relationship. The married guy was the first time in years I considered having an actual *boyfriend*."

"And then you came to New York, vowing to change your ways."

"Basically, yeah."

"What do you get out of sex, Kelly?"

"I don't know. I guess it takes me to a place where I don't have to think, I just feel good." I ball the damp tissue in my hand, waiting for Jean to tell me I'm every bit as screwed up as I think. "I just love it when a guy really *wants* me that way, you know?"

She sets her notebook down on the ottoman

beside her and leans over her lap with her arms crossed. "Kelly, have you ever considered what happened the night you lost your virginity was a form of rape?"

I blink several times before asking, *"What?"*

"It's considered 'date rape' when someone you know has sex with you, without your permission."

"For all I know, I told him it was okay." I shake my head. "I was so drunk I probably would've agreed to get a tattoo on my face."

"That's not an excuse. When you're intoxicated to that degree, even if you drank willingly, you weren't responsible. And this man was older than you. What he did was also likely considered statutory rape."

I balk at her, unable to process what she's saying. Wordlessly, she hands me another tissue. I didn't even realize I had started crying again.

"I'm normally not much of a crier," I say with a peaked laugh, dabbing at my eyes.

"That's because you seem to be a strong young woman, Kelly. By no means are we done with these sessions, but I'm starting to get a good handle on what's going on in your head. It appears sex with Erik took you to a place where you could avoid your feelings. You felt pleasure while doing it, then guilt and shame came afterwards. It seems to me that you've conditioned yourself to want sex with attractive men while somewhere denying yourself the chance to have a real relationship. What we need to work on now is finding a way to break that cycle."

"So I'm fixable?"

Jean laughs, giving me another one of her genuine smiles. "Yes, Kelly, you're quite 'fixable.' It'll take some time, and we're going to have to set some boundaries on any relationships you want to try in the future. First thing I want to do is focus on getting you back on your feet and making you confident. The fact that you're here and you've recognized your sexual activity isn't healthy is already a huge step."

My head swarms with her revelations as she stands. I bolt to my feet and crush her with a hug. "Thanks for listening to me. I know it's your job and everything, but...just...*thank you*."

She laughs quietly and pats my back. I'm sure I've violated some kind of doctor/patient rule, but for the first time in months, I don't feel completely broken.

Chapter Fourteen

THE FIRST DAY OF FALL, I move into the apartment above Flanagan's just in time for Adam's cousin Davis to take over my spot in Jewels and Adam's guest room. It only takes two trips up the rickety old stairs by Jewels, Adam, Chloe, Davis, and myself since my new room is so small, forcing me to leave a few boxes with Jewels until I can find a bigger place.

I don't have time to unpack before starting my very first shift as a waitress. Dressed in leggings and a v-neck t-shirt with the bar's name on the back, my hair slicked into a high ponytail, I cross my arms as I appreciate the room. There's a faint odor of mildew lingering from a burst pipe that once ruined the ceiling, otherwise it's suitable for my needs. With the quilt my grandma made before she passed away and some framed pictures of me with Jewels from college, it actually feels cozy. Maybe I can find a chair small enough to jam in the corner for times I actually find a moment to read. I feel a rush of pride knowing that I'll be making my way without relying on anyone else's generosity.

I'm thrilled when I discover Mick and a sprite-looking little thing named Stella have been tasked with the job of training me in. They're both astoundingly patient with my limited knowledge. By two a.m. I'm keeping up with them, and hardly ever need to ask for help.

The next few weeks go pretty much the same, burning through the long days of September until they're just a distant memory. I work long shifts until the bar closes at ungodly hours, sleeping half the following days away before a long run through Central Park, a quick shower that leaves my new roommates, Felicity and Avery, ample hot water, either a visit with Jewels and Chloe if their schedules allow for it or an appointment with Jean, then back to work.

There's hardly any time to ponder if Theo's ever thinking about me, or if he's moved on to someone else, though I do run through Central Park the same hours he normally goes in hopes of crossing paths. I'm plagued with disappointment each time I visit Jewels at her place and he's not there.

No matter how much time has passed since the night Theo kissed me, it's still so fresh that memories of the way his lips felt and the taste of his tongue come rushing back at the most unexpected of times. I sometimes catch myself running my fingers across my lips whenever I think of him—which turns out to be quite often. I didn't realize how ruthlessly hard I had fallen for him until he walked out of my life.

I run into Erik one time as he's leaving a coffee shop. It's awkward as hell, resulting in stiff smiles and very few words. My heart pounds whenever his steely gaze meets with mine. Though he looks considerably well, I'm relieved to say I don't feel the aching need to pull him into the nearest building and break the progress I've made with Jean. It seems there's something else he wants to say to me, but he final mumbles something about having to go and lifts his hand to his side in a final goodbye.

Oddly enough, without Theo and Erik in my life, my sexual urges are close to null. I took the new vibrator from Erik's apartment when I left without bothering to replace it. Jean encouraged me to masturbate on a regular basis, or whenever I felt the need for a release. She went into detail when explaining how orgasms are beneficial to a woman's health, and that I shouldn't feel any displaced feelings when doing it, other than simple pleasure. I was quick to let her know I got the gist of her lecture. It was like listening to my mom all over again when she explained safe sex to me as a teen. The feel of something electric bringing me to orgasm is far from the satisfaction I get from a man. Still, I don't spend as much time thinking about sex as I had in the past.

Jean also encourages me to set boundaries with the other men in my life who could be a potential sexual partner. I was quick to let Mick know after he seemed to be flirting the first couple of days that I won't let anything come between us as it may jeopardize my job. Although he claimed to be heartbroken, he proceeded to give me what he called a "nuggie" on top of my head, and said I'd be more fun as a younger sister he could pick on. From that point on, it became easier to be around him without worrying that our flirting has gone too far.

Early November, Chloe finally gets her own station at the tattoo shop. It's only the second time I've asked for a night off—the other in October to stay with Jewels when Adam was hospitalized overnight with an infection from his new insulin pump. Tess doesn't even bat an eye when I ask off. Instead she compliments me on how hard I've been working, and says she thinks the bar has gained a following of new male customers since I started.

Our now tight group of friends gathers at a brand new club in SoHo to celebrate Chloe's accomplishment, proceeding to blow what little "fun" money

I've stashed away for the month. I've come to terms with just how expensive living in this exciting city can be, and I'm improving on my budgeting skills. Still, it's sometimes difficult when I'm constantly trying to keep up with Jewels's rich boyfriend, and Chloe, who works enough jobs to make decent money.

Until tonight it's been relatively easy not to let my sexual inhibitions dissolve with liquor, as Jean suggested. I've been working nearly every single night straight, and Tess is strict about no drinking on the job, even if the customers buy me one—which happens all the freaking time. It's been a fine line between keeping my sexuality in check, and dressing the part to get outstanding tips.

Far too many drinks and shots of tequila later, I search the club until I find Chloe chatting it up with a heavily tattooed bunch, two of whom are her band-mates, and another I recognize from the tattoo shop. I come at Chloe with my arms extended, my purse tucked under my armpit. "Give me a hug, baby girl. I gotta head out. I've spent my limit in booze *and* money."

Chloe holds her hands up like a traffic cop, stop-ping me. Her button-sized eyes swarm, trying to focus. "Nuh-uh. Your fabulous ass isn't leaving this party yet, miss *thing*. Terina wants to take us to see *strippers*! You can't miss it when you're dressed like that! I know you're struggling to stay away from the guys, but sweetheart, have you *seen* yourself tonight?"

I roll my eyes. The snug halter dress was a bargain Jewels and I found at a second-hand shop on a trip to Jersey. It's cut very low in the front, and barely covers my ass. Jewels insisted I buy it, saying the pale color make me look tan. It's the first time I've dressed like my old self in months. "No strippers for me. I traded an earlier shift with Stella tomorrow so I could come hang with you tonight." I push her arms down so I can crush her to me. "I can't wait for you to pop my tattoo cherry!"

A few of the guys beside us snicker. Chloe's hands trail down my butt, stopping to tug my hemline down as far as it will go before releasing me. "You know I love ya, chica, but you gotta keep that juicy ass covered up if you don't want to attract the men. You got money for a cab? I sure hope you're not planning to take the subway alone."

"Yeah, I've got it," I insist, bending down to kiss her cheek. I slip a $20 bill between her exposed breasts. "Get yourself a lap dance."

Beckett, the hot bassist from her band who's pretty full of himself, loops his arm around Chloe's shoulders. "I'll give you one for free, baby. Those guys ain't got nuthin' on me."

Chloe looks highly amused by the gesture, so I wave goodbye, leaving her to flirt. Since Jewels and Adam left over an hour ago, I make my way solo to the exit through the never-ending sea of sweaty bodies jumping in lazy synchronicity to a techno remake of Justin Timberlake's latest tune. Getting tussled around doesn't bother me the way it once would, when I was afraid I'd lose myself if a guy were to touch me in a suggestive way. I barely flinch when someone touches my arm.

"Cavenaugh?"

I become completely unglued with the sound of the his voice. Holding a hand out at my side to steady myself, I take my time turning around, knowing damn well what the sight of his dark eyebrows and sexy green eyes will do to my well-being.

I wish I could say he looks distraught or lovesick when our eyes meet, but in fact, I don't think Theo's ever looked better. He's almost unrecognizable with hair longer than usual, grown out just enough that I could slip my fingers through it and hold him to me. There's a healthy glow to his face, and I can't stop staring at his damn lips now that I know what they're capable of. The dark gray t-shirt he wears beneath a thin leather jacket showcases the ridges of his muscular chest and stomach. When I steal a glance down, I'm thrown off by the delectable way his tight jeans show off his toned legs. In all the time we spent together, he was always wearing shorts.

Autumn dressed Theo is even hotter than the guy I spent half the summer lusting over. But my feelings for him have evolved light years beyond lust—he's also a valued friend. Until seeing him in the flesh, I wasn't aware of just how much I've missed him, or how ruthlessly deep the ache went. My chest twinges painfully.

"Theo! You look…great." I try to hide the longing in my voice as I feign a smile. "I love your hair."

His eyes lock on my cleavage, and he presses his lips together. "Wow." It seems to take him forever to finally meet my gaze. "You look amazing in that dress."

"Thanks. I was here celebrating with Adam and Jewels. Chloe finally got her own booth at the shop."

He nods. "So I heard. I sent her a gift."

Before I never once thought about how it would hurt him to stop hanging out with Jewels and Adam times like this, though there have been plenty of nights when I was working that he could still get together with them.

For a moment we stare at each other, unsure what to say. The fact that he hasn't smiled at me yet makes me uneasy. If it weren't for the glimpse of longing I catch in his eyes, I'd think he was *annoyed* to see me.

I finally turn to the side, ready to bolt. "So it was good seeing you again. I gotta head out. I work an early shift tomorrow."

He grabs my arm. "Wait! Who are you leaving with?"

A white-hot surge flares through me from his touch, jumpstarting my already precarious heart. I set my hands on my chest, trying to breathe normally. "It's just me. Adam and Jewels already left, and the others are staying."

Frowning, he leans in to the guy closest to him and says something before tipping his head towards the exit. "Let's go. I'm taking you home."

"*Theo*. It's *fine*. Seriously. I'm taking a cab."

"Cavenaugh, I'm going with whether you walk on your own will, or I have to take you over my shoulder and haul your stubborn ass out of here." I see a brief flash of the fun guy I fell for when he finally smiles. "Your choice."

"Fine," I grumble. "Let's go."

His hand rests on the small of my back as we weave our way out to the street, making my heart skip like crazy. When we reach the curb, he taps out something on his iPhone. "My driver will be here in a few minutes."

"For the record, I would've been perfectly safe in a cab." I cross my arms, suddenly wishing my dress wasn't quite so low. His partially hooded eyes keep flickering back to my breasts, stirring the passion I've worked so hard to keep at bay. "I've managed to survive the last couple months without you taking care of me."

"You should've put more thought into what you

were going to wear tonight...unless you weren't planning to go home alone."

I flex my jaw, stopping myself before I blow up. "You mean if I was going to hook up with some random guy?"

"*What?*" His eyes flash wide. "No! I meant if you weren't going to catch a ride with Jewels and Adam! I don't like the idea of strangers ogling you when you're all alone."

As my face grows hot, I wish there was something I could hide behind. Once again, I jumped to the kind of conclusion Jean is attempting to help me shatter. It's as if I can feel *months* of progress slipping out from between my fingers from only spending a few minutes with Theo. "They don't exactly live in my neighborhood. It wouldn't make sense for us to share a ride."

We both pause to peer out into the busy street. Cars whiz by, honking and changing lanes, while pedestrians wait in hordes at the crosswalks. I can always count on New York to be animated, encouraging me to move forward rather than dwelling on the past. I don't imagine the sight of everything all lit up at night will grow old, and can't wait to see the transformation once the Christmas celebrations begin. Chloe warned us the city can have brutal winters once the wind comes whipping off the water. I shiver with the thought.

"You cold?" Theo asks. He removes his jacket

before I can tell him otherwise, so I accept it gracefully. When he places it on my shoulders, the scent of leather and Theo envelop me like a warm burrito of pheromones, dampening my underwear. The sight of his toned forearms out in the open don't help any, either.

I have Jean on speed dial, and seriously consider finding an excuse to break away and call her. Then I hear Mick's voice telling me only I can control my own destiny and decide against it. *I can handle this on my own.*

I study Theo's stunning side profile, anxiously wondering if I'll ever see him again after tonight. Now's my chance to make things right. Who knows if I'll ever have this kind of opportunity again?

"I got that bartending job I mentioned. I'm living in the apartment above the bar."

"Adam told me. Congratulations." The lopsided grin he gives me does nothing to cool me down. "I'm glad to hear things are going well for you." He looks down to check his watch.

Although I'm suddenly worried he's eager for his driver to come pick us up and end the torture, my body's alive, still buzzing from his grin. "Did he tell you I started seeing a psychologist too? She's been really helpful." I swallow several times, my throat suddenly bone dry. "And I haven't been with anyone since you kissed me."

His head snaps in my direction. "Really?"

Is that disbelief I hear? Or is it my self-doubt creeping in?

"Yeah, really. I've resolved to make a lot of changes in my life since that night you left me. I never got a chance to tell you what happened, the whole reason I moved to New York."

Eyes sparkling with interest, he opens his mouth, then shuts it. Then his beautiful, magical lips part again. "I know you said you need to get home, but would you at least have time to grab a cup of coffee? We can stay out as late or as early as you want."

"Coffee sounds good," I say, nodding. Despite my promise to myself to stay hard and not give in to him, my lips curl with a wide smile.

We engage in small-talk in the back of his private car until we stop at a quaint coffee shop open 24 hours that's closer to my apartment. My stomach surges excitedly with the dense aroma of specialty flavors. There aren't too many customers yet as the clubs are still in full swing, so we're given a peacefully quiet place to talk. Theo chooses the small table closest to the windows, balancing the cups in one hand, and pulling my chair out with the other.

I begin by telling him more about my new job and my roommates, and he launches into stories of his work and his family life. I knew his dad was in the entertainment business, but I wasn't aware that he stays in shape because his mom died of a heart attack at a fairly young age when he was a teen, and that his younger sister I've heard him speak of many times before lives with his aunt in the Bronx. My heart warms the way he openly shares his personal life with me, like I'm an old friend even after he declared he was through with me.

Our coffees are gone when Theo's smile fades, and he reaches for my hand. "Damn it, I've missed you, Cavenaugh."

"I've missed you too." Not wanting him to take his hand away, I lace my fingers with his. An unmistakable look of hope seizes his features with my gesture. "I suppose it's time for me to explain some things."

"Only if you're comfortable doing it." He flashes me a flat smile that stops at his lips. His eyes are dull in trepidation.

Here goes everything.

I suck in a deep breath of courage before telling him of my sexual history, even spilling nearly every detail of my tumultuous relationship with Erik. I give him the long version of my "affair" with Brad, wrapping it up by telling him about my sessions with Jean, and how her advice has helped me stay on track.

Theo occasionally rubs his thumb across the back of my hand as I ramble on, but otherwise he remains stoic. He doesn't even flinch when I tell him that the same night we first bonded in Jewels and Adam's backyard was immediately after I slept with Erik. Honestly, I don't take it as a good sign.

Clubs must be closing by the time I'm finished, because the coffee shop begins to fill with boisterous patrons dressed to the nines. Theo seems lost in his thoughts, processing my confession.

"I hope now you understand a little better why I freaked when you suggested I try out for that acting part. My therapist helped me understand that you were just trying to help me. I was too focused on how everyone back home would see it—getting a part when I was dating the producer of the show. It would've just fueled the rumors, and that was the kind of image I was trying to undo."

Theo watches me with an unusual, eerie calm. Either he's in shock, or he's disgusted by the truth.

Sighing, I look down. "I don't expect you to understand everything I've done. But I really like you, Theo. I mean, I love how I feel when I'm around you. You know, genuinely *happy*. I meant it when I told you that I wanted to try dating. I know I'm seriously messed up, and maybe you don't want that kind of drama in your life. I'll totally understand if that's the case. If you don't want to start over and give this exclusive thing a try, I hope we can at least continue to hang out together with Jewels and Adam. I don't want you to feel like you can't be with your friends because of me. And I definitely don't want to lose you as *my* friend, either. You mean a lot to me."

The band of muscles in Theo's jaw jump to life. His hazel eyes turn to stare at the surge of traffic outside, shuttling the die-hards home from the clubs.

Knowing it's over between us, I start to pull my hand away from his. "I'm really sorry."

He squeezes my hand. "Stop," he commands, drawing his eyes back on me. His thumb goes into overdrive stroking the back side of my hand. "I'm sitting here trying to rationalize why I shouldn't hunt this Brad asshole down like the animal he is."

Tears spring to my eyes. I was sure he'd be done with me after he knew all the dirty details, the ugliest parts of my life. I never dreamed he'd have *this* kind of reaction.

"I'm sure his life was ruined when everyone discovered the truth," I say quietly.

"I don't know why you were so afraid to tell me what happened with that jerk. It doesn't sound like what happened was your fault. What kind of *man* cheats on his dying wife?"

"Everyone automatically assumed I knew he was married. I was afraid you'd think I did, too." I shrug. "It's one of the things I'm working through with my psychologist. Did I mention I'm messed up?"

Theo tilts his head down to his side. "Come over here."

With my heart pounding, I drag my chair around to his side of the table. Once I'm close enough, he wraps me in his bear-like grip, and buries his face in my hair. "Even though the Erik thing really pissed me off, I don't think you're messed up. Someone should've listened to you back home. I'm sorry I didn't give you more of a chance."

I let him hold me for a long time, soaking his shirt with my silent tears.

Chapter Fifteen

Eventually Theo and I leave the coffee shop, hand-in-hand, each of us taking a moment to breathe in the now chilled air. I snuggle into his jacket, finally appreciative for its warmth.

"My place is just a few blocks down if you want to walk," I tell him.

"You're not too cold?"

I shrug with a smile. "It's not that bad. Maybe in another month or I'd rather take the car." I bite down on my lip. I'm assuming we'll be together that long when nothing has been decided. I need to slow it the fuck down before I push him away.

"Okay. I'll let my driver know."

He drops my hand to approach the passenger's side of the sleek black card parked a few yards down. It gives me the opportunity to appreciate what a great back end Theo has, similar to that of professional football players. Now that I see a spark of hope that we still have a chance, I let myself fantasize how phenomenal he'd be completely naked. The guy's like a work of art. I've never asked if he does more than just run, but as toned as he appears, he must go to the gym on a regular basis.

It's just dark enough under the street-lights that I don't think he sees me flushing when he returns to take my hand. We're quiet as we walk, each of us mindful of our thoughts. Part of me is afraid that if I open my big mouth, I'll ruin everything. Still, I can't imagine anything more tantalizing than walking the city streets at night with Theo at my side. When we reach the bar, his ride is already waiting at the curb.

"This is it," I say, tilting my head to the unlit sign over the bar.

Theo takes both my hands. "When can I see you again?" His beautiful eyes search me eagerly, like he wants to kiss me. "I want to finally take you on this mystical date."

"I don't have a lot of time off yet. I had to switch my schedule around just to go out tonight. Tomorrow I'll be done by nine, though. I could be ready by ten if that isn't too late." It probably sounds desperate to offer such a late time, but then again, this is New York and I'm trying to fit in with the locals.

"I can make tomorrow work." He draws his finger

up to my jawline. "I'm so glad I found you tonight. It killed me that we didn't speak all this time."

My lips part with his touch, and I close my eyes. I can't speak.

"Remind me what your therapist said about kissing."

Flipping my eyes open, I grin and move closer, wrapping my hands around his waist. "Kissing's okay as long as I feel under control and it's in a safe place where it can't lead to unplanned sex." I take a sweeping look around the neighborhood and grin. "As long as *you* can promise to control yourself, I'd say we're good to go."

He takes me in his arms and crushes his lips down on mine. Our mouths simultaneously part to allow our tongues to tango, mixing the remnants of coffee and lingering booze. He holds me so tightly against him that I'd be gasping for air if he wasn't breathing more into me. I wrap my arms around his head, finally tugging at his long locks that have been making me insane since we first ran into each other. He lets out a low moan of approval into my mouth and deepens the kiss, moving his lips harder, making longer strokes with his tongue. My stomach flutters wildly, as if ready to take flight.

Our bodies meld together, his erection pressed against my belly, my nipples hard with the friction of his chest. Between my legs I'm clenched tightly, swollen and ready. A low, guttural moan resonates from his throat. Realizing how desperately I want to do more with him, I lighten my end of the kiss and slip away a fraction of an inch, bringing my hands up to hold onto his face.

Theo catches on immediately, making his kisses feather-light. He cradles my face in his hands with a throaty hum before breaking the connection. Then he takes me in his arms and kisses the top of my head. "We need to stop now or we're going to break all the rules."

I breathe heavily against his chest. "For the record, you're totally worth breaking the rules for."

He chuckles, the vibrations of his chest against my body driving me wild all over again. "Be careful what you say to me. I'd take you up to your room if I didn't respect what you're trying to do."

I bury my face against his pectoral muscles, breathing him in. "This so going to be so fucking hard," I whine.

He kisses me with one last, lingering yet innocent kiss before heading to his car. I'm beaming as I watch him open the door. Before sliding in, he pauses, grinning at me.

"This will all be worth it, Cavenaugh. I promise."

Morning—or at least the end of my abbreviated slumber—comes far too soon. I text Jewels and Chloe as I'm heading down for my shift, sharing an abridged version of my night with Theo. My phone buzzes repeatedly as I set it on the bar. I don't read their messages since I'm officially on the clock.

"It's alright if you're on your phone when there aren't any customers who need waitin' on," Mick reminds me, wiping the bar down at my side. "It would seem someone's eager to get your attention."

I wave a hand through the air, laughing. "It's my friends. They can wait."

"You look awfully chipper this morning," he says in a teasing tone. "Weren't you out late celebratin' somethin'?"

"I didn't get home until nearly five this morning, actually. I was busy taking charge of my destiny." I throw him an over-the-top wink.

"Well good on ya then. That's my girl."

The regulars are waiting outside when Mick unlocks the doors. Half an hour later, Chloe and Jewels come bounding in, the look in their eyes a mix of excitement and irritation.

"I have *twenty minutes* until I have to leave for my next class, so you better make this snappy," Jewels says, hopping onto the barstool directly in front of me. She flutters her thick lashes expectantly.

Chloe claims the stool next to her. "You know it's not polite to just text someone vague details and not respond to their questions and shit afterwards. Your Midwestern manners are slipping."

Mortified that they're expecting me to spill the

details while I'm working, I look over to where Mick stands at the register. "I'm sorry, I have no control over my friends. It's understandable if you decide to throw them out."

He laughs with good spirits, the only way he knows how. "It's alright. You're allowed to converse with the customers." He looks to Jewels and Chloe, his eyebrows raised. "Are you goin' to introduce me to these lovely ladies?"

"Jewels, Chloe," I nod at each of my friends as I say their names, "this is Mick *Flanagan*. As in *the brother of the owner*. So mind your manners."

Mick approaches them to shake each of their hands. "Ah, the friends I've heard so much about. Kelly didn't mention you were just as beautiful, but I suppose good lookin' people tend to stick together." When he takes Chloe's hand, he pauses. "What about you then, sweetheart? Have we met?"

The way Chloe uncharacteristically giggles like a school girl makes me glance at Jewels with wide eyes.

"My band played here once. I don't remember when exactly, maybe a year or so ago. I remember *you*, though—you sang to your girlfriend. Ungrateful thing ran out of here, leaving you hanging. I personally think it was one of the most romantic gestures I've ever seen a guy make, even if you couldn't sing worth a lick. But you were a real trooper, and didn't let her get to you. A lot of guys don't have that kind of class."

Mick brings his hands up to his chest like he's been shot. "I was hopin' no one would remember that night. About killed me, she did." He drops his hands to the bar, grinning. "Now I remember the way you bounced around, playin' the guitar. I couldn't believe somethin' so little could could produce that kind of noise with her voice. You drew in a great crowd, but your style wasn't for my sister's liking. If it were up to me, I'd hire you back in a heartbeat."

"Don't worry about it," Chloe tells him, waving her hand. "Our style isn't for everyone. I'm into all kinds of music myself. I swear half the money I earn goes toward concerts at the Garden. You'd think they'd start cutting me a deal after all the money I've dumped there. You ever go to any concerts?"

"I'm a bit of a music junkie, m'self," Mick answers, beaming. "I may not be able to sing, but I can play a bit of the guitar. I'm more into the classic like Cash and Zeppelin."

Chloe brightens with his confession. Jewels and I watch mutely, holding back laughter as the two of them banter, deep into discussion on their favorite musicians, and dissecting different genres of music. Jewels, being a serious music junkie herself, tries to jump into the conversation, but finally just sips on the water I give her. I wait on our three customers when needed, letting Mick and Chloe continue. Soon it's time for Jewels to leave.

"Well this was productive," she tells me under her breath. "I guess we'll just have to get together again. Don't make me ask Theo for the juicy details, Kelly Cavenaugh. I mean it. You have no idea how awkward it is, listening to him elaborate on past make-out sessions. *Especially* now that it's with my bestie."

"Anything I should know about these past experiences?" My stomach flutters with jealousy. Just because I gave Theo a detailed account of the men I've slept with, does it mean I want to know how many women he's been with?

"Would you lighten up? I was just messing with you." She braces herself over the bar, leaning in to kiss my cheek. "*Enjoy* your date tonight! Just relax, and remember Theo wants to be with you even after he's heard your darkest secrets. I don't see anything that could screw it up between you now."

Chloe watches our exchange with wide eyes. "Is it time to go already? It feels as if we just got here." She reaches into her studded leather bag to grab a business card, slipping it on the bar between her and Mick. "If you ever decide to get that tattoo we talked about, I know a wicked talented artist who could draw up the perfect one. She won't even charge you full price. Her number's on the card—you should really give her a call."

Mick takes her hand to kiss it. "And I know a bartender who would love to take you to see a band one night. I'll be callin' ya."

Chloe actually *flushes* when she reclaims her hand. She's tongue tied, only passing me a wave before following Jewels out the door.

I turn to Mick with my hands on my hips. "What just happened? You totally made my most talkative friend mute *and* blush. In all the time I've known her, I haven't seen her do either one."

Winking, he says, "It's called Irish charm, sweetheart."

By a quarter to ten, I've tried on nearly every piece of clothing I own just to deem them all too revealing. I called Jean on my break to tell her of my big night out with Theo, and she advised me to wear something that won't lead Theo's imagination too far ahead. Theo already sent a text earlier saying that I should eat a light dinner and wear something casual, so I guess it works.

"I'm going to need a new wardrobe," I sigh, looking at the discarded pile of shirts and skirts spread across my mattress.

"You talking to me?" Felicity asks from the hallway.

I turn to see her lingering in my doorframe, her spectacled eyes expectant. Of the two girls I'm living with, Felicity's my favorite. She's way more interested in studying and reading fiction in her spare time than she is into guys and never brings anyone home I'll bump into half-naked the next morning. She's quite pretty with warm brown skin, a round face that draws you in, and smooth black hair she knows how to style a thousand different ways. If I dressed her up for a night on the town, she'd likely break a few hearts. But Felicity's shy and reserved with the wardrobe to prove it.

"Felicity!" I exclaim, grabbing her by the shoulders. "Can I borrow something to wear on a date tonight?"

She draws her brows together, giving me a complete once-over. "I thought you told me I need to spice up my wardrobe. Is this some kind of a joke?"

"No!" I say with a blatant laugh. "This is me deciding I need something that doesn't make me look desperate for attention. I just want to look pretty...like you."

My roommate lights in excitement. "Oh, this is going to be fun!"

I'm downstairs and appropriately dressed in time to see a dark sedan pull up to the curb. I check to make sure Felicity's white sweater sits on my shoulders properly, not showing any skin beyond the leopard-print scarf she also loaned me. Paired with my favorite skinny jeans and tan riding boots, I actually feel quite comfortable. The tan suede coat I grabbed for later matches my outfit perfectly.

My heart thunders against my rib cage as I wait for Theo to step out of the car. Instead Charles, the elderly driver who took me to see Theo at work, steps out of the car.

I smile brightly. "Hey, Charles, looking sharp!"

"As do you, Miss Cavenaugh." He opens the back door of the car. "Come along now. You don't want to keep Mr. Roberts waiting."

"Where are we going?"

"I'm afraid I've been asked not to share any details of the night with you. Be assured that he's done a splendid job of preparing for your evening."

I run my hand along my carefully styled wavy locks, suddenly nervous. I didn't ask Theo where we were going. What if he's taking me somewhere classy? "Charles, please, help a lady out. Am I under-dressed?"

His kind eyes wrinkle with another bright smile. "You look brilliant. Rather fitting, I might say. Mr. Roberts will be pleased."

Charles keeps the divider open between us at my request, calming my nerves with stories of his daughter and new grandson. Time flies by quickly, and in no time we come to a complete stop. I peer out the tinted windows as Charles steps from the car. For a moment I'm not able to place what buildings and trees are visible beneath bright lights. Then it finally clicks into place—we're at a zoo, parked in front of a sign that reads "EMPLOYEE ACESS ONLY."

I balk at Charles as he opens my door and I step from the car. "The zoo's open this late on a week night?"

He smiles warmly, the deep lines in his face settling. "I don't believe so."

A slender woman wearing safari gear appears at the gate. "Good evening, Miss Cavenaugh. Come this way."

Charles winks. "I'll be seeing you later. Enjoy your evening."

Stunned, I follow the woman through the gate and down a path leading through two cement buildings. We come upon a nook designed to look like a jungle with bright flowers, dense ferns, and palm trees. A small table clad in a white linen cloth and a dozen candles has been set up in the center of it all. The dank smell and occasional sounds of lions and monkeys in the distance make it feel like we're actually in Africa.

Theo stands next to the table dressed in a gray v-neck sweater that compliments the green of his eyes and tight-fitting enough to show off his rigid arm and chest muscles. Between his snug jeans and dazzling smile, I have to stop myself from rushing forward to ravage him. He looks amazing.

"Enjoy your evening," the woman tells us as she walks away.

Theo strides my way, confident and in charge. "You look beautiful as always, Cavenaugh."

I hold my breath as his lips graze my cheek, thrilled by the feel of it. "How did you arrange for this?"

"Generous donations will get you pretty much whatever you need in life." He slips his hand into mine and checks his chunky, platinum watch. "Let's eat, I'm starving. And we're on a schedule."

We're barely seated when a stout, dark-haired woman in her 50s, wearing a white apron over a floral dress, sets a plate before each of us. "Good evening," she greets me, beaming. "Theo tells me you like my manicotti. I wanted to give you a proper salad before your meal, but he tells me there isn't time for that. Honestly, I don't know where the boy's head is half the time."

My stomach bursts with joy when I look down to see the same manicotti Theo had ordered the day I stormed from his office. Once again, the smell is heavenly.

"I'm pretty sure it's the best I've ever tasted," I say, grinning.

With a chuckle, Theo pushes his sleeves up. "Kelly, this is my Aunt Carmela."

The woman takes my hand, beaming. Her hand is warm and doughy. "It's a pleasure to finally meet you, *tesoro*. My boy Theo has told me so much about you."

I don't try to hide the surprised look on my face. "Theo didn't mention he ordered from a *family* restaurant." Suddenly it makes sense why Theo seemed so tight with the kid who delivered our food that day.

"My boy works hard, makes good money, and he's generous to those he loves." She releases my hand to pinch Theo's cheek with gusto. "My sister taught him to be proud of where he comes from. I'm sure it slipped his mind."

Theo squirms away from her. "Ow, Aunt Carmela. Enough already."

The way the two of them interact, I can suddenly picture Theo as a little boy before the big muscles and tattoos. I cover my mouth to muffle a quiet laugh.

Carmela crosses her arms. "I'll leave the two of you alone now. Kelly, I hope you'll come by for family dinner one night soon. Theo's baby sister is dying to meet you."

I raise my eyebrows at Theo, and his face turns beet red. "I'll bring her by, Aunt Carmela. I promise. I can't wait for everyone to meet her. Thank you again for doing this for me tonight."

"Anything for my boy." From the twinkling spark to her eyes, it's obvious she's happy for her nephew.

My heart warms to know that she seems to approve of me at least. "Good night, you two."

"It was nice to meet you," I tell her. When she's gone, I turn to Theo. "That was definitely a surprise. When you said you were ordering the best Italian in the city, you never mentioned it was from your aunt's restaurant. Any other surprises you'd like to throw at me while we're on the subject?"

Taking a bite, he gives me a crooked smile. "Eat your manicotti before it gets cold, Cavenaugh. The surprises for tonight have just begun."

Chapter Sixteen

I'M in an Italian-induced coma when Theo leads me away from our empty plates. The restless noises of animals settling in for the night are alive all around us. My pulse races with the possibilities of where he's taking me next. I highly doubt he brought me here just for the jungle-like ambiance. My love for animals and the possibilities have already made this the best night of my life.

Theo strides with energy at my side, playing with my fingers and flashing me his deepest-set grin. A few months ago, I would've tackled him into the bushes and had my way with him. I still want to, but I resist.

We enter a gray cement building that smells like a vet clinic—a sharp mix of medicine and animal. I hear the soft muttering of a gorilla before we see it.

"Good evening, I'm Veterinarian Jackson," a

round-faced man in a white doctor coat and square glasses greets us. He stands beside a black gorilla nearly half his size that's resting on her knuckles and chewing on something. "Theo tells me you're interested in pursuing a career in animals, and thought maybe you'd like to see some of the behind the scenes action."

"*Oh. My. God*," I whisper, wrapping my arm around Theo's waist. He pulls me into his side with a light squeeze.

"Serena, here, seemed to have a tummy ache, so they brought her in for an exam," the vet explains. "She's harmless. Just be sure to use a calm voice and slow movements around her so she doesn't get overly excited."

Theo and I watch on silently as the man interacts with her, as if examining a person. A few times her eyes fall onto me, and it's like staring at another human. It's a total rush standing so close to an animal without a fence separating us. I feel myself glowing with excitement. More than once Theo bends down to kiss the side of my head while I just stand in awe, taking it all in.

After the exam, the vet wraps his stethoscope around his neck. "It seems she just has a little indigestion. She'll be just fine."

The gorilla makes a quiet little noise, and reaches her arm out to me.

"Serena seems to like you," the vet tells me with

a bright smile that glows against his dark skin. "Would you like to come over and say hi?"

I look up at Theo, who laughs. "Go ahead. This is why I brought you here." He kisses my head again before releasing me.

I slowly approach the large animal with my heart in my throat. "Hi, Serena."

The gorilla first touches my hair, then brings a handful up to her nose for a long sniff. On instinct I reach for the roots of my hair so she won't pull too hard and laugh softly. She meets my gaze as if watching for my reaction. Then she releases my hair and reaches out to touch the top of my head, gently picking her fingers along my scalp as if looking for bugs.

I laugh again. "She's beautiful."

There's a soft click of the door opening behind us. The woman who brought me into the zoo appears. "Sorry to interrupt, but Zahara is crowning."

The vet nods. "I figured that'd happen about now. I'm sorry, folks, but we're going to have to wrap this up. Our newest addition to the zoo came to us pregnant, so I wasn't one hundred percent sure of the timing. Susan, would you please take Serena back for me?" He removes his rubber gloves before reaching for another pair. He pauses, turning back to us. "If you'd like, the two of you could come along to watch from the other side of the gates."

I open my mouth to answer, but can't find the words. Theo rubs my arms. "We'd be honored."

Exhilarated with the prospect of seeing an animal give birth, I don't even think to ask what *kind* he's leading us to as we wind through the trails of the zoo and into another gray cement building. I stop in my tracks when we come upon a group of elephants grazing inside a pen with thick cable wires. One of them seems to be more on edge than the rest, pacing and trumpeting in short blasts. A slimy white sack hangs from between her legs. It's both disgusting and intriguing.

I squeeze Theo's hand and whisper, *"Hole. E. Shit."*

"You two wait here, and try to stay quiet," Vet Jackson tells us as he opens a door to the pen. His eyes dance with excitement. "Don't blink an eye. It will happen very quickly."

We watch in bewilderment as the elephant paces around, a group of zoo staff hanging back incase she needs help. Theo slips his arms around my waist, resting his cheek against my forehead. I can feel the tension in his cheek from a wide smile.

The vet has hardly stepped foot inside the pen when the elephant takes on a galloping speed. The white sack falls out from beneath her, its contents of blood and fluids exploding everywhere like a full bathtub falling from the sky. I cover my mouth to stifle a small cry of surprise.

The staff is quick to release the baby elephant from its sack, and rouse it to life. Tears spring to my eyes as we watch the little animal take its first steps, lifting its hooves out in front in the world's cutest baby elephant march.

"Having fun yet, Cavenaugh?" Theo whispers with a little chuckle.

In the back of the private car, I'm still stunned into silence, sitting at Theo's side. He squeezes my hand after a long silence has passed. "You okay?"

I turn to him, shaking my head. "That was by far the most amazing first date in the history of dates. Meeting the gorilla...seeing that baby elephant coming into the world...it all felt like some kind of a *dream*."

"I'm glad you liked it."

"*Liked* it?" I touch his arm and shake my head. "That's an understatement. It's the sweetest thing anyone's ever done for me. How are you going to top that? How could *anyone* top that? You've ruined me. I'll never see dinner and a movie the same way again."

Chuckling in his deep voice, he takes my face in his hands and kisses me, soft and slow. He presses his forehead to mine, his lips still lingering inches away. "Good. I won't have to worry about losing you to some schmuck who promises you flowers and candy."

"Flowers aren't my thing, but you'd be amazed what I could be enticed to do with a bar of chocolate," I tease, stroking his face with my fingers. "Keep this up, and I'm going to have a reason to let myself give in to my desires. You're incredible, you know that?"

"I have my moments." He pulls away with a confident smirk. "Hold on, Cavenaugh. Our date isn't over yet."

Before long, Charles pulls the car into an underground garage. I raise my eyebrows at Theo. "Is this the part where he leaves us alone so you can have your way with me? Please say yes."

Theo laughs. "Grab your jacket." He pulls me out of the car. We take an elevator up to the top level of the building, and exit onto the roof where we're blasted with cold air and the chopping sound of helicopter blades.

"Really?" I turn to him and say, my hair instantly covering my face. "You're unreal."

He removes the hair from my face and tightens his grip on my hand before leading me to the sleek black aircraft awaiting us. A man in dark-colored flight gear and a headset stands waiting, holding the back door open. Theo helps me climb inside, shaking the man's hand before joining me.

"Good to see you again, brother!" the man tells him.

It's not as loud once we're all situated inside with our designated headphones adjusted in place. "Let's ride," Theo says, his voice flat inside the headphones.

"Roger that," the pilot answers before launching into radio talk.

The helicopter slowly rises, taking my rolling stomach along with it. It reminds me of peaking at the top of a roller-coaster when you know you're about to plummet. I reach for Theo's hand, smiling with a burst of giddy delight. "Why am I not surprised you happen to know a good pilot?"

With a rolling laugh, Theo brings my hand up to his mouth, kissing it. "He's an old buddy from the Corps."

We stare down on the city, all aglow with twinkling lights of varying colors. Everything appears smaller and impossibly dense from above. Rows of cars go on as far as the eye can see in a dizzying cluster of white and red. It's easy to make out the top of the Empire State Building: its top lit up in a mix of red and white for whatever occasion I'm clueless to.

Theo holds my hand as we fly over the Statue of Liberty, a football stadium all lit up, the loading docks of several barges, and a close buzz above downtown Manhattan.

I take the city in with a new appreciation, realizing I truly am in my home now. There are moments in my life when I've felt a discomforting nag because I thought I had made a wrong decision, but this isn't one of them. For the first time in a *very* long time, I feel as if I'm on the path I was meant to take, living the life that was destined for me. Whether or not that means Theo is meant to be a part of it weighs heavily in the back of my mind.

As the car rolls up beside Flanagan's, we face each other, grinning. Theo brushes my hair over my shoulders, his gaze burning with wanton need. I feel the same desire burning through my veins. More than anything, I want to stay with him and let him hold me through the night.

The partition between us and Charles cracks just a smidgen. "I'm going to run across the road and grab myself a cuppa coffee. Would either of you care for one?"

"No, thank you, Charles," Theo answers.

"Goodnight, Charles," I pipe in. "It was good seeing you again. Enjoy that baby grandson of yours. Next time I hope to see a few pictures."

"Of course, Miss Cavenaugh. Good night."

After Charles leaves, Theo's fingers trail up my neck, brushing across my lips. "I suppose since this is our first date, I should kiss you like a gentleman and tell you goodnight."

"This date was a long time coming." I curl my fingers around a loop in his jeans. "We're far beyond first kisses."

"Refresh my memory on these rules again," he says in a thick voice.

I close my eyes and sigh. "What rules?"

"Cavenaugh, look at me." When my eyes flip open, he grins, his fingers still trailing across my lips. "I don't see us going anywhere but forward together. I'm confident there will come a day when you're ready to share yourself with me. Until then, I plan to play within your boundaries, whatever you want them to be. And when I say 'play', I mean *play*."

He draws me into his arms, kissing me with a heat that burns into my core. I fall into the kiss eagerly, swiping my tongue against his and letting out a throaty moan. I climb into his lap and straddle him, giving me an unobtrusive angle to kiss him without reserve. He cups my ass, bringing me as close as our bodies will allow.

I stop to bring his sweater up over his arms and sigh before running my hands over each of his exposed muscles on his stomach, taking in what I can see of his sublime body in the dim light. "Holy shit, you're so gorgeous."

I can't resist leaning in and running my tongue

along the dark ink running along his pectoral muscles, pleased when his nipples shrink and harden from my touch. His hands are all over me at once, slipping up my sweater.

"Is this okay?" he asks, his fingers pausing at my bra clasp.

"I'm still in control," I say quietly, slipping my sweater over my head before removing my bra from my arms. When he discovers my nipple rings, an epic look of surprise and lust seizes his features.

"You wanted to play," I say, breathless. "So go ahead, *play*."

His eyes meet mine. "Are you sure?"

I'm not sure of a lot of things anymore, but I trust Theo enough to continue. "Just don't let me lose control."

He doesn't hesitate in taking my nipple in his mouth, giving the other ring a turn with his tongue. He brings his mouth back to mine, this time feeling as if he's claiming me. I'm stuck between holding on to resolve and giving into lust when I unzip his jeans. His immense erection springs to life inside his boxer shorts.

"*Cavenaugh*," he groans between kisses. "*Wait*."

"Tell me you won't think I'm cheap once I step out of this car," I whisper, stopping to meet his gaze.

He takes my face in his hands. "I'd *never* in a million years think that of you. And like I said, I can't wait for you to meet my family. This thing between us is *real*." He strokes the side of my face, a tender look claiming his features. "We can stop now if you're not ready for anything beyond kissing. I don't want to go too far and make you regret it tomorrow."

"There's no way I'll regret doing this with you. As long as we don't have actual sex, everything else is fair game."

As I assess his gorgeous body, all mine for the taking, I realize it's going to take a miracle to hold back. After all, we're half naked and alone in the back of a parked car.

This is so dangerous.

Knowing there's no way I can straddle him like this without things going too far, I climb down and slip my hands beneath his boxers, stroking him. He grunts against my ear, flexing his hips with the movement while biting and pulling at my nipples. My body's on fire. I may not be able to fix Theo's long run without sex just yet, but there are other ways to satisfy him. The minute he's detached from my nipples, I slip down to the floor of the car, taking his glorious erection in my mouth.

"Are you sure..." he begins to ask just as I take him deeper. Then he wraps one hand in the thick of my hair, tugging on one of my nipple rings with the other. I become incredibly excited myself with his pleasurable groans as he comes to a shuttering climax. "*Damn*. You feel so fucking good, Cavenaugh."

He rests his head against the back of the seat, panting. I move up to sit back at his side, running my hand across the ban of tight muscles across his chest. Soon he's grinning at me like the Cheshire cat. "Is it okay if I take a turn now? I'm dying to get a taste."

"Be gentle," I plead, tracing my fingertips along the pattern of his tattoo.

He unzips my boots and removes my pants with torturously slow movements, stopping every few seconds to flick his tongue against my nipples, letting his teeth click with the metal bars. Once to my leopard print undies, he runs his large fingers along the lacy band. Just as I'm sure I can't handle it any longer, he touches my throbbing parts. The explosion of a million nerves bursting from his touch. Gasping, I arch my back, eager to feel more of him.

It's scary as hell knowing I'm letting myself go this far. Then I stare into his eyes and remind myself I'm only doing this because it's *Theo*.

He finally pulls my undies down over my legs, running his fingertips along the insides of my thighs. The anticipation is total torture. I want to grab him and make him come inside me. Instead he moves his mouth down between my legs, his breath so hot on my swollen lady parts that I think I'm about to melt.

I cry out with the introduction of his warm, large tongue, swirling and licking against my bud with precision.

I feel ready to burst when he stops, his breaths heavy between my legs. "God you taste like candy." When he takes me in his mouth again, I pull his hair with both hands, screaming his name among obscenities. He reaches up to play with one of my nipples, his reserve from earlier gone as he yanks so hard that I see white. His other hand presses underneath my butt cheek, bringing me closer to his talented mouth. My body's aglow with sensational nerve endings. As I find sweet euphoria, I suck in a deep breath, arching my hips up to the roof of the car.

Theo trails kisses up my body, from the curves of my hips and stomach to the side of my breast and neck, relaxing his hold on my nipple as he goes along. His lips brush with mine, his tongue slipping inside to mingle the taste of our sexes. I twist my fingers through his hair, deepening in the kiss. Before now, I'd never experienced an orgasm that left my feet violently twitching.

"We definitely need to plan more playdates." He runs his hand up and down my bare side. "You're fucking amazing." Then he reaches for my sweater, throwing it over my chest. "Now get dressed before my resolve breaks and I take you in the back of this car."

"I'm not so sure I would mind," I say, eyeing his

naked body. Although I've been able to keep my sexual beast in check, the need deep inside has resurfaced, craving more of him. I run my hand along his chest, admiring his ink.

"*Cavenuagh*," he grunts in a dark tone, rolling away from me. "You're treading in dangerous waters."

Before our eyes make contact again, we both quickly throw our clothes back on. I'm crushed when I no longer have access to the hard ridges of his chest and stomach, but he still takes my breath away, even fully dressed.

Grinning like it's the best day of his life, he wraps his fingers with mine. "Now let's get your sweet ass out of this car so I can walk you to the door like a gentleman."

With my heart still racing, I follow him out the car. We stand underneath the Flanagan's sign, staring into each other's eyes for a moment of silent reflection.

I finally take his face in my hands and give him a soft kiss. "Thank you for this magical night, Theo. Everything was...perfect. I don't remember the last time I've been this happy. You don't know how much it means to me that you decided to give us another chance."

"It was worth it to see you light up around the animals tonight. *You* make *me* happy."

I wrap my arms around him, pressing my face

against his chest and enjoying the pounding of his heartbeat. "Hang in there, big guy," I whisper. "I have a feeling you're going to be the first one to claim my heart."

He presses his face to the top of my head, inhaling. "That's good to hear, because you've already claimed mine."

Chapter Seventeen

THE NEXT FEW weeks I'm higher than a stoner at a Snoop concert. Our schedules don't allow us to spend much time together, but Theo constantly calls and sends thoughtful texts whenever we aren't able to make time for another date. He even sends random pictures throughout the day, although I'm disappointed that they're all PG.

I've dissected our first date a millions times—it was epic on so many levels. The fact that he arranged all of it with a day's notice, and took so much care in finding something he knew I'd love speaks volumes. Theo's the total package, just as I always suspected. I'd be a fool not to recognize that. Each time I recall our steamy night in the back of his private car, my skin warms to dangerous levels.

Our dates since have been on a much smaller level, usually involving getting to know each other better over dinner at various restaurants, or carryout in Flanagan's. It's too dangerous for us to be alone at his place, and we've backed down on our near-sexual encounters. I find myself wanting him more and more with each time. I'm afraid I'll lose control before I'm completely sure that I'm in love with him.

There have been nights when I'll lay in bed wondering what would've happened if I had stayed with Erik and never given Theo a second chance, or if I hadn't come to New York at all. I guess sometimes it's the little decisions in life that lead to the future meant for you, even if you're unaware how significant they'd become at the time you're forced to choose. If ever there was a time I would believe in fate, or the alignment of stars, this would be it.

The day before Thanksgiving, when I'm to meet Theo's entire family, I'm finishing my shift at the bar as a cheerful young guy brings me a delivery in a large white box. I'm pleased to discover instead of flowers, it's a large "bouquet" of chocolate candy bars.

"Someone's smitten with ya," Mick remarks, admiring the gift from behind the sink.

"You have no idea."

With an ear-splitting grin, I read the card.

Can't wait to see what I can get you to do with this much chocolate. XOXO THEO

.   .   .

I clutch the note to my chest, feeling a blast of fluttering in my stomach. "Mick, there's something about this guy. I don't want to jinx it, but....I think I'm actually *in love*. I can see myself having an actual future with him."

"Sound like you're happy with the lad." Mick stops washing the bar to wink up at me. "And to think this is comin' from someone who was once ready to trade her life for a new one."

Right on time, Theo strolls into my room early on Thanksgiving morning with a delicious smirk, his eyes more alive than I've ever seen. "Hey, Cavenaugh."

I left the door to the apartment unlocked so he could come up while I was getting ready. Beneath a leather coat and gray scarf, he wears a similarly snug-fitting sweater and jeans as the night of our first date. I grow warm all over when reminded of how he looked *without* them as well.

Oddly enough, I've begun to see him as being even *more* attractive than the first time we met. He hasn't changed much aside from his hair being longer, but now that he's finding his way into my heart, it's almost like my lungs can't deal each time he steps into the room. The rush I get around him is

271

better than any drink, or even the pot I tried last year at a concert.

After Jewels returned this summer from her trip with Adam and told me she was in love, I noticed so many changes: the way she carried herself, the change in her voice when she said his name, the bright spark to her eyes whenever he was around. I wonder if anyone has noticed those changes in me. I wish I would've known this kind of joy much sooner.

Theo scans the room, without *really* looking, as if nervous or incredibly preoccupied. He's up to something. "It's definitely a downgrade from the last place. I'm just glad you have *female* roommates this time."

I finish securing my earrings and turn to him. "*And* they're both pretty decent. They aren't home much, though, and they went to stay with their families last night. I'm not sure when I'll get a chance to introduce you."

My heartbeat anxiously rakes my body. The temperature of the room spikes with Theo standing so close, and his musky smell mixed with the leather of his coat nearly sends me over the edge of control. Usually there's some kind of distraction when we're together, or the threat of someone walking in on us to keep things from going too far. We've purposely avoided hanging at each other's places so there wouldn't be any added temptations.

We're completely alone with a bed in the room.

I dig my fingernails into the palms of my hands and sit on the mattress.

Theo pulls a silver gift box from the pocket of his leather coat, a little bigger than his hand and tied with a red bow. "I got you something."

I take the expensive looking box, my eyes still locked with his. "Since when did it become customary to exchange gifts on *Thanksgiving*?"

Removing his coat, he stands at the edge of the bed at my side, suddenly appearing shy. It's incredibly hot, and I have to resist throwing him down and have my way. "Just open it."

"Should I check to see if it's ticking?" I ask, holding it up to ear. "Seriously, you're acting like a twelve year old without his Adderall."

"Cavenaugh, you're killing me."

"Okay," I concede, removing the ribbon and opening the box. I pull out a clear plastic container with the word "Amant" written in gold cursive above a small, silver bullet. A tan cord runs from a small, silver bullet down to a plastic box. I glance back at him.

His eyes sparkle mischievously, like they're made of diamonds. "I know we've backed things down because you're afraid of losing control, but you mentioned you're allowed to masturbate. If it's okay with you, I want to give you another memory to work with until you're ready to take this to the next step."

"Oh," I say, letting his words run through my head. "*Oh!* You mean, you want to..."

I can't choke out the rest of the words.

"Do you trust me?" he asks. When I nod, he leans down, letting his lips brush against my ear. "Lay down, sweetheart. I promise I won't let you lose control."

The rest of my body heats to dangerous levels. The idea of him touching me sends a title wave of shivers racing down my spine. I reach for the package to pop it open and place the small, smooth object in my hand. His cool fingers reach out to take it from me, letting his pinkie drag across the palm of my hand. I'm already so turned on I feel as if I'll erupt.

Theo's gaze darkens. The hint of a smile tugs at the corners of his mouth. "If we're going to do this, you have to take your jeans off."

I swallow, though my throat is suddenly paper dry. Shimmying my skinny jeans down to my ankles, I struggle to yank them off before settling my head against the pillow. As terrified as I've been that I'll give in to Theo, I'm also thrilled to know that I can put my complete trust in his hands.

His intense green eyes lock with mine. "I'm going to make you come now, Cavenaugh."

He flips the switch, bringing the bullet buzzing to life. I become so hot that it's a struggle to swallow.

Just thinking about what he's going to do makes me throb eagerly.

"Halfway there already," I manage to squeak out, bending my legs and flexing my hips seductively.

"Save it for me."

He lowers down to the mattress, sitting by my knees. His free hand reaches for my undies, brushing his fingers over the material with a feather-light touch, turning my senses insane with need. Gasping, I bite down on my lip. He removes my undies before pressing the vibrator to the sweet spot that throbs with anticipation. When the cool metal vibrates against my warm folds, I close my eyes and cry out with instant pleasure.

"*Holy...*" I gasp, clutching his arm. "How many megawatts are in that little thing? I mean...*damn*."

His eyes are lit with satisfaction and excitement. "Be quiet and let it happen."

I gulp down a squeal as the vibration sparks a warm feeling that spreads down my legs, shooting into the sensitive nerves at the base of my feet. I dig my fingers into his hair, bending my back and moaning his name.

As the electric glow builds between my legs, Theo slips his free hand under my shirt, finding the piercing on my nipple. With a firm tug, I teeter over the edge of bliss, losing myself in a mind-numbing explosion that rakes my body. Bending back, I cry out so loudly that I'm sure whoever's working in the bar downstairs can hear.

Once the convulsing waves have subsided, I turn my head to grin at Theo. I didn't even notice he had already removed the bullet. Instead he lazily runs his bare hands along the inside of my thighs.

"You're totally amazing," I say, touching his cheek. "You know that, right?"

The look on his face speaks loudly of content and pride. "Damn it, Cavenaugh, you are one sexy woman. I really want to kiss you right now, but I made you a promise, and I don't think I'd be able to stop there." After kissing my forehead, he rises from the bed.

I glance down at my low-cut top I covered with another one of Felicity's scarfs. If anything, I still look like a Midwestern girl trying to blend in with the fashionistas. What if his sister thinks I'm some kind of hick? "I should change. I don't know that I'm wearing the right thing."

"I would agree with you there." He chuckles, eyebrows raised. "If my cousins see you half-naked, I'll have to spend the entire day fending them off, never-mind what Aunt Carmela would think. I'd suggest putting your panties back on, at the very least."

I shoot him a "very funny" look while slipping back into my clothes. "I just mean I wish I would've found something...I don't know...more impactful. I want to make a good impression on your family."

"Cavenaugh, you could slap water on your face and show up in sweats, and it would still take everything I've got to keep my hands off of you." Crossing the small distance between us, he takes my hand to help me back on my feet and grins. "Trust me, my family will be totally smitten." He presses a sweet kiss against my lips.

New York is a complete madhouse with the Macy's parade in full swing. Theo directs the driver to stop by for a part of it on our way to his aunt's so I can experience a bit of what it's like to see the parade in person. We only watch a few floats pass by before I decide I've had my fill. As much as I've come to love the city, I prefer it when the entire population isn't attempting to jam into one section.

Theo's aunt lives in a clean, upscale neighborhood in the Bronx. When we pull up outside of the two-story, Tudor-style home with peaked roofs and meticulous landscaping, a dozen cars already line the driveway. One's a sparkling Mercedes, but the rest are otherwise average and well used. As we step out of the car, my eyes fall on the handicap ramp leading up to the front door.

Theo takes my hand. "I'm going to apologize in advance for anything my cousins say to you. They're a rowdy bunch. Aunt Carmela does a decent job of keeping them in line, but they're sometimes like a bunch of wild animals."

I squeeze his hand with a blunt laugh. "Sounds like my kind of people."

I don't ask about the handicap ramp as we side-step it to enter the house. Theo walks in without knocking, leading me into a world of chaos and a blend of heavenly smells. The house, spacious and open from one room into the next, is divided only by pillars and clusters of Theo's animated relatives.

"Theo!" someone yells above the racket.

A young woman comes at us, unmistakably Theo's little sister with the same eyes, except her dark eyebrows are waxed down and perfectly shaped. She has his other features, only in a feminine size, and her long flowing locks are in the same brown hue as her brother's. The navy dress she wears is simple, yet trendy. She rolls along in a high-tech wheelchair like she's been doing it her whole life.

"Gwenny!" Theo bends down to take her in his arms, lifting her from the chair by a few feet before carefully setting her back down. He kisses her forehead before standing at her side, beaming down on me. "Gwen, this is Cav—er...I mean...*Kelly*."

"Holy shit, *it's about time!*" Rolling her eyes, Gwen pulls on a belt loop of Theo's jeans. "My big brother here *finally* gets himself a good girlfriend, only he hides her away from our family like he's afraid we'll ruin it."

"We haven't been together that long," I assure her.

Gwen draws her eyebrows down in an expression very similar to her brother's usual confused look. "Aren't you the friend who came here from Wisconsin? I've been hearing all about you for *months*."

I flash Theo a look of surprise. He's been talking about me for that long to his little sister? I guess he wasn't kidding when he first claimed he was interested in more than a one-night stand. My spirit warms with his responding smile, and suddenly I feel the surge of a pang deep in my chest. For a minute the room takes on an unnatural slant, and my legs feel as if they're about to give out.

I'm so in love with this guy that it scares me.

Before any of us can say more, we're surrounded by a gang of their male cousins who are eager to introduce themselves. They're all basically as handsome as Theo with dark eyebrows and sharp features, making it clear Theo got his looks from his mother's side of the family. They're loud and constantly speak over each other, bringing the noise level of the house up by several decibels. Still, I can't stop taking my eyes off Theo who beams proudly at his sister's side, laughing and bantering with his family.

The way I feel each time I look at him, I'm confident it won't be much longer before I give in and allow myself to be with him.

After spending the entire day with Theo's boisterous family, enjoying his aunt's sinfully delicious cannelloni and listening to his cousins' wild stories of family reunions gone bad, we decide to call it a night. I'm exhausted from working a long shift the night before, plus keeping up with Theo's family. As sweet as they were, being around that much energy was draining.

Outside of Flanagan's, Theo steps out of the town car, holding the door for me. The clamor from inside the bar spills out in a muffled mix of bubbling laughter, live music, and shouted conversation. I peer inside, finding it packed. Sometimes it's nearly impossible to fall asleep with so much noise below my room and I have to wear my noise-canceling headphones to bed. It looks like tonight will be one of those nights.

I turn back to Theo. "I had a lot of fun today. Your family's amazing." Then I bite my lip and reach for his fingers, lacing them with mine. "You never mentioned your sister was in a wheelchair."

"I try not to make a big deal out of it," he shrugs and glances down at our hands. "She wants everyone to act as normal as possible around her, and not dwell on the fact that she lost the use of her legs shortly after she turned eight." When he looks back up at me, I can see layers of concealed hurt and pain. "Some *asshole* struck her down while she was riding her bike to the pool. She had a brain-stem stroke after it happened and her leg muscles quit working."

I touch his chest. "Shit, I can't even imagine what it's like for her. Or you. I'm so sorry."

"It's one of those things in life you have to accept, I guess." His lips purse in a mock-smile. "Nothing we can do about it now."

"You're so sweet with her. The two of you seem close."

"Someone had to take over after our mom died. Our dad was too involved in his work to help, and would be gone for months at a time. We lived with Aunt Carmela. She was the best parent she could be while trying to run a busy restaurant. Our dad offered to hire a full-time nurse, but I didn't want a stranger raising Gwen. That's about the extent of the relationship we've had with him." He reaches up to ruffle his hair, something he did earlier in the night when he was talking to his sister about some guy she was seeing. "I only went into the Marines because by then she was strong enough to do just about everything on her own whenever our aunt wasn't around. And she insisted that I sign up because she knew it was something I always wanted."

Looking into his beautiful eyes, a world of emotions well up inside. There are so many layers to

Theo, each one more amazing and complex. To think I once saw him as someone who just wanted to get laid and nothing more. Jewels always claimed he had a heart of gold, but I had no idea it was this big or this full of compassion for those he loves.

Taking both of my hands in his, Theo smiles wide. "It's just like I thought, my family adored you." He leans in to press his lips to mine, bringing his hands up to my face and deepening the kiss. Before we get a chance to make it all hot and heavy, he pulls away. "Then again, what isn't there about you to adore?"

"I could say the same thing about you." I reach up to brush his lips with my thumb, sending my hormones into a tumultuous ride. "I don't know what I did to deserve this kind of life. You make me feel like a freaking princess."

"I'll tell you exactly what you did." He steps in closer, sweeping me into his arms. "You stole my heart, Cavenaugh. I've never felt this way about anyone, not even Brooklyn, and I let her move in with me. You make me want to be a better man."

"There's nothing about you that could get any better," I whisper.

Once again, he crushes his lips to mine. I barely respond, too caught up in my thoughts. Is he saying he's in love with me? By now I'm sure the wild anxiety stirring in the pit of my gut all night is love as well. It'd be so easy to give myself wholly to Theo.

He goes out of his way to make me happy and knows exactly what to do in the bedroom—or at least it seems from our other escapades anyway. The way he doted on his sister all night just proved he's the real deal.

Theo's kisses, gentle yet eager, feel so differently than the passion-fueled make out sessions we've had in the past. It's as if he's getting ready to make love to me, wanting all of me and passing his feelings along through his lips. His tongue lazily brushes with mine as his lips take control.

When we part, he holds me close to his chest, rubbing my back. As much as I want to confess that I'm in love with him, I decide to hold off. When I finally do tell him, it's the kind of thing I'd like to plan an entire night around. I want everything to be perfect.

I could easily avoid the madness inside by taking the side door up to the apartment, but instead I decide to see how Mick and the rest of the staff are holding up. I doubt I'd be much help at this point if they needed it, considering how exhausting it is to simply push my way through the energetic crowd, but I can at least wish them a good night and maybe even have a drink to help me slip into a blissful sleep.

Stella, one of my favorites to work with since she's always full of humorous stories involving her over-active toddler, spots me from behind the bar. Her eyes light up. "Ah, Kelly! Good to see you out on your night off! You alone?"

"Just coming back from Thanksgiving with Theo's family!" I yell over the loud rock, claiming one of two free barstools. "Thought I'd stop in to see how you guys are doing!"

She hands change to one of the patrons before settling in front of me, her arms folded over the bar. "It's been a crazy night. The band brought in a bunch of the college crowd. I guess they're pretty popular on campus." She suddenly slaps her hand over my wrist. "Oh shit, I almost forgot! Mick about had to kick some poor schmuck out earlier. He was going on about being your friend, said it was urgent that he talk to you. I didn't catch his name, but he was a complete mess. Tall guy, gorgeous eyelashes and sultry lips, kind of looks like the Wall Street type. Not sure what he's doing here. This doesn't seem his kind of crowd."

I balk with my jaw dropped. *Erik?* Why would he want to see me? "Is he still here?"

Stella tilts her head to the side. "Last I checked he was sitting in one of the tables in back. Mick decided to give him a break since he said he knew you, and made him drink a cup of coffee to sober up."

"Thanks," I tell her, sliding off the stool.

I haven't had a real conversation with Erik since

moving out. My heart hammers in my chest as I finally squeeze through the group dancing around to the band and reach the far end of the bar. Erik's slumped over a coffee mug, dressed in a dark button-down and jeans, his usually perfectly styled hair just as despondent as he seems. I can only see part of his face since he's looking down.

Taking small steps his way, I ask, "Erik? What are you doing here?"

His head pops up. His eyes are blood shot, red-rimmed and wet, but grow wide when he sees me. "Kelllly," he slurs, rising from his chair and knocking it over.

"Hold on," I say, hurrying over to his side.

He collapses against me, burying his face in the crook of my neck. The stout odor of whiskey oozes from him like he bathed in it. I struggle to stay upright with most of his weight on me. His arms wrap around to my back, crushing me to him.

"I'm so glad you're here," he mumbles into my skin.

The sudden hug and his lack of control with booze frighten me. I've never seen him this way. I'm about to ask what he's doing here when I feel something hard pressed against my stomach. Eyes wide, I back away from him to confirm the wild thoughts racing through my head.

He has a gun.

Chapter Eighteen

I CAN HARDLY BREATHE with the sight of the black handle peeking out from Erik's rumpled shirt. My first instinct is to find Mick or call the police, but I'm too terrified to make a move. Plus for whatever reason Erik has a gun, I don't want to do anything that will upset him. He's already in a terrible state, which could be dangerous in itself.

I struggle to help him stay upright without knocking us both over. "You need to sit down."

"I don't want to *sit*," he snaps, pulling me back to him. "I want to hold you."

A group of women behind us begin to stare, giggling. I need to shut this down before he causes a big commotion and we're surrounded by people. The best ideas I can come up with are to either call Adam, or ask Mick for help. I can't just leave him in a bar, drunk with a deadly weapon.

I finally get him to sit down. While he sulks with his hands on his head, I try calling both Adam and Jewels, only to get each of their voicemails. They didn't have any plans after the parade, except to order takeout and watch movies all day. Knowing them, they've already gone to bed and put their phones on silent. One of these days they're going to miss an urgent call. *Like this one.*

I search above the bouncing bodies for any sign of Mick, but it's so packed that I can't even see the bar from this angle.

Erik's drunk enough that I could possibly grab the gun from him. But then what? I'd be the one with a deadly weapon in public, and that doesn't seem incredibly wise, either. Plus he's bigger than me, so it wouldn't take much for him to overpower me if I tried. I can't just send him home in a taxi, wondering if he's going to lose it on his way home and shoot someone. With the state he's in, we wouldn't make it more than two blocks on foot, and he lives over seven away.

"C'mon," I say, looping my arm around his back. We're only a couple dozen feet from the door leading up to my apartment. I help him to the stairway where he stumbles over the first few steps, falling to hands.

I help him back up. "Okay, here we go."

The bar noise becomes muffled when the door closes and I suddenly feel like I can actually formulate a plan. Unlocking the door to the apartment with my free hand, I help him through the doorway and flip the light on. Erik wiggles out of my hold to take the place in, running into walls like he's a bumper car. He continues down the narrow hallway before ducking into the bathroom, slamming the door shut behind him.

I bang my head against the doorframe to my room, welcoming the sharp pain that follows. Erik is incredibly drunk, possibly high on who know *what*, carrying a weapon, and obviously has some kind of ax to grind, and now we're alone in my apartment. I've officially reached expert level in making mistakes of epic proportions.

How'd I let this happen?

I'm reaching for my phone to call Theo when the toilet flushes and Erik emerges from the bathroom. He brushes past me, disappearing into my bedroom. I stick my phone back into my pocket and let out a long, frustrated sigh before following him in. He stands hovering over my things, reaching out to touch everything he sees.

I try to keep my distance from him. "Are you going to tell me what you're doing here?"

"Considering my brother doesn't want anything to do with me, you're the only other person who ever gave a shit about me. Or at least the only one who was ready to give me a chance." He finds my red-laced bra on the dresser and sticks his finger through the strap, dangling it in front of his face. "You should model this for me."

I pull the bra from his hands and set it back down. "Did something happen?"

"Apparently I happened." He begins digging through my things again. "I went over to confront him once and for all, tried to tell him how I feel about that night I tried to shoot him, but he didn't want to hear it. Kicked his own little brother out. On Thanksgiving."

Fear strikes my core with lightening fast speed and I whimper. *He went over to see Adam and Jewels with a gun? Is that why neither of them will answer their phones?*

"What'd you do to them?" I whisper, my stomach flipping around to the point of nausea. "Jesus, Erik, you have to tell me what's going on."

He flops on the bed next to me. The gun pokes out from his waistband. "I didn't do *anything*. He wouldn't give me a chance. He told me I'm a spoiled asshole, and that if I really felt remorseful then I'd tell our parents what went on that day."

With my breath stuck in my throat, I don't move my eyes off the gun. "Why do you have a gun? What were you planning to do with it?"

"Your pretty little friend and my brother are fine, if that's what you wanna know." He blows out a long breath before pushing his face into my neck and trailing his lips up my skin. "I need to feel the inside of you again. We had a good thing, baby. You make me feel *good*. I want to feel that. I need to feel *something*." His hands spring into action, one reaching for my breast and the other cupping my ass. He's quick to press his mouth over my lips, jamming his tongue down my throat.

"Stop!" I plead between his kisses, trying to pull away. "Erik! I said *stop*!" I finally break free from his tight grip. "I'm with Theo now! I won't do this with you!"

Something flashes across his drunken gaze. I can't pinpoint what, exactly, but it most definitely isn't the look of understanding or even comprehension. "I should'a known you wouldn't wait for me to get my shit together. You're too good for me. I knew it the first time I saw you. At least there's a way you can help me." He wraps his hand around mine, bringing it to his waistband, resting over the gun. "Apparently I'm too much of a coward to do it myself, but you could pull the trigger and end this thing. We'd all be better off—you, me, my brother, even my parents. No one would probably even fucking notice."

Feeling as if I'm about to have a heart attack, I slip my fingers around the barrel of the gun and pull it out with shaking hands. I've never held a gun before. It's warm from being down Erik's pants, and much heavier than I expected. Terror renders me breathless.

"That's right, baby." Erik's lips trail up my neck,

and his hand returns to my breast. "You can do this. Make the pain disappear."

With the gun clutched in my hands, pointed at the floor, I jump from the bed. "I'm *not* going to fucking shoot you, Erik! I can't believe you even asked me! You obviously need help!"

Bending over, he runs both hands through his hair. "Don't do this. *Please* don't do this. I just want...you gotta help me."

"I am helping you. But I'm not giving you the gun back. I won't call the police if you can promise me you won't do anything stupid." I sneak over to my small closet, never taking my eyes off Erik. I'm suddenly grateful for Mick's suggestion to invest in a small safe for my valuables. He assured me they had never been robbed, and that his sister trusted my roommates, but he reminded me Avery was known to bring strange men home and didn't want to see me cleaned out. I quickly punch in the code to the keypad and set the gun inside like it's made of dynamite.

Erik's crying softy into his hands by the time I return to him.

I cradle his head against my chest. "I'm sorry you're dealing with this all alone. Sometimes it just takes certain people a little longer to let themselves forgive someone who's hurt them so deeply. Once Adam hears about this, he'll know just how sorry you really are. You have to give him more time. You can't quit this easily."

I allow Erik to cling to me until he passes out.

I wake to a persistent knock on my door. Erik lays at my side, cuddled up into a fetal position, his mouth slightly parted, eyes fluttering in his sleep. As upset as he was the night before, I decided it was safest to stay by his side incase he decided to get up and find something in the medicine cabinet to make the pain stop.

I prop myself on my elbows and grab my phone from the nightstand to see it's after ten. As exhausted as I felt after calming Erik down, I still can't believe I let myself sleep in so late. There's a string of missed calls and texts from Theo. He had asked the night before if I wanted to join him for a run in Central Park, and I know he's usually finished by nine.

"Shit," I mutter to myself. Then I call out, "Yeah?"

The door opens. Avery stands in the doorway with wide eyes.

Theo, dressed in cold-weather running gear, stands at her side.

Fuck.

Theo's thick eyebrows draw down as his eyes dart between me and Erik. I can't muster the words to explain what happened. I'm so astounded with the sight of Theo standing in my apartment, catching me in such a compromising position that I can only sputter fragmented sentences. "It's not...this wasn't...not what it looks like."

Erik stirs at my side, running his hand over my stomach. I try to wrestle his arm away, which wakes him. His eyes fall on mine, filled with all the emotions of someone who wanted to kill themselves and now regrets it. Even though Avery and Theo can't possible understand what it's about, I'm sure to them, it's an extremely intimate look.

Double fuck.

I look up in time to see Theo throw me one last glare of the upmost disappointment before storming away. My heart plunges with his disgust.

"Wait!" I cry, jumping from the bed and racing past Avery. "Theo, it's not what you think! Please don't go! *I love you!*"

Theo stops in the doorway, his back to me. "I was in love with you, too, Cavenaugh."

He slips out of the apartment without looking back.

Together Adam and I are able to convince Erik to check himself in to treat his drug addiction and fragile mental health. Adam calls their parents, who are quick to buy tickets for the first flight out to visit their troubled son. It's late afternoon before Erik is situated in the treatment facility and I'm free to absorb my own complications.

I sit in a ball of misery on Jewels's couch, my arms wrapped around my legs. Silent tears disappear into my hair. Theo won't respond to any of the dozens of texts I've sent, trying to explain what happened and saying I love him too much to hurt him that way.

Of all the things I've fucked up in my life, this was by far the most damaging to my spirit. I'll never be able to erase the hurt look Theo shot me before walking away or the way he said he "was" in love with me. It overpowers all his beaming smiles and the lust-fueled moments we shared. I can't even blame him, considering what he thought he walked in on.

Jewels sits by my side, rubbing my back and shooting Adam weary glances every so often. "What can we do, Kel? It kills me to see you like this."

"It doesn't matter," I whisper. "It's over."

"Finally!" Adam cheers excitedly, looking down at his phone. "He answered me. He's saying he doesn't want to talk, but I'm going over there anyway." He grabs his coat and bends to kiss Jewels on the forehead. He glances at me. "Don't worry, I'll fix this."

I shake my head. "He thinks I lied to him. He'll never forgive me."

"I'll make him understand what happened. This is

my fault. If I had listened to Erik, maybe invited him in, he wouldn't have gotten loaded and come looking for you. I promise you, Kel, I'll make this right."

He's gone mere minutes before Chloe appears. My two best friends pop in a horror movie to get my mind off the fact that Adam's the only hope I may have to reclaim the heart of the first man I've ever loved. I curl up into Jewels's side, eventually falling asleep.

As the movie credits roll, Adam returns with very little to report. Although he was able to get Theo to listen, there was very little emotion in response to my side of story. Theo thanked Adam and asked him to leave. It reminds me of the night I told Theo everything about my past: he took it all in with almost nothing to say before he confessed that he was angry with the man I slept with.

Chloe and Jewels eagerly try to convince me that I need a night out, but I refuse. All I want is to go back to my apartment and sleep.

In the days that follow, snow begins to accumulate, and the winter chill Chloe warned us of sets in. It doesn't really affect me as I spend most of my time either working or hiding out in my room. I don't even care that I'm missing the Christmas lights throughout the city that I had been eagerly looking forward to.

I haven't heard from Theo since the night he walked in on Erik in my bed—not a single text, tweet, or old-school phone call. I spend my free time scrolling through pictures of us together, and all the snapshots he sent me in the past weeks of himself. It's the final twist of the knife piercing my heart. I was strong enough to stand on my own the first time he left me, but this time it's different, because this time he took my heart with him.

Chloe, Mick, and Jewels make several attempts to pull me from my funk without success. My parents even offer to pay for a flight home so I can spend Christmas with the family, but the thought of faking a smile while surrounded by a room filled with happy people burns through my insides.

My heart has shriveled up into a black mass and died.

Before I know or care, December has arrived. My roommates set up a Christmas tree, and I'm forced to help decorate Flanagan's with obnoxious red bows and clusters of ivy even though the Christmas spirit is dead to me.

Jewels and Chloe come stumbling into the bar one afternoon while I'm finishing up my early shift, patting the snow from their bodies with their mitten covered hands, and stomping their boots. I swear each of them looks like they've stepped from a fashion show the way all their winter gear matches and their hair is perfectly in place. I haven't done more than brush my hair and throw it into a ponytail since I last saw Theo.

"Ohmigod, this is one crazy-ass blizzard!" Chloe declares, removing her hat from her head and shaking her hair. "I haven't seen this much snow since three years ago when half the city was shut down for a week! You wait, there will be accidents like crazy starting today. You'd think people would learn to take it easy in the snow, but it's like there's some kind of challenge in seeing who can still get around in record time."

"Hey, guys," I greet them in a monotone voice.

Stella waves at them from my side behind the bar. "Hey, ladies."

Chloe takes a sweeping glance of the near-empty bar. "Where's Mick?"

"He took the day off," Stella answers with a shrug.

"I suppose he's entitled to one or two of those," Chloe says.

When she miraculously doesn't say anything more, I exchange a surprised glance with Jewels. Chloe and Mick have started texting each other, and I even saw them friend each other on Facebook. Otherwise, I don't think either of them has made a move, although they both seemed pretty interested. Maybe if I wasn't busy wallowing in my own sorrow, I'd do something to nudge them a step closer.

"We've come to take you out for the night," Jewels tells me, setting her mittens on the bar between us.

"I told you—" I start to protest.

"Nuh uh!" Chloe scolds, clamping her hand over my mouth. "There won't be any of that tonight! We're not taking you to a club, we're going to watch them light the tree in Central Park. All I've heard since we first met was how much you couldn't wait to see the Christmas lights. While you've been hiding in your room—losing far too much weight, I might add, because you're starting to look like a bean pole—they've been lighting this city up in the way you were looking forward to. This is one of those things you have to witness *once* in your life if you're going to be a true New Yorker."

Stella sets her hand on her hip. "I didn't know there was a big ceremony for the tree in Central Park. When did they start doing that?"

"It's not as big as the one in Rockefeller," Chloe explains, flapping her hands as she speaks. "You probably haven't heard of it because there aren't that many people that go. It's less of a tourist thing and more for locals from the area. You know, people who live near the park. You'd be surprised at the low turn out. At least it isn't as chaotic. You can actually get up close and personal."

"C'mon, Kel," Jewels whines, taking my hands across the bar. "It'd be ridiculous for you to miss it, and it won't be the same without my bestie at my side. It's our first Christmas in the city together. We have to go." She bats her thick lashes at me, looking as ridiculous as a great dane trying to mimic a newborn puppy.

Knowing Jewels won't stop until I agree to go, I finally give in, complaining the entire way. My friends insist on primping me for our night out, probably because they're tired of seeing me looking like a bum off the street. Admittedly, it makes me feel just a smidgen better to actually wear makeup and have my hair done up in loose curls by Chloe. I slip into one of my favorite old sweaters, pleased how the bright blue stands out against my dark hair and brown eyes. Once I've slipped into skinny jeans and my heaviest boots, I feel like a real human being again. Maybe even a tad womanly. I step outside into the snow-filled sky with my friends, surprised when they lead me to a dark town car at the curb.

Jewels shrugs, a bright grin stretched across her face. "Adam wanted to treat us since it's your first night out in awhile."

Though it was a sweet gesture on Adam's part, memories of steamy nights with Theo in the back of town cars quickly douses the good mood I had almost achieved since my friends appeared. Thankfully, it's a short ride to Central Park. The driver drops us off on a road inside the park. Lights shine in the distance over the rink packed full with skaters. I haven't seen the skating rink yet, though Jewels has been trying to entice me to go with her either there or in Rockefeller. My eyes focus on a large tree next to the rink, strung with white lights.

"Looks like we missed it," I tell the others, pointing to the area.

Jewels knocks my hand down, pulling me in the other direction. "Nope. Wrong tree."

There aren't too many other stragglers walking through the park this late at night. The three of us huddle together, warding off the cold wind and letting any muggers know we aren't going down without a battle. My lashes are covered in snow by the time we ascend the stairs leading down to the fountain.

The lights are all out, leaving it dark, cold, and barren. Like my life has been.

"You guys definitely have the wrong place." I turn to my friends, who have both suddenly fallen back. "Guys?"

They point at the same time to something behind me, grinning. I reel around as the entire fountain erupts in Christmas lights, some white and twinkling, some a combination of reds, greens, yellows and blues. The lights follow the wide mouth of the pool beneath the fountain and run all the way up the base of the statue, the angel on top glowing from them.

I'm so impressed by the beautiful display that I hardly notice Theo standing beside it.

Chapter Nineteen

"Hole. E. Shit," I mutter under my breath. I swivel around to face Jewels and Chloe, finding them huddled together, giggling at their clever antics.

"We'll just be....*gone*," Jewels tells me, leading Chloe back to the stairway. "We expect a call tomorrow!"

Collecting myself, I turn back to find Theo striding toward me in quick, confident steps. My breath sticks in my chest the closer he becomes. The black knit beanie he wears covers his forehead, accentuating his dark eyebrows, and the wool, gray pea coat fits snug against his big muscles. I've never seen him look better.

Momentarily, I forget how to speak.

"Cavenaugh," he greets me once the puffs of our breaths are commingling. "I didn't think calling you on the phone would be enough."

I stand with my hands pressed to my chest, still touched by the gesture, and his gloved hands hang lifeless at his sides. There's an air of excitement passing between us, but it's as if our bodies aren't sure how to proceed. I press my lips together, letting myself fade into the glistening of his eyes.

He licks his lips and glances over my shoulder before meeting my gaze again. "Before we started dating, you told me you were screwed up. I told you I didn't care. Then you told me what happened with that guy back in Wisconsin, and with Erik, and I acted like it rolled off my back. But it didn't. I was filled with a blinding jealousy I'd never felt before. It killed me to know you had been with those guys. It ate me up inside that you had slept with *anyone* other than me. I knew it wasn't realistic, but I couldn't help it. The more time we spent together, the more I wished there was a way to go back and change your past, especially when I realized how much I was falling for you.

"I put all my trust in my last girlfriend, and she let me down. I know you're not her, but the minute I saw that preppy fuck in your bed, it just reminded me of the night I found Brooklyn with her tongue down some exec's throat. I became unhinged and didn't even want to consider there'd be a reasonable explanation. All I knew is that I trusted you despite my reservations, and you let me down."

"It wasn't like that," I say with a tear slipping down my cheek. "I swear."

He presses a gloved finger to my lips. "Would you let me finish, Cavenaugh? I'm sorry it took me so long to cool off. I should've called you the next day. I meant to, then I kept putting it off until another day had passed. It wasn't until Jewels and Adam came knocking on my door last night with a letter from Erik that I finally considered your side of things."

Gasping, I pull his hand down. "Hold on. Erik wrote *you* a letter? What'd it say?"

"It wasn't to me, it was to Adam. It was a long, handwritten apology for all he had done to his brother, and even the crude things he had said to Jewels. He also went into great detail on how he manipulated you while you lived together, even though he knew you were trying to keep things platonic and dealing with your own issues. He explained how you saved his life that night when he came to your door, loaded on booze and cocaine. I called in sick to the office today because I couldn't deal with anyone. I'm pissed at myself for not listening to you earlier. I'm no better than your family and friends back home who believed an ugly lie without giving you a chance. I decided if I was going to give you my heart, I had to stop wrestling with demons from my past and comparing you to Brooklyn." He removes his glove from one hand to rest his bare palm against my cheek. "I *love* you, Kelly Cavenaugh."

My cheeks nearly split with a smile. I set my mittened hand over his and close my eyes, forcing more half-frozen tears to spill. A million different emotions swirl through my gut, each one louder than the last. Not knowing what to say, I remain quiet.

Theo's thumb brushes my tears away. "Lately when I think about my future, I've started to picture you in it, at my side. And that means I have to accept your past, just as you'll have to accept mine. You once told me people don't always know how to forget, but if they have any kind of a heart at all, they can at least try their damnedest to forgive. I know you have a big heart, and I'm asking you to forgive me. I'm asking you to move on from our pasts together, as my girlfriend, and hopefully one day as something more. I'm asking if you could try to love me back, despite everything we've been through."

I touch his jaw, smiling. "Are you crazy? I *already* love you back. More than you can ever comprehend."

His eyes close, and he presses his forehead to mine. Unable to resist him any longer, I wrap my arms around his neck and bring him close, kissing him with tears still rolling down my cheeks. He hoists me into the air by my waist, knocking the wind out of me. Fueled with raging passion, he eagerly kisses me again as I slip down against him.

My heart skips merrily. There's a good chance we'll be okay after all.

Theo breaks the kiss before I'm ready, setting me back on the ground. "Your face is freezing."

"Not when you're kissing me." I dust my lips over his, teasing them with my tongue.

"This isn't the only surprise I have for tonight." He slips his glove back on before taking my hand. "The next place is *much* warmer, I promise."

Pulling my phone from my pocket, I snap a few pictures of the light display before pulling Theo in for a few of us together. I kiss his cheek in the last one.

"Thank you," I whisper, kissing him one more time. "This was all incredibly sweet."

"Cavenaugh, you haven't seen *sweet* yet." Chuckling, he wraps his arm around my waist. "Just you wait."

I walk in step with him, resting my head against his chest. "You know you don't have to keep trying to outdo yourself. You already won me over with the trip to the zoo. As your girlfriend, it's okay if we simply *hang out* instead of you trying to impress me all the time."

"Trust me. You're going to enjoy this surprise." He kisses the side of my head before we slide into a town car waiting in the road and weave our way out of the park.

I sit as close to Theo as the backseat will allow,

running my bare hand underneath his layers, across his hard chest. "You know, since I've come to the conclusion that I'm head over heels in love with you, I think I'm emotionally ready to allow myself the pleasure of sex again."

A low grunt rumbles through his throat. "And here I thought I was going to have to wait a while." He stops my wandering hand, looking down on me with a smoldering gaze that makes my insides quiver. "You really love me, or was that just something you felt you had to say, given the situation?"

I move across his lap, straddling him, and taking his face in the palms of my hands. "I love that you're close with your family, and raised your sister when no one else could. I love that you were so incredibly sweet to Jewels when she was alone in the city, and I couldn't be there for her. I love that you're confident, and sexy as hell when you call me by my last name. I love that you go out of your way to make me happy, even though I don't deserve it. I love that you served your country and branded your body with the Marine symbol. I love that you're always trying to make me laugh or smile. I love everything about the man that you are when we're together. It's safe to say I'm a hundred percent sure that I am, in fact, crazy ass, *in fucking love* with you, Theo Roberts." I kiss him gently then pull back, smiling wickedly. "And I can't wait to hear you scream my name when I finally break your sexual dry spell."

The car slows to a stop.

Theo runs his hands up and down my thighs. "Cavenaugh, you're killing me. How do you expect me to make it upstairs with a hard-on the size of Texas?"

"Like the saying goes, God bless Texas." I kiss him on the nose before sliding off his lap.

Theo joins me on the sidewalk, turning to take an armful of bags from the driver. We stand outside a tall glass skyscraper across the street from the park, lights filling less than half of the rooms. There's a large, steel globe nearby that looks familiar, but I can't quite place. I eye the building with curiosity as Theo takes my hand, seeing "Trump International Hotel and Tower" written above the entrance.

The lobby is a blend of gold and black marble, chandeliers and glowing lights classing it up even further. I sigh happily, not only from the warmth of the hotel, but the knowledge that Theo wants to be with me in every way possible. He turns, kissing my cheek. "Wait here."

I watch as he speaks with the graying man behind the counter. A bellhop appears at Theo's side to take his bags before he returns to me. "All set."

I take his hand. "You could've given me a heads up this time, at least that we were spending the night. I'm afraid you'll run when you see me without the essentials."

"When are you going to get it through that beautiful head of yours that you don't need any of that crap? You weren't wearing makeup the day we moved Adam and Jewels into their place, and it didn't change how badly I wanted you." He looks down at me, beaming. "Besides, Jewels and Chloe packed your things while you were getting ready earlier tonight."

"Those *traitors*," I tease. "I should've known they were up to something the minute they breezed into Flanagan's."

We follow the bellhop up the elevator and into our spacious room where we're greeted with a panoramic view of the city lit below. The room itself is extremely upscale and beautiful—everything top of the line from the cream colored bedding and headboard to the winged armchairs surrounding the modern fireplace—but I'm more focused on Theo as he pays the bellhop, closing the door behind him. So many out-of-control sensations rage through me that I feel ready to explode into a million tiny pieces.

He spins around, flashing an enticing grin. "We can start a fire, or—"

I run at him and claim his mouth, digging my nails into his scalp with a primal urge so raw it's as if I'll rip in half. He pulls away, chuckling in a coarse voice, though his eyes are full of the same kind of sexual energy raging through my veins. "Are you sure you don't want to take it slow? We've both waited a long time for this."

I unzip his coat slowly, my eyes locked on his. "I'll go at any pace you choose, baby. This night is all about *you*. I want you to *feel* just how much I love you."

He tosses his coat to the floor and helps me shimmy out of mine. I reach for his sweater, yanking it over his head. We both laugh when it temporarily sticks to his arms. The sudden humor almost comes as a relief, considering there's an electric vibe in the air that feels as if we're both about to combust with pent-up anticipation.

Bare-chested, Theo pulls me back for another slow, blazing-hot kiss. I take a minute to run my fingers over the ridges of his chest and stomach before pulling my sweater over my head. He removes my boots and jeans with the same kind of slow precision he did the first night we messed around in the town car. Although downright torturous, it's sexy as hell the way he stops to appreciate each part of me once I'm standing in nothing other than my lace underwear and bra. His eyes fall to my breasts spilling out.

"God you're so sexy. I can't wait to have all of you, Cavenaugh."

Love and desire swell up inside of me with the force of a rocket as I unzip his jeans, brushing my fingers across the swelling hard-on straining against his black boxer briefs. His breath stutters. He kicks his boots to the side and strips down to his underwear. My breathing hitches at the sight of him nearly naked.

"Go wait for me on the bed," he says, his eyes overflowing with yearning.

As I move toward the king bed, Theo flicks the light switch. The room falls dark except for the exciting glow from the city lights below. I stop to gaze out the windows, feeling a rush knowing how exposed we'll be once completely naked. It's almost as breathtaking as the sight of Theo stripped down.

He sneaks up behind me, wrapping me in his arms. "I wanted to make love to you somewhere as amazing as you are. This was the best I could come up with."

Spinning around, I kiss him deeply, sighing as his warm hands trail all over my body. At first he responds with light, playful kisses, and I'm sure he's decided to take this slow, but then he unhooks my bra and pins me up against the window with light, yet demanding force. I gasp with the sudden chill to my bare skin from the glass. He bends down to slowly remove my underwear, waiting patiently for me to step out from each side. I'm left to stand completely naked against the cold window, shivering from both the temperature and the lustful way he takes in every inch of my body.

I reach for his boxer briefs, pulling them down with the same delayed speed as he did mine. My hands trail up the sides of his body until I reach the top of the complex tattoo stretching from between his hips up to his shoulder. I run my tongue over the design, pleasure spiking through me when he grips my hair in his fists, quivering. He moans when I get to the bottom of the tattoo.

With heavy breaths, I stretch back up to hover my lips beside his. "You have no idea what you do to me. I love you so much it almost hurts."

"I don't want you to hurt. I don't want to ever hurt you again," he whispers in a choked voice, setting his hands on either side of my face. "I promise to love you with everything I've got. No more pushing you away. No more bullshit."

Spellbound with desire, I run my fingers across his warm back. "Make love to me, Theo," I whisper, each word a breathy effort. "I feel like we've waited a lifetime already."

He swallows and nods once, dropping his hands from my face and leaning down to his discarded jeans.

I pull on his arm, stopping him. "Wait. I've never been with a guy who wasn't wearing a condom. I'm on the pill. I want to really *feel* you."

Although he looks stunned, he rises back to his feet, claiming my mouth. He lifts me to balance against his hips and spins around to give me a full view of the brilliant light display. With his hips flexed to keep me upright, he spreads my thighs wide and cups my ass. We moan in unison when he enters me inch after delightful inch. An explosion of sensations fills me to the brim of pleasure with his warm, large girth.

It seems Theo is using an incredible amount of strength to make upright sex happen. The way his square jaw sets in concentration makes him so incredibly hot I can hardly contain myself. As he guides me back and forth, he bends down to flick my pierced nipples with his tongue.

Gratification of new levels rips through me and I set the palm of my hand on the glass, fixing my eyes on the lights as I feel the blissful build of my very first orgasm during traditional sex. The sublime intensity builds like a fire deep down, building its way up through every nerve ending. Clawing at Theo's back, I gasp inside his mouth.

As if sensing the way I clutch around him, Theo brings his eyes up to meet mine. "Cavenaugh, you're so fucking beautiful. Come for me, baby."

I shake my head and pull on his neck, bringing his face up against mine to bite his bottom lip. "You first."

His grip on me tightens and he moves over to the bed, gracefully setting me on my back as if I'm a carton of eggs. He crawls over me slowly, tugging on each of my nipples, biting the skin on my neck. Our eyes lock with an intensity that makes it difficult to hold myself off until he's satisfied. I can literally feel how much he loves me as he moves with strong, precise thrusts, never breaking eye contact.

With just a few thrusts he's done for, yelling with a great, fantastic roar. He collapses next to me, breathing heavily as he brings me into his arms, kissing me with another lazy, meaningful kiss. "That was fan-fucking-tastic. It was *so* worth waiting for you, Cavenaugh."

We burn the midnight hours making love two more times, finally creating a chance for me to reach that place of pure bliss. We eventually pass out in each other's arms on the hotel floor.

The next day we both call in sick to work and hide away in Theo's little corner of Murray Hill. From the minute I walk into the swanky bachelor pad, I feel right at home. It's not modern like Erik's apartment, and it doesn't have an impressive view. Instead it's incredibly classy and warm with dark floors, beautiful paintings, a granite fireplace, cream-colored couches, and a gorgeous kitchen with upscale appliances. Theo proudly explains how he recently renovated the place, taking his time to show me every detail before taking me into the master bedroom where we christen his new, luxurious bedding.

The weeks to follow, I'm so consumed by Theo that I keep forgetting it's Christmastime unless I see the accumulating snowfall or festive decorations outside. The rare instances we both have time off from work, we lock ourselves away from the world in his brownstone. Aside from picking out a live tree and decorating it together, our activities are restricted to his bedroom, kitchen, and living room—one time even the stairway. Our lovemaking only seems to improve with each experience. Theo's the best lover I've ever had, and before long I find myself hoping he'll be the last.

On the afternoon of the 23rd, Chloe and Jewels join me to battle the crazy crowds on the streets of the city. Though Theo insisted that I don't spend any money on him for a present, I want to buy him a little *something*, and there's no way I'll show up at his aunt's on Christmas Eve empty handed. My friends harass me endlessly about never having time for them anymore, but I can tell they're ecstatic that Theo and I are officially together, and in the kind of over-the-top love that leaves me to feel like I'm walking on clouds.

We decide the liquor stores are the safest place to shop without getting trampled and duck into a large one we come across on the edge of Chelsea. Chloe darts to the far back end of the store, on her own mission. Jewels and I take our time strolling through the store. She stops to hold up a bottle of white wine with a questioning gaze.

I shake my head. "His aunt runs an Italian restaurant. She probably knows way more about wine than

I do. I was thinking maybe some top shelf tequila. Theo mentioned she loves margaritas."

Jewels sets the wine down with a roll of her eyes and we continue walking. "I've never seen that big guy act so jacked up over anything. Nights you're working, he's usually sulking at our place. Maybe you should see if there's still an acting part available so you guys can spend every day fawning over each other."

"What's that saying again?" I tap my chin lazily. "Something about a kettle and a pot, and something black?"

Her eyes fall down to the floor. "We aren't as hot and heavy lately."

I reach out to stop her. "Something going on?"

When she looks back up, there's a hint of desperation in her expression. "They're taking the pump back out next week. Adam hasn't been able to fight off the infections that keep reoccurring from the incision made when they put it in. It's okay, I mean he'll be okay without the pump. It was more a thing of convenience. But he's been really irritated ever since they told him. Davis is going to fly out here over Christmas to see if he can somehow lighten his mood."

I fold my friend into my arms. I've been so busy living in my own blissful world that I failed to notice hers is crumbling down around her. "*Damn*. I'm sorry, hun. What can I do?"

"I don't know. He's been so fucking distant, just like the last time when he was sick. I'm so terrified that he's going to push me away again." She shakes a little against me as she lets out a small cry. "I can't take it again, Kel. I'm not strong enough for that."

"Well we all know he isn't good at dealing with his feelings, and I can't imagine he'd be dumb enough to push you away again. Maybe he's just trying to deal with the news in his own way, without bringing you down." I arch away from her. "Do you want me to have Theo talk to him about it?"

"He'd be mortified if he knew I sent Theo."

I shrug. "So I'll tell Theo not to let on that we sent him. Maybe it can just be a casual kind of conversation. You know, 'how are things, I'm sorry about the pump, by the way if you hurt Jewels again there are a line of us who will kick your ass.' That kind of thing."

"Okay, *fine*." She giggles, pushing me away. "I guess Theo can talk to him. I don't know that it will do any good, though."

I sling my arm around her neck. "I'm sure you're reading too much into it. He's probably just pissed that he has to go through *another* procedure. He loves you, Jewels. Everyone can see how much you mean to him. I don't think he's about to throw away what the two of you have."

My gut stirs with unease. I just hope I know what I'm talking about.

Chapter Twenty

CHRISTMAS EVE at Aunt Carmela's is just as lively and exciting as Thanksgiving, only with the addition of presents and festive music that his cousins dance around to. Aunt Carmela gives me a statue of an angel and squeals like a school girl when she opens the bottle of tequila Jewels and I picked out. I'm embarrassed when Gwen gives me a beautiful silk scarf as I didn't buy her anything until Theo tells me later that he bought it at her request.

I actually feel like I'm a part of Theo's family this time, slipping into natural conversations and throwing harmless jabs at his cousins when they relentlessly try to flirt. We're so wrapped up in the excitement that it's nearly midnight before we head back to Theo's brownstone where we make love by the fireplace before passing out.

On Christmas morning, we Skype my parents.

It's strange seeing them on a screen during the holidays instead of indulging in my mom's cooking and catching up with my sisters. They're thrilled to "meet" Theo, and announce that they're considering paying for me to go to school in New York as soon as I'm ready to finish working toward my animal science degree. All four of my sisters budge in for screen time, barraging Theo with embarrassing questions and giggling like a gaggle of dorks. Although I've talked to each of them individually since Glori visited, gracefully accepting their apologizes, it's the first time since this summer that things between me and my family felt almost normal again.

Once we're done with my family, I give Theo his present: a small print of the fountain in Central Park where we professed our love to each other. Though he was first a little annoyed I spent money on him, he seems rather touched by the gift and kisses me deeply after telling me we'll pick out a frame together.

We spend the remainder of the day in bed, watching old Christmas movies and making love until we're too exhausted to continue. After eating the manicotti—also in bed—that his aunt sent home with us the night before, Theo disappears into the other room for awhile. I fall asleep while he's gone, waking when he returns completely naked except for a wide grin. He holds one of his hands behind his back.

I sit up in his bed with my arms crossed across my exposed breasts. "That wouldn't be a *present* behind your back, would it? I thought we weren't doing that."

"I said *you* weren't spending any of your hard-earned cash on me, Cavenaugh. I reserve the right to do whatever I want with mine." The way he can't stop grinning, I know he's up to something big. "You didn't listen to me anyway."

"Getting to see your glorious body naked is enough of a gift in itself. And besides, I don't need any more toys now that we have a green light for you to do whatever you want to me. So get in here already and *do* it."

His eyes light with poorly restrained mischief. "Present first."

My heart races as he comes at me. He's acting so insane that I don't know what to expect. He sits on the mattress at my side, resting his free hand on my bare thigh, his other still held behind his back. "It's ridiculous that you're paying rent for your shoe-box sized room when we'd both rather have you stay here full time. But I did the live-in girlfriend thing before, and it didn't end up so well. I don't want to make that mistake again. Besides, you're different. *You and I* are different. This is real."

I don't know what to say. We never really discussed moving in together before now, so why is he telling me this if he doesn't want it to happen?

He swings his arm from behind his back, presenting me with a small velvet box. Inside there's a princess-cut diamond the size of my knuckle on a wide band glittering with tiny diamonds that catch against the bedroom light.

"*Theo!*" I gasp, bringing my hands to my mouth.

He smiles warmly, his eyes lit with sincerity. "I want to marry you, Cavenaugh. I know we haven't been dating that long, and you're still trying to find your way, but I've never felt this way about anyone. I don't see the point in dragging it out. It already seems like I've waited a lifetime for someone like you to come along. After talking with Adam the other day, I realized just because he has health problems doesn't mean the rest of us are going to outlive him. I don't want to waste any time when I already know you're the one I want to spend my life with. You're the only thing I know for certain when I think about my future. It'd be my honor and privilege to have you as my wife."

He takes the ring from the box, slipping it on my finger. It fits perfectly.

"What do you say, Cavenaugh? Will you marry me?"

Tears spill from my eyes when I nod. "Yes. A million times, yes."

He pumps his fist in the air and hollers in a booming voice, "Yes!"

Laughing, I wrap my arms around his neck and

bring him to me for a deep kiss. I lean back, meeting his gaze. "But you do realize that means you're going to have to stop calling me Cavenaugh, right?"

He buries me in his hold, kissing the side of my head over and over. "*Never*. You'll always be my Cavenaugh, even if you *do* take on my name."

"My family is going to *freak*!" I say, biting my lip.

"I Skyped them back while you were sleeping to ask for their permission." He pulls back, grinning sheepishly. "I was worried your sisters' screams were going to wake you and spoil the surprise."

I touch his face, running my thumb against his lips. "Holy shit, you are perfect."

"I wasn't until now." He crushes his lips against mine, sealing the deal on the best Christmas of my life.

At first I'm reluctant to share my news with Jewels until Theo assures me she'll be okay. I run by her place to tell her on the way to work the next after-noon, but she seems far from "okay" with the fact that I became engaged before her. I can sense her old cheerleading abilities kick in as she squeals in a flat tone and draws me in for a hug. Despite the warm smile she flashes as I tell her the details of her proposal, her eyes are flat and lifeless.

The days leading up to New Year's Eve are excep-tionally busy at Flanagan's. I give Tess notice that

I'm moving out of the apartment, and later that night Mick gives me his blessing, even buying the entire bar a free round of shots to celebrate my engagement.

While we're in no hurry to set a date and actually get married, Theo and I agreed that it made sense in every way for me to move in with him as soon as possible. I can hardly believe how much my life has changed in just six months. I've gone from having nowhere to live and being in constant turmoil over my life to having an amazing fiancé who constantly tells me how he plans to spoil me for the rest of our lives.

Adam spends the night in the hospital for observations after they remove his pump. Chloe, Davis, and I camp out on the couch with Jewels, doing our best to take her mind off the fact that Adam insisted she didn't spend the night at his side. It was Theo's idea for us to go over and cheer her up. He continues to insist things will be fine between them, though I really start to question his confidence in the matter.

On New Year's Eve we walk to Jewels and Adam's brownstone with appetizers and champagne for after we watch the ball drop in Times Square. Although we know the code to their place, we ring the doorbell as we often do when we know they're both home. Chloe answers the door, her big eyes even larger than usual.

"About time you got here," she whispers. "Shit's

going down in here, you don't even know. Davis told Adam that Jewels locked herself in the guest bath and won't come out. She won't answer me when I tried talking to her, but I could hear her moving around. Theo, you get your sexy ass in their room to help Davis with your buddy, and we'll go up and try to talk J down."

"Wait." Theo grabs my arm before I can go with Chloe. "Whatever happens, you make sure she knows it will be okay."

I sigh. "Why do you keep saying that? How do you know?"

"Because Adam swore to me that he wouldn't push her away again. He's been under a lot of stress since the infection, but he'll snap out of it eventually. You have to trust me on this one, Cavenaugh. I know what I'm talking about."

"I'll always trust you," I say, leaning in to give him a quick kiss.

Chloe hums as we climb the stairs to the second level. "You guys are so damn sweet. You're as bad as Jewels and Adam, when they aren't having problems like this, of course. When am I going to find myself a hunk who treats me like that?"

"Soon," I promise with a smile, knowing it won't take much to get her and Mick together. I knock on the bathroom door. "Jewels, sweetie, it's me. What's going on? Talk to me."

"I'm fine," she calls back after a beat. Her voice sounds little and soft. "I just need a minute."

"Chloe says you've had the door locked for a while." I close my eyes, hoping that my best friend hasn't done anything to hurt herself. She doesn't answer.

Chloe sets her head against the door. "We have to get going if we're going to find a good place to watch the ball drop, and I know you don't want to miss it. As crazy as everything will be, it's epic when they release the confetti and everyone around you is kissing. You *have to* see it to believe how unreal it can be. It's like something straight out of a movie."

"Let us in so we can help you get ready," I add, watching Chloe hopefully.

"He's either getting ready to leave me, or preparing to die all over again!" Jewels's voice cracks. Her quiet sobs seep through the door. "He's been quiet and weird, and he keeps talking about *my* future and *my* dreams as if he's getting ready to give up again! I don't care about the stupid fucking New Year! Just go without me!"

Chloe frowns as if waiting for an explanation. I just shrug.

"I don't know what's going on, Jewels, but Theo promises it's going to be okay. He wouldn't tell me anything more, and said we have to take his word for it. He seems to know what he's talking about, and I know he wouldn't lie to me about something like this. We have to trust him. Adam must just be having a hard time and doesn't want to bring you into it." I knock on the door again. "C'mon, sweetie. Open the door so we can talk about this. We're not going anywhere without you."

After a drawn out pause, we hear a click and the door springs open. Jewels stand in her pjs with snot running from her nose and her eyes swollen. *"I can't lose him,"* she whispers, her shoulders shaking.

I take her in my arms, making room for Chloe to join in.

By the time we convince Jewels to let us doll her up for the night and then fight the insane traffic, it's past eleven when we're near Times Square. The limo Theo hired can't even get us within two blocks. After we park on a side street, Theo excuses himself to make a call.

Adam and Jewels sit next to each other on one of the short ends of the limo. Though Adam has his arm wrapped around her shoulders, Jewels quietly watches the snow fall outside, unresponsive to his affection. He occasionally flashes tight, nervous smiles while we wait. Chloe taps away on her phone, her face aglow from the screen. I twist my giant engagement ring back and forth around my finger.

Davis rubs the palms of his hands along his faded jeans at my side. Since he's an artist, I figured he'd hit it off with Chloe, but the two haven't shown any interest in each other. He's so tall that his ear-length, sandy blond hair brushes the limo's roof. He reminds me of a misplaced surfer the way he's always so relaxed, both in the way he dresses and acts. It's the only thing that keeps me from thinking of Erik each time I look into the intriguing blues of his eyes, or the succulent curve of his lips. All the Murphy boys were blessed with the same handsome genes.

"So this is killer, right?" he asks, most likely trying to break the awkward tension. "I was here five years back with some artists who had made the big time. Turns out they were high on some messed up weed, so I wandered away from them and brought in the new year with a group of beautiful blondes from Norway." He flashes his perfect teeth in a bright smile. "Best night of my life, bro."

"Okay, how many times have you *been* here?" I ask, amazed. "You could almost one up Theo with epic stories of New York, and we all know how nearly impossible *that* can be."

His long shoulders lift. "Dunno. Lost count a year or two back."

"Why don't you just move here already?" I ask when no one else jumps in. I keep hoping Adam or Jewels will snap out of it since they're both close with Adam's cousin.

"Easy. If I stuck my inheritance into a place out

here, I wouldn't be able to afford traveling around the world on a regular basis, and I don't think I was meant to stay in one place for too long. Guess it's why I never put much effort into finding a girl as good as Jewels, either. My cousin is one lucky S-O-B."

Adam leans down to kiss the top of Jewels's head. "You got that right."

The sad smile she gives him in return makes me want to jump across the limo and shake them both, reminding them how good they have it together.

The limo door finally reopens. Theo leans in, holding his hand out to Jewels. "C'mon. I got us into the party at Marriott."

Chloe nudges me as we watch Jewels, Adam, and Davis pile out. "How's it feel to know you're marrying someone with so much influence? 'You want a ride in a helicopter? No worries, I know a pilot. How about a pass into the biggest party on New Year's? Sure, go right ahead.' The way the guy snaps his fingers to get what he wants you'd think *he* was a celebrity, or some kind of fucking prince."

"Hey. He's *my* fucking prince."

I slip out after her. Theo stands outside the door, holding out his hand and flashing me his million dollar smile. "Hi, my beautiful fiancé."

"Hi." My insides turn to mush with the sight of his dark gaze. He makes me immensely proud with all he's accomplished, and all he does for his friends and family. It doesn't hurt that he's crazy hot in his knit hat with snow melting into it.

I take his hand and he brings me into his arms for a long, slow kiss. I dissolve against his hard body, wishing we were alone in his brownstone so I could do so much more than just kiss him back. When we part, he takes my hand, winking. "Get ready, Cavenaugh. You're going to like this."

Inside the hotel, the six of us squeeze into the already cramped elevator. With my bestie looking so hopelessly crushed, it's hard to get excited about Theo's puzzling comment. Part of it's probably due to the fact that she's not very fond of heights, however. I worry that she'll come apart once we're high up, looking over the crowd.

Cold air blasts into us when we step outside onto the balcony, making it hard to catch our breaths for a moment. Once the oxygen returns to my brain, I look from the crowd gathered back to Theo with my jaw dropped.

"Uh...what's going on?" Jewels asks quietly.

Her mom and dad stand next to the people I recognize from pictures as Adam's parents. The two moms, bundled in stylish winter gear, hold hands like they're lifelong best friends. Jewels's mom, looking no older than thirty-five, has tears in her large blue eyes. Adam's mom, standing with perfect posture, beams at her son and Jewels.

When Jewels spins around, Adam bends down on

one knee. Chloe and I gasp along with Jewels, who holds a hand to her chest as if she can't catch her breath.

"*Hole. E. Shit,*" I say quietly.

Theo wraps his arms around my waist from behind and rests his chin on my shoulder, chuckling quietly. "This is why I promised you that everything would be okay," he whispers.

"Baby, I'm so sorry that I've been moody lately," Adam tells Jewels, his eyes intense. "I've been so nervous for this moment that I haven't been able to sleep. For the longest time, I wasn't sure this is what you wanted, knowing I may never be able to give you children, or that I can't promise you a happily ever after. But then I realized you wouldn't have fought so hard for me to have the transplant if you thought you could one day walk away. After all you've done for me, I owe you my life. I'm probably not the man you dreamed of marrying when you were little, but I promise to love you with all I've got, and take care of you for however long the rest of my life will be." He reaches for the inside pocket of his winter coat, pulling out a ring. Then he takes Jewels's hand. "Jewels Elizabeth Peterson, will you be my wife?"

Jewels breaks down sobbing. Adam quickly rises up to hold her. She throws her arms around his neck, saying "yes" a dozen times into his chest. The rest of us laugh and cheer, exchanging hugs and high-fives. We all hoot and holler when Adam dips Jewels backwards in the middle of a long kiss. She breaks away to throw an arm around each of her parents, huddling with them in a tearful display.

Theo spins me around, grinning madly. He was obviously privy to Adam's plan this entire time. "Are you disappointed I didn't make more of a grand gesture like this when I proposed?"

"Are you kidding?" I brush my finger against his jaw. "Proposing in the nude was just my style. I wouldn't have it any other way." Holding his face in my hands, I stand on my tiptoes to give him a deep, surging kiss.

"Okay, we get it, you're in love," a familiar voice nags at my side. "Do you *have* to rub it in our faces like that?"

I move away from Theo to see my sister Glori standing next to me. My parents, my other three sisters, and my brother-in-law file out behind her, surrounding us.

"Surprise, Cavenaugh," Theo whispers in my ear.

I squeal along with my sisters, running to hug each one individually, then collecting them all for a long, group hug. Finally, I approach my dad, then my teary-eyed mom. She brushes the snow from my face, smiling sadly. "I'm so proud of you and the life you made for yourself, my baby girl. I'm so sorry I let my faith in you lapse before."

"It's okay, Mom," I say, hugging her close. "I've already forgiven you."

"Now let's see that ring!" my sister Megan shrieks, tugging on my arm.

Once again, I'm swarmed by my four sisters who "ooh" and "holy shit" the hell out of my diamond. Mick and James slip into the crowd at some point, popping bottles of champagne and passing their congratulations to the four of us. Among the madness, Theo explains that his aunt and sister send their love, but didn't want to deal with the city on such a crazy night. My dad and Jewels's dad each make a heartfelt toast at one point, bringing everyone to tears.

After more hugging and high-fives from my sisters and parents, I finally make my way to Jewels. We laugh and fling our arms around each other, squealing. "Holy shit, this is insane!" she exclaims. "Can you believe the guys arranged all of this to surprise us? I never dreamed we'd both be engaged by the end of the year!"

"I think our adventures together are just about to begin," I say, laughing happily.

Everyone joins in when the official countdown begins, yelling the numbers at the top of their lungs and eyeing each other with giant smiles. When the ball drops, everyone couples up as best as possible for a kiss. As I move to kiss Theo, I catch Mick bending toward Chloe and laugh when her eyes grow impossibly wide.

"Happy new year, Cavenaugh," Theo whispers,

drawing me in with his burly arms. "I can't wait to give you a proper welcome to our new future when we get home."

Laughing, I kiss the man I love with everything I've got, surrounded by my friends, family, and a billion pieces of confetti floating through the air.

I can't believe this is my life. Half a year ago I was lost and angry with myself for playing into the image perceived of me by others. I almost let them break me down, and forever mar the strong woman I seem meant to become.

It feels necessary to pinch myself on a daily basis when I realize Theo's all mine, and that I'm the one he chose to spend the rest of his life with even after he discovered every detail of my sordid past.

As overjoyed as I feel, I don't allow myself to cry, even if they *are* happy tears. Because I'm Kelly Fucking Cavenaugh...at least for a little while longer.

Keep reading for a preview of *Chloe's Dream*, book #3 in the NYC Love series (now available)!

Chloe's Dream

Kelly Cavenaugh

If someone told me at the beginning of last summer that I'd soon be engaged to a gorgeous man who spoiled me rotten, living in a beautiful brownstone in New York City, planning for not only *my* wedding, but my best friend's at the same time, I'd most likely ask what kind of medication they're on and if they had any left to share.

Watching my beautiful blonde friend emerge from the upscale dressing room to parade around in front of the wall of mirrors in a dizzying blur of white tulle and sparkles makes everything so surreal that I have to sit down in one of the plush armchairs next to Chloe to collect myself. *We're getting married.* At times I wonder if I'll ever have to stop reminding myself of the fact.

"Oh my god you look like a freaking princess!" Chloe declares, clapping her hands together at the 3-way reflection of Jewels staring back at us. "Only you could pull that look off, J. Your waist is so tiny, and your boobs look amazing. I mean, that dress isn't my style, of course, but *you*, *you* would probably look good in anything. We could be here for months trying on every dress in the store and you'd rock every single one."

I can't stop myself from laughing at Chloe's rant. Even though more than half a year has passed since Jewels introduced me to her, I'm still amazed by our "little" friend's spirited quirks and how adorable she is: from the bright blue streaks in her bangs against her dark black hair to the way her heart-shaped mouth and big brown eyes stand out against her petite face like a sexy cartoon character, she's one of the most enduring people I've met. I never used to be into music as much as Jewels, but my new favorite past time has become following Chloe's hard rock band through New York bars. You'd never guess someone so little could belt out songs the way she can, plus she really knows how to rock a guitar.

"What *would* be your style, Chloe?" I ask with a smirk. "I'm having a hard time picturing you in anything sparkling. Or bright white."

With her tattooed arm, she gestures to her light blue camisole and short skirt. "*If* I ever get married, what I wear on my wedding day would probably look something like this. But I say *if* with a capital 'I F' because it would take the perfect guy to make me settle down and commit to something that big. No offense, because the two of you have definitely found your Prince Charmings and they're both amazing in their own way, but I have a really high set of standards. They can't just be sweet and good-looking. They have to know how to rock a guitar and carry a note because he'll probably go on the road with me when I make it big, so we may as well start a band together. It's one of the reasons you've never seen me date anyone."

I nudge her, grinning. "What about Mick? He always asks me about you. Don't even pretend like you didn't kiss him on New Year's, either, because I saw it."

Chloe's face turns crimson red with the mention of my coworker. Although Mick and Chloe met at Flanagan's last fall and really seemed to hit it off with their mutual interest in music and concerts, their only interaction that I know of was to add each other on Facebook and the brief kiss the night Adam proposed to Jewels on a rooftop overlooking Times Square.

"What do you want me to say? The guy's a total sweetheart. I wouldn't mind getting to know him a little better, though I think if he felt the same he would've made a move by now. I *did* give him my number, and it's been months." She waves her hands through the air in a "never-mind" gesture. "Besides, I barely have time for *you two* outside of the band and the shop. I don't know where a guy would fit into all of that. I can only be stretched so far. You can tell him next time you see him that I say hello anyway."

An older woman with white-blond hair slicked back into a pretentious bun, wearing a long dress and a name tag pinned to her chest, appears at my friend's side. "Well, what did we decide? You look delightful in that dress, my dear."

This is when I realize Jewels is standing with her hands set firmly on her hips, staring holes into me. Oh, right. I haven't said anything about the dress.

"It's pretty, but it's not really you," I say truthfully, gesturing to the nest of tulle. "I've never seen you wear anything so...*girly*. I see you in something long and elegant. Maybe something with a higher waistline and a sleek skirt. Flowing. Less bling. You know, classic."

The saleswoman purses her lips when looking my way, obviously dismayed by my lack of approval. But Jewels is the free-spirited type who likes to fight her way to the front of the crowd at concerts. As beautiful as she looks in the princess-style dress, it's not her style.

"Yeah, you're probably right," Jewels concedes, frowning at her reflection in the mirror. "I guess I just wanted to see what I'd look like in something like this."

"You look freaking gorgeous, of course," I tell her. "Still, as your maid of honor it's my duty to help you pick the *perfect* dress since your mom can't be here. And that, my friend, is definitely not it."

"She's right, you know," Chloe chimes in. "Always listen to your bestie. She knows you better than anyone else. Me, I could sit here and tell you that you rock every dress you try on. I'm sure Adam will lose his shit no matter what you choose. Your wedding is going to be exactly like a fairy tale, I can see it now."

Jewels inhales sharply as she looks my way. "*You should try this on, Kel!*"

I laugh bluntly. "Except that sparkles aren't really my thing either. And I'm so not wearing *white* white."

Truthfully, I'm terrified to actually do something that will move the wedding forward. Sometimes I worry Theo and I moved too fast with the marriage thing even though I know in my heart he's "the one" and I can't envision a future without him. I fell so hard and fast after he finally understood my twisted past of trysts gone wrong that it seemed right when he proposed to me on Christmas. It's just that I don't know if I'm ready for the responsibilities that come with being a wife. I feel young, not to mention the fact that I'm new to this big city life and have so much to experience. What if married life makes us dull? I can't bake worth a shit, gardening seems so boring, and I have no interest in sewing anything. Aren't those things expected of a good wife?

So far the good news is that Theo told me he doesn't know if he sees himself becoming a dad one day, so at least we're on the same page when it comes to children. There are days I'm amazed that I can take care of *myself*, and can't imagine being responsible for a tiny, helpless human. Yet I've caught myself fantasizing at random times over what beautiful babies we'd make together, so there's that.

Jewels raises her eyebrows at the woman. "Could you maybe find her something like that? And maybe something with a bunch of lace, too. With her awesome backside, she could pull off the look."

"I'll gather some different styles together," the saleslady tells Jewels, her tan skin appearing orange next to her artificial smile. She throws me a terse glance before turning on her heels and leaving us with our Barbie-esque friend.

"Why does that lady keep looking at me like I'm going to pee on something?" I ask my friends once she's gone. "And why did you sell me out like that, Jewels? Seriously, I wasn't going to try anything on today. This isn't about me, it's all about you."

Since we haven't set a date, I didn't plan on actively shopping for a dress. Jewels has been with Adam a few months longer than Theo and I, plus they've had to deal with Adam's medical issues that come with being a brittle diabetic. Neither of them has said it out loud, but I think they're anxious to get married while he's relatively healthy.

Jewels touches my arm. "Except we're *both* getting married. I'm so not letting you out of this shop until you try something on with me. It's not like you have to *buy* something today. It'll be fun trying them on together!"

Less than ten minutes later, the woman returns and ushers me into an open dressing room with quilted benches and draping white cloth among a jungle of white flowers that give off the fragrance of a funeral home. Four dresses hang against a wall, one with a full lace skirt and heart-shaped bodice; a long, tame number with a lace covered front and funky lace detail on back; a dress similar to the one Jewels tried on with silver jewels instead of sparkles, and a champagne-colored number with more of a tame tulle skirt and big, chunky jewels on the bodice.

"You've *got* to be kidding me," I say, tapping my fingers against the wall and blowing a big breath of air out.

None of the dresses are remotely *close* to anything I'd pick out. Then again, I have no freaking clue what I *would* choose. Until I hooked up with Theo, I was more a short skirt and low-cut top kind of girl. I still occasionally dress that way when we hit the clubs. Otherwise I've become conservative since doing away with one-night stands.

Jewels closes the door behind me, her eyes dancing with mischief and excitement. "This is awesome! You may as well start trying them on. I'm camping in here until I see you in those dresses."

"I really wish we'd go somewhere else to look," I tell Jewels. "Are you really going to give that snob out there commission? Did you see the dirty looks she kept throwing me and Chloe? She probably thinks we're just trying dresses on for the hell of it. Either that or she's worried they'll stain with our redneck juices."

Jewels clicks her tongue after a little giggle. "Just try these on, and we're out of here."

She helps me slip into the lace number first. Though it's elegant and regal, it isn't my style. I don't even bother popping out to show Chloe. "Moving on," I say, quickly stepping out of it. I skip over the next two and pause before taking the champagne-colored dress off the hanger. The sweetheart bodice and color are actually gorgeous. I just don't know about all the tulle.

When I slip into it, however, watching my reflection in the mirror as Jewels zips me up, I have to cover my mouth. I'm struck with a vision of myself walking down a sandy beach with a large bouquet of red roses in hand as Theo waits for me in a casual suit, button on his shirt gaping as he gives me the kind of grin that melts my heart. And I can see him peering up at me from beneath all that tulle once the reception is over, and we're left alone to ravage each other.

Jewels steps back to admire me, her eyes wide. "Hole. E. Shit. Kel, you look *stellar*. That dress is *amazing* on you!"

A sudden wave of tears prick my eyes, even though there's no way I'm about to allow myself to become *soft* in front of my bestie. I promised my three sisters and mom that I would wait until they were in town later this spring to shop for a dress. What if this is *the one*? How in the hell can I find the perfect one after only trying on two?

Jewels pokes her head out the door. "Chloe, get your tiny ass in here!"

Our friend skips into the dressing room with the saleswoman at her heels.

"You're a vision of pure beauty in that dress, my dear," the saleswoman says, touching her chest in what I can't decide to be mockery or sincerity.

"*Damn*, Kelly!" Chloe exclaims, holding my arms out at my sides to get a better look. "I know you aren't a fan of sparkle and fluffy shit, but this is perfect on you! It's like you stepped right off the pages of *Vogue*!"

"It could work," I say cryptically. I'm not about to tell them just how much I'm in love with the dress. I can't try on a mere *two* dresses if I'm only going to do this marriage thing once. Besides, I have no interest in telling the woman just how much I like something that she picked out. Yet there's something deep down that tells me this is the dress I'll be wearing when I marry Theo. My stomach flutters in anticipation.

"I'll write down the information so you'll have it for later," the saleswoman tells me, her smile a bit more generous as she leaves the dressing room.

"Seriously, Kel, you look *amazing*," Jewels gushes, beaming from ear to ear. She peers down inside the bodice of the dress at her boobs, frowning. "Now someone needs to help me out of this thing. I think all this bling is giving me hives."

The three of us celebrate the first, though unsuccessful for Jewels, wedding dress search with drinks at Flanagan's. It was my idea to hit the bar in hopes that Chloe and Mick would reconnect. When we walk in, however, my co-worker Stella tells us he left for a family emergency.

"I guess it's nothing serious," she assures us while pouring our drinks. "He said he might be able to come back in later."

The Irish pub I've come to cherish for so many reasons is fairly quiet for once as there isn't a band. I belly up to the bar between my friends, enjoying a rare night off. Flanagan's has become a second home of sorts and not just because I once lived in the apartment over it. Mick and the other bartenders have become my second family.

Theo has been on me to find a different job with hours similar to his so we'll see more of each other. I agree it needs to happen, though every time I walk into the low-lit building, seeing the worn wooden bar and beams overhead with the smell of stale peanuts and beer wafting through the air, I'm reminded of how I changed my life all on my own when Mick offered me the job, and I don't have the heart to quit.

A full hour later, I've just taken my first sip of the second round of Jameson when the strong arms I could ogle and stroke for hours on end slip around my waist. The tantalizing scent of my beautiful fiancé surrounds me like a cloud.

"Did my smoking hot bride-to-be find her dream dress today?" Theo asks, his husky voice letting me know just how much he missed me while he was off at work. God, his affection for me will never grow old. Neither will the blazing desire I feel for him when he's near. My underwear become damp with just the sound of his voice and fell of his warm body hovering near mine. I'm drawn to him like a moth to a light.

"Hmmm, I think she was too busy exchanging flirty texts with her fiancé to bother with such trivial things," I say over my shoulder with a coy smile. "Besides, it was all about Jewels. She's on a deadline." I'm not about to tell him this early on that I think I may have found the perfect dress. Besides, I don't want him to think I'm suddenly eager to set a date.

Theo brushes my hair off to one side and leans in to whisper, "If it weren't for the fact that my aunt and sister would murder us both if we didn't have a traditional wedding, I'd take you to some private island where we could marry in the nude and consummate our love right on the beach." His soft lips brush against my jaw. "Over." He kisses the corner of my mouth. "And over again until we collapsed from exhaustion." He runs his nose along the ridge beneath my jaw before pulling away.

With a turned-on quiver, I make a strange sound that comes out as a blend of laughter and choking. "Somehow I don't think my sisters and friends would be excited about it either. Especially when I've already asked them to be in the wedding."

"A man can fantasize." He makes a low grumbling noise as he kisses the spot beneath my ear and pulls back. "And believe me when I say that I do. All. Day. Long."

Running my fingers over his rigid muscles, I turn to bring our lips together, allowing him just enough time to slip his mouthwash-flavored tongue into my mouth. I lean back with a satisfied grin, taking in his hazel eyes sparkling beneath his low eyebrows and the devilish smile against his square jaw. My gut stirs excitedly. More than anything I want to pull him somewhere private and have my way. I'll never grow tired of our intense make out sessions or the chance to do naughty things with the beautiful man.

For the first time I realize Theo didn't come alone. Adam stands behind Jewels with his arm slung loosely around her neck, whispering into her ear. She clings onto his arms with both hands, giggling. They've become even more adorable since the night he proposed, though she may have mentioned the same about me and Theo. Several times.

Chloe clears her throat at my other side. When I turn to her, she's sliding off the barstool. There's something off the way she blinks numerous times and holds her mouth tight. "Today was fun as always being with you girls. As much as I'd love to stay for another drink, I have a few errands to run before jamming with the band. If I don't leave now, I'll be late. Last time I was late, Beckett threatened to find a new lead singer. I know he was only joking, but you never know with that guy. His ego's bigger than all of us put together."

"Hey, you okay?" I ask, touching her arm. Have we grossed her out with all the canoodling? I figured she'd be used to it by now and it never seemed to bother her before.

"It's all good. Like I said, I have to go." She flashes me a tight smile and squeezes my arm. She tips her head at Jewels. "See you tomorrow, J."

Everyone throws her a "bye" as she races to the

front door without looking back. For a moment I consider going after her. Something's definitely up.

"What was that about?" Jewels asks, running her hands along Adam's arms and frowning. "Chloe usually doesn't 'do' jittery like that. Should call her?" she asks, glancing down at her phone. "Make sure she's okay?"

"She'll call when she's ready to talk about whatever's bothering her," I say, holding a hand out above the bar. "Hey, Stella, can I get another beer and something for the guys?"

"Sure thing," Stella answers, sliding over to take orders from Theo and Adam. As she's filling a glass at the tap, she grunts and tips her head to a table near the entrance. "I see Mick's back. I don't know what his emergency was, but it looks like everything is more than okay now."

I scan the crowd before I find Mick sitting incredibly close to a stunning brunette who apparently feels no shame in showing her oversized breasts to the world, much like I did before meeting Theo. The black lace of her bra peeks out beneath the neckline of her slinky, emerald green dress. *Seriously*. It's well below zero degrees outside and the girl's dressed like it's the middle of summer. I can't help but wonder if she's desperate for Mick's attention as she touches his chest with one hand, laughing brightly with her head tipped back. Mick smiles from ear to ear, his eyes filled with light, obviously pleased to see Big Tits humored by whatever he said.

"Shit," I mutter under my breath, nudging Jewels. "I think I know why Chloe was so upset. Check it out."

Jewels narrows her eyes on Mick and the woman. "Shit," she parrots, pursing her lips.

Chloe's Dream, Book #3 in the NYC LOVE series, now available on Amazon!

Note from the Author

Mental health is not something that can be neglected. If you're secretly fighting your own battles and need someone to talk to, don't ever think twice about asking for someone's help, even if it's from a total stranger online or through a crisis hotline. We've all been through hard times, and it's nothing to be embarrassed about. There's always someone in your life who cares, even if it may not seem that way to you.

For more information on mental health disorders and ways to seek help,
visit http://www.mentalhealthamerica.net

Acknowledgments

To each and every one of the readers and bloggers who bought *Adam's List*, making this series what it is, I wish I could tackle hug you! I never imagined it would have this kind of success. It truly warms my heart to know so many people fell in love with my characters, Theo especially. I hope I made everyone happy with his heartwarming story. Having come from a family with a strong military background, I have a special place in my heart for anyone who has served our country, and wish I could thank each and every one of the US soldiers in person.

Once again, a big thanks to my superstar cover designer, Najla Qamber, for knowing how to give me exactly what I had imagined, even though I can be flaky at times!

Thank you to my patient and very knowledgeable editor, Christopher Vondracek, for agreeing to stay on and help me improve my skill with each book I write. I wouldn't be where I am today if you didn't continue to challenge me and my motivations.

A sincere thank you to my beta readers Sydney Aaliyah, Maria Monteiro, Leesa Bow, Lilly Christine, and Corrie Hanson for your incredible support and invaluable feedback. I'm honored that all of you agreed to take the time to help me out so early on!

Thanks a million to my dear friend across the pond, Emma Meade, for helping me to perfect Mick's Irish accent. Once again, your knowledge was priceless. Can't wait for the day when we finally meet in person!

Again, a special shout out to my sweet cousin, Hope Domeier, for sharing with me your brutal experiences of being a Type I, brittle diabetic. I love you, and hope life continues on the upswing for you.

Special thanks to my lifelong friend, Heidi Schiltz, for letting me pick inside the head of a psychologist to properly treat poor, confused Kelly. Looking forward to our next "session" for book #3... this time I'm buying all the drinks! You're the best!

To all my friends who continue to buy my books and support this crazy adventure of mine: you guys rock! Seriously, you're what keeps me going. Having friends like you to let loose with on my down time keep me sane. Sorry to those who are weirded out by my sex scenes, but just remember, IT'S FICTION!

To my family who puts up with my career and the rumors that you're related to someone who "writes porn", a million apologies. It's far past time to educate the public on the different between the erotica involved in books like *Fifty Shades of Grey* and healthy sexual activity between consenting adults.

Like someone recently told me, "Everyone does it. If they didn't, we all wouldn't be here."

To my dear husband: I know I wouldn't be able to do what I love if it weren't for your hard work and support. Thank you for all you do for our family, and thanks for putting up with my odd work hours/moods. You're truly one in a million.

ABOUT THE AUTHOR

With over 45 captivating titles spanning various genres, Quinn Avery honed her talent for crafting intricate puzzles through her smart and quirky Bexley Squires mystery series. Her contemporary suspense thrillers, often set in her beloved locales such as Mankato and Lake Shetek, are nothing short of addictive, leaving readers spellbound with their mind-spinning twists. When Quinn and her husband aren't off on adventures, they enjoy the tranquility of their Minnesota acreage and lake home in their newfound empty-nest phase.

Quinn also writes romantic suspense as Jennifer Ann and children's picture books as Jennifer Naumann. For all the latest on her work, visit www.QuinnAvery.com